EQUINOX

The Kemkabi Strike

Jeff and Lilly Sayre

This book is dedicated to all the fallen warriors of the Light. There's a place in heaven for each one of you.

Much Love to Everyone,

Jeff and Lilly Sayre

Table of Contents

Jayna's World

It's a beautiful night. The stars are sparkling in the sky like beautiful gems, and all is peaceful in the city.

Today is December 24, 2019. My husband, Landry, and I live in a city named Sirius, and we're on a planet called Sekhmet. Planet Sekhmet is located in the Alpha Centauri solar system. The Sekhmetians don't celebrate Christmas like we do back on Planet Earth, but it is a beautiful night just the same.

How I wound up on another planet in another solar system is a long story.

It began in May of 1966 when I was eight-years-old, and my parents entered me into a talent contest. My parents' names are Natalie and Marcello Valdarsa. We lived in Brooklyn, New York, in a limestone building in the Prospect Park area.

They said I was a funny child, and they wanted to test my comedic skill.

The competition was held in a hotel in midtown Manhattan. The room looked like an auditorium with a theater platform and chairs for the audience. There was a man at a piano on the stage, ready to play songs for the contestants. Two judges sat in the front row, one man and one woman. Their names were Spencer and Marci, and both were well known actors. The contestants sat in the back of the room behind the audience. I was slightly agitated because it seemed like I had to wait forever for my turn. When it finally came, I walked on stage and introduced myself to the judges.

"Hello, my name is Jayna Valdarsa and I come from Brooklyn, New York."

"Hello," the judges said to me.

"What would you like to share with us today Jayna?" Marci asked in a sweet voice.

"Well," I said, "I would like to do a number for you today."

"Okay," Spencer said, "what song would you like to sing for us?"

"Hound Dog" by Elvis Presley."

"Hound Dog," it is!" Marci said.

The music began, and I started singing my song and doing my little dance. I did my best impersonation of Elvis Presley, except with extra vibrato in the singing. The dance moves were exaggerated as I swayed and dipped to the beat. The next thing I knew, the audience was clapping with my singing and the judges were laughing.

I always could bring down the house with this routine. I performed it for family and friends, and it always made people laugh. I loved the fun it created, and this group of people seemed to like it too.

At the end of the song, the audience applauded, and I thanked them and left the stage.

"Jayna," Dad said, "you were wonderful!"

"Yes, Jayna," Mom said, "you did well. We're so proud of you!"

"I know," I said. "I've seen that I'm going to win."

Mom said to Dad, "Honey, she's having another one of those moments."

"I wish she'd have one of those moments with the ponies," Dad said.

"Behave Marcello," Mom answered.

The next contestant walked up to the stage and performed their routine until all the contestants were done. There were twenty-five contestants in all. This competition had three winners, first prize, second prize, and third prize. The third prize was $100.00, the second prize was $300.00, and the first prize was $500.00, with an opportunity to compete in a national talent competition.

While we were waiting, I whispered to Dad which contestants would win second and third prize. When the competition was finished, Dad and I moved to the front of the room to be closer to the judges. They took a break to make their final decision. Everyone waited anxiously until they returned to the room.

When they finally returned, the room was silent. The judges gave a short speech about how enjoyable all the acts were and how hard it was to select three winners. Then, the moment came. We held our breaths. They announced the third prize winner and then the second prize winner. My name was not mentioned. Dad looked down at me with a puzzled look on his face.

"You were right," Dad said.

"Yep."

The other two contestants were standing on the stage by Spencer. They seemed happy with their prize, but I could feel the emotions they were hiding.

"Ladies and gentlemen," Spencer said, "now we would like to announce our first prize winner. After much deliberation, Marci and I came to a decision.

And the winner is…"

The man on the piano plays a little tune.

"Jayna Valdarsa."

With that, the audience clapped, and I walked up to the stage. I addressed the judges and the audience and said, "Thank you. It was so much fun performing for you, you are a great audience. Thank you one and all."

I paused a moment and turned to the other two contestants and said, "I enjoyed your performances. You both did a great job!"

I walked off the stage, and Mom and Dad hugged me. I could see their joy; they were so proud of me!

Everyone left the room, and we waited for the judges to speak to us. They gave us the information about the next competition. It would be held in New York City again, and there was no need for us to travel. The show would be in six weeks, so there was time to prepare another routine.

This competition had eight contestants, and they were from all over the country. The winner would appear on a network television variety show. Quite a prize indeed!

I was thrilled to win the talent show. It made my summer vacation even more enjoyable. Mom was telling the neighbors how well I performed and about the next upcoming competition. Dad was happy as well. I was able to play with my friends from school in the park, and the days went by quickly. The following talent show was approaching in the next few weeks.

Take The Bully By The Horns

My friends were happy for me, but not all the kids wished me well. Tony, an eleven-year-old that lived down the street, was one of these people. After I won the competition, Tony began poking fun at me. I ignored him at first, but then he started to bully me physically. Whenever he saw me, he pushed me to the ground and laughed.

"Look, it's Hound Dog girl!" Tony said as he laughed.

"Why don't you leave me alone, Tony!" I snapped. "I haven't done anything to you."

"What are you going to do?" Tony asked. "Cry all the time?"

There were other kids around, and they were giggling as Tony mocked me.

Without thought, I said, "At least I don't pee the bed!"

Tony screamed and said, "I don't do that! Who told you that?"

I said with a grin, "I know things!"

He said, "You need to shut up." With that, he shoved me to the ground.

I stood up and said, "You better not do that again, Mr. Peepeepants!"

With that, the kids started giggling, which made Tony angry. He rushed up to me and slapped me on the side of the face. The kids all fell silent. I was angry and afraid. Tony was older and taller than I was, but I wasn't going to let him treat me this way. I pushed my hand towards him and felt a rush of energy go through me. Tony was knocked off his feet and fell to the ground even though my hand did not make contact with him. He sat there and looked bewildered.

I heard my mother's voice coming from behind, "What's going on here?"

She looked at the children and said, "You kids need to go home."

Tony had made it to his feet by this time, and my mother asked him, "What do you think you're doing picking on my daughter?"

"I,..I,..I was just, uh, uh,…" Tony said.

"Just being a big meanie!" I interrupted.

"Mrs. Moretti called me and told me you were up to no good." Mom said.

Tony turned and ran down the street.

Mom said, "Jayna, why is your face red?"

"Because Tony slapped me." I answered.

"I'm going to call his father and have a talk with him," Mom said.

On the way home, Mom asked me to tell her what happened.

"I called him 'Mr. Peepeepants' and he got mad and hit me," I said.

Mom asked, "How do you know he pees his pant?"

I answered, "When he shoved me to the ground, I saw an image of him in my mind where he got up out of bed with wet pajamas."

Mom had a puzzled look on her face and said, "You're not normal."

After we got home, I heard Mom talking to Tony's father on the phone. She said, "So your boy likes to shove little girls on the ground and then hit them in the face?"

I could hear Tony's father yelling at him over the phone. He said he would deal with Tony, and he was sorry for his son's behavior.

When Mom hung up the phone, she said, "Tony's Dad told me that Tony said you used magic on him. What happened?"

I answered, "I put my hand out and I felt this energy go through me and it made him fall down."

"You have to be very careful. You could hurt someone very badly," Mom said.

"It would be better if you stay closer to the house so I can watch you."

"That's fine," I answered, "I'll just practice more. The talent show is coming up soon."

"That's a good idea," Mom said.

I didn't see Tony again for the rest of the summer. I was able to practice my next routine for the upcoming competition. I was excited and getting impatient to perform. Mom and Dad were eager to see how I would do in the following event.

Stepping Stones

When the day of the competition arrived, Mom and Dad took me to the Javits Center on the west side of Manhattan. The seats in the audience were all filled, and there was a lot of excitement in the air. I prayed for help with my routine. My sole desire was to make the audience laugh.

The front row was filled with judges, six in all. Three men and three women. They were all personable and relaxed the contestants. When my turn came, I walked on the stage and addressed the judges.

"Hello, my name is Jayna Valdarsa. The song I picked out to sing for you today is "Do You Love Me Now That I Can Dance" by The Contours."

The judges smiled at me and wished me good luck. The music began, and I started my routine. I used the most robust voice I could muster and the most animated dance moves that I could imagine. The next thing I knew, the audience was laughing. At the end of the routine, I received thunderous applause. I thanked the audience and walked off the stage. Mom and Dad were laughing hard. I was overjoyed that everyone was having fun.

I did win the competition, which brought government agents' attention as they kept track of all public figures and potential public entertainers. They are concerned that any given celebrity could have significant influence on the public, so they are sure to follow all rising stars to control the situation.

The agents interviewed my parents and discovered I had a psychic gift as well. This was their primary interest in me. After much testing, it was concluded that I could accurately predict the future, and I could also reveal the hidden past. The government agents said they would contact us at a future date to tell us how my special abilities could be used to help our country.

While we were waiting for the government to contact us, my parents decided to go about our lives as usual for the time being. We decided I would go to another audition. This one was for a role in a TV series.

It was a warm spring afternoon when Dad and I took the subway to the audition and left the car at home. We arrived at the studio in midtown Manhattan. It was a three-story brownstone with steps leading up to the entrance. The door had glass panes, and we were able to see that the studio was filled with parents and children. We got there late, and many of the children had already auditioned. We filled out an application and sat down and waited for our turn. I noticed a dark-haired man with blue eyes walk out of the audition room and head towards the front door.

Within a few minutes, a lady called my name, and I went into a room with the casting director. She was a red-headed woman in her fifties and was very kind and personable. She gave me a script to read, and I proceeded to do so. Dad came with me but remained silent. My audition went well and after I finished, the casting director said they might contact us.

As we walked down the steps exiting the building, I asked Dad, "So, do you think I have the part?"

"Well, Jayna," Dad replied, "it's entirely possible. You did very well. Now we have to wait and see if they call us back."

He's right, I thought. But I was so excited that I couldn't wait to find out.

As we walked to the subway station to go back home, cars were parked all along the sidewalk. We headed to the crosswalk. Dad watched the intersection to see if the traffic was heavy. A large dark blue sedan pulled up and double-parked.

A man quickly exited the rear door of the car and grabbed me by the arm.

I panicked, and my heart pounded rapidly in my chest. "Dad! Help!" I yelled.

I tried to pull away from him as hard as I could, but he kept dragging me to the car. Dad quickly moved and grabbed the man by the arm.

"What do you think you're doing, pal?" he said. He punched the man with a hard right to the jaw. The man's knees buckled and he released his grip. I ran behind Dad.

He punched him again, hitting him in the nose.

"You picked the wrong girl, fellow!" Dad said.

The man staggered backwards and pulled his arm from Dad's grasp. He then jumped in the back door of the waiting car and sped away.

I looked up and recognized the dark-haired man from the audition. He ran up to us. "What's going on?"

"The one man tried to grab that little girl!" a nearby lady said.

Dad walked over to me. "Are you alright, honey?"

"Yes," I said.

The lady who was standing nearby said, "She's a brave little girl!"

"She sure is!" Dad answered.

I tried to hide that I was petrified. I could feel myself trembling and was in a cold sweat. It all happened so fast.

"Dad," I said, "I want to go home. Can we leave now?"

"What's that on your hand?" the dark-haired man said to Dad.

I saw a blue liquid smeared on my Dad's hand.

Dad raised his fingers to get a better look. "I don't know," he said.

I leaned closer to Dad to get a better look.

"The guy must have had a pen in his pocket," Dad replied.

The dark-haired man pulled out a handkerchief and handed it to Dad. "You can clean it off with this."

"Thanks!" Dad said. He wiped off his hand and returned the handkerchief to the man.

"I'll walk with you to the subway station, if you don't mind," the dark-haired man said.

"Sure," Dad said.

"Do you want to call the cops?" the man asked.

"Did anyone get the license plate number?" Dad answered.

"It all happened so fast, and I don't know if anyone got it.

In any case, you didn't waste any time; you really let that guy have it!"

"I used to be in the Merchant Marines and I boxed for a while. I've been in a few rough places in this world, but I really didn't expect anything like that here."

"What's your name sir?" I asked the man.

"John Tinkerman is my name," he answered.

John started to walk through the crowd and asked if anybody had gotten the license plate number. No one seemed to have any helpful information.

We walked to the train station and parted ways when we got there. Dad thanked John, and we said goodbye.

When we got home, Dad told Mom what happened. She was distraught.

"Marcello, this is not good. Jayna could have been kidnapped! Maybe we should rethink her getting into show business."

"Natalie," Dad said, "we don't know what this is about. Let's not jump to conclusions."

Mom turned to me, her eyes wide with worry. "Jayna, do you want to keep doing this?" Mom asked.

"Yes," I answered. "But I want Dad to come with me. Is that okay?"

"Yes, he answered.

I didn't know at the time that the government was one step ahead of us. The next day we received a phone call from them.

Dad took the call, and a secretary told him one of their representatives was coming to introduce himself to us. He was going to be talking to us about a particular government program.

When he arrived, Dad and I were shocked. It was John Tinkerman! He said he was assigned to this project.

My parents spoke with him privately and I wondered what was going on. They went into the dining room and closed the door. I stood by the door and listened, but their conversation wasn't loud enough for me to hear what they were saying. So, I sat on the couch and concentrated and tried to use my psychic ability to listen to their conversation. My mind was racing, so I couldn't hone in on their conversation. I waited until John left the house and then approached my mother.

"Mommy," I asked. "What does John want?"

"Honey, the government is interested in your psychic abilities, and want to bring you, your father and me into a government secret program. We had to sign a non-disclosure."

"What's a non-disclosure?" I asked.

"It means we cannot tell people about this," she answered.

I was utterly speechless, as though I had forgotten how to speak. I couldn't wrap my mind around what Mom said. She just looked at me with motherly concern and gave me a reassuring hug.

My parents waited for about a month before they brought up the secret government program to me again. They sat me down one night to explain precisely what the government was asking of us.

"In our meeting with John, he shared a great deal of information with us, and it is extraordinary," Mom explained. "There are beings on other planets in other solar systems that the government exchanges information with. The government wants to use your psychic abilities to help Planet Sekhmet. In exchange, they will give the United States government technological information.

The US government has many agreements with various races throughout the galaxy and have human settlements on many planets. In some cases, if the humans have a valuable skill to offer the extraterrestrial race, an exchange takes place.

The government also sends its citizens off-world to live in settlements simply to have humans in diverse places, so that if for some reason Planet Earth does not make it in the long run, there'll be people from our planet already living in many other places throughout the universe."

"Why wouldn't our planet make it?" I asked.

Mom said, "There could be a nuclear war that could wipe out our planet."

"There is so much to understand about what goes on in this universe," Dad said. "We still have much to learn. From what we've been told, all this information has been kept from the public. There seems to be a battle behind the scenes between two groups of people. There are those who want humanity to know our true history, and there are those who want to keep us in the dark so they can continue to dominate our culture, and make money from us."

I spoke up and said, "But what about my auditions?"

"Do you want to make people laugh, or do you want to help people?" Mom asked.

"I would like to do both!" I answered.

"Jayna," Dad said, "there are opportunities in the settlement."

"Dad," I asked, "if we go to an off-world settlement, will we be safe there?"

He answered, "I asked the same question to the government representative, and he assured me we would be safe. However, we'll all have to make a significant adjustment to adjust to a new environment successfully. There are many things to think about.

Before we commit to this program, we want to be sure that you're okay with it. We don't want to push you to do anything you would not want to do. Please think about this, and we'll discuss it again."

***

For the next few days, I couldn't bring myself to go outside and play with my friends. This put a damper on my summer break from school. This information was going round and round through my mind day and night. I couldn't believe this was happening to me. There were so many unanswered questions. How does one begin to understand how off the charts amazing this all really was? And how could we find out more about what we would be getting ourselves into?

The next time John came over to our house, Dad and I met him at the door. Dad took him to the living room, and I followed them. John sat down on the couch. Mom went into the kitchen and started to make fresh lemonade. Dad sat down in his chair and started talking to John.

"John," I asked, "how about my auditions here and being able to make people laugh. Can I do that there?"

"Possibly," he answered, "but it may not be right away. "There is a TV station with actors on the other planet."

"So, what do you think, Jayna?" Dad asked. "Would you like to give it a go?"

"Are you going to have a job there, Dad?" I asked.

"Well, John explained to your mother and I that we would receive a large sum of money plus living expenses. And, there's opportunities for businesses as well."

"Dad, you're such a good cook; why don't you open up your own place?

"We'll see."

Mom entered the room with a pitcher of lemonade and four glasses on a serving tray. She set down a glass on a coffee table for each one of us and poured us a drink.

Dad continued with a question to John. "How will we get to another planet?"

"Through the Cosmic Fountain!" he replied.

"What?"

"Let me explain. Millions of years ago, a technologically advanced culture from Planet Manji, located in the Whirlpool Galaxy, traveled through the universe. They are a pure energy race that lives in the fifth dimension, a dimension of energy. They can take any form in the third dimension, the physical dimension, including humanoid. They created a system of portals to go between planets, solar systems, and galaxies, and they called it 'the Cosmic Fountain.' It's a machine that's used to take you from one location to another, and with no limit to how far in the universe you can go as long as there's a Cosmic Fountain on the planet. This energy creates a wormhole that connects you to another Cosmic Fountain. It folds space-time so that you can move through space effortlessly.

"The Manjins put at least one Cosmic Fountain on every planet in the cosmos, and on some planets even more. Earth has a total of four since there was so much interplanetary travel to this planet through the years. Pretty neat, huh?"

We were dumbfounded and could not speak for a few minutes.

Dad finally got the courage to say something. "That is one of the most amazing things I have ever heard."

John smiled. "Wait, it gets better…"

My parents were so shaken up over all of this, and now I understand why. It all seemed so surreal. Could this really be happening? I asked John for more information.

"Now I'm going to tell you about your destination," John answered.

The History of Sekhmet

"Sekhmet is a planet that is located in the Alpha Centauri solar system that orbits Proxima Centauri as its sun," John said.

"What's the difference between the two planets?" Dad asked.

John answered, "Sekhmet is a larger planet that has more land mass than Earth. Since the planet is larger, that means the rotation is a little slower, which causes each day to increase the number of hours in a day. Also, the planet has more density than Earth so the gravity is higher."

"Will that hurt us?" Mom asked.

John answered, "It will be uncomfortable at first, but your body will adjust to a new gravity. There's medical technology that will help in the adjustment."

"What kind of people live there?" I asked.

"The race that lives on the planet is called 'Sekhmetians,' John said. "They are a humanoid hybrid species that have both feline and human characteristics. They have a human body with a proportionally balanced lion's head. The males have thick tan-colored hair with a matching colored beard resembling a lion's mane. Their eyes are large and yellow, and they have a wide-shaped feline face. The males' faces are wider and more rugged, and the females' faces are softer and more streamlined. The women have long hair that they traditionally wear braided or cut short. The males stand about 5'8" and the women about 5'5". The women are both athletic and feminine, but not as muscular as the males."

"They sound kind of scary," I said.

"They can be intimidating when you first meet them," John said, "but they are surprisingly kind and compassionate too."

"That's good;" I said, "at least we know we don't have to be afraid of them."

Mom asked, "What other characteristics do they have?"

John answered, "The Sekhmetians are powerfully built. They have retractable claws on their hands and feet with excellent muscle tone, and look very formidable. The Sekhmetians are highly intelligent like humans, but ferocious like lions. They've been on the planet since what would be the early 1800s in our time."

Dad said, "I'm glad they're on our side!"

"Yes," John said, "it took a number of years to build a positive relationship with them."

John continued, "The Sekhmetians originally came from the time-space dimension, which is an alternate reality of ours, space-time. The two worlds interact with each other on a regular basis. At certain times of the year, portals open up, and any being can cross over at that time. These overlap events explain how travel is possible back and forth.

"In time-space, they are aware of us, but most people in our culture are not aware of them. Creatures like elves, fairies, gnomes, unicorns, dragons, and other mythological beings live in this alternate reality. When the portals open up, there are some creatures that cross over. There are many in our world who claim to have seen one or more of these beings."

"I want a unicorn!" I said.

Dad answered, "Jayna, you can't have a unicorn the same way as you can't have a pony."

"On the new planet," I said, "we might have some place to keep them!"

Mom interrupted, "Please you two, listen to John."

Mom looked at John and said, "Can you please keep going?"

"Certainly.

"In situations where ships, airplanes, and other types of vehicles have disappeared without a trace, it is believed they crossed over through an open portal and are living the rest of their lives out in time-space.

"Yeah," Dad said, "like the Bermuda triangle!"

Mom asked John, "so that's how they got there. Then what happened?"

John answered, "They waited until the pathway between the dimensions opened up, and the military escorted a group of 500 people to their new home on Planet Sekhmet.

I asked, "Why did they go there? Did they think that going there would be fun?"

"No, I don't believe so," John responded. "They had another reason to go there.

"Approximately two hundred years ago, they wanted to start a new civilization in the space-time dimension, which would allow them to see the effects of space-time on their technology. They would then be able to research the elements and properties of this universe. They desired a lawful and disciplined culture that would support personal progress, both scientific and spiritual.

"The Sekhmetian culture was peaceful and prosperous. Like their home planet, personal liberties were crucial. You had the freedom to do what you would like but could not infringe upon others' rights with criminal activity. The Sekhmetians' judicial system was swift and decisive, and serious criminal and dishonest activity were not tolerated.

In most cases, doing anything of this nature would end in losing the perpetrator's life. The Sekhmetian people achieved the proper balance of love and discipline, and their people flourished and realized their full potential.

"It sounds like they were trying to create a Utopia," Dad said.

"Yes, I would say so," John answered, "but it only lasted for a short time.

"In the early 1900s, Planet Sekhmet was visited by the Draconians. They were from Planet Reptilia Draconis, located in the Draco Constellation, and were an opportunistic race of beings. The Reptilian Draconians had turned so evil; they were thrown out of the Draco

Constellation. They then broke up into factions and separated, and started looking for worlds to exploit.

"What do these people look like?" I asked.

"The Draconians were a human/reptile hybrid and were as evil as they were intelligent. They had a humanoid body with a reptilian face, large green eyes with slits for pupils, and dark maroon-colored scaly skin. Throughout the rest of the solar system, they were notorious for mind-control technology. There also were some Draconians that were genetically modified to shapeshift. One of their factions came to Sekhmet.

"What did the Sekhmetians have that they wanted?" Dad asked.

"They were interested in the precious metals that the Sekhmetians produced from the planet. They manipulated the Sekhmetians into allowing them into their society and slowly took over their government and military. They presented themselves to the Sekhmetians as benevolent peace-loving space travelers. However, this was not the case.

"John," Mom asked, "the Sekhmetians were really strong people. How did this happen?"

"They used ancient spiritual technology that had been corrupted and turned into black magick to control the minds of others. They used this to take over government officials in key positions, and they were able to change the laws to benefit the Draconians. The Sekhmetians were being manipulated into believing that the rules were being changed to help them. But in reality, they were losing their sovereignty and had lost their rights to free speech and self-protection. The Draconians had become part of their armed forces; and had succeeded in taking positions of power which led to their society's downfall.

Mom said, "That's heart-wrenching!"

"Since the early 1900s, they tyrannized, plundered, and oppressed the Sekhmetians. The Sekhmetians were exhausted and at the end of their rope. They met in secret to discuss their options.

"Life was so painful for them. Freedom and prosperity were distant memories of the past, and the Sekhmetians longed for happier days. They organized resistance cells and searched for an answer to their dilemma.

"How did they take back their planet?" Dad asked.

"They had a device given to them from the Arcturians, the blue-skinned beings that inhabit Planet Arcturus. It's called the Crystal Cube. It's a three-inch by three-inch cube made from an alien crystal that is etched on the surface with geometric shapes and Arcturian writing.

"It has extraordinary abilities. The Cube is an invention that can help to retrieve information quickly. It's a repository of information, or in other words, a portable library. It stores all the information known to intelligent life in the universe, and the Arcturians are the only race in the galaxy capable of such technology.

"A Sekhmetian named Katet used the Cube to find a weapon that could take out the Draconians, but not to destroy the planet. He did find such a weapon, but it came with a serious warning. The weapon was called the scalar weapon. This device changes molecules in any given form of matter to any other desired form of matter."

"What happened?" I asked.

"Katet sought out the best Sekhmetian scientists to produce the scalar weapon. They did so, but all did not go as planned."

"And then?" I asked.

"This is what I was told years ago about Katet. It was the early 1900's on Planet Sekhmet. This hero was destined to liberate Planet Sekhmet, but he did not know it yet..."

On the day that Katet began the journey to free Sekhmet, he walked down the hallway toward the Arcturian ambassador's office. Boxes lined the side of the hall. The Draconians had ended communication with Arcturians weeks ago. The ambassador was to leave Sekhmet as soon as possible.

Two Draconian guards stood at the entrance of the ambassador's office.

"Why are you here?" the guard on the right asked in a gruff hiss. "Show me your ID."

Katet reached into the pocket inside his coat. He fumbled a moment getting the ID. Sekhmetians had to wear gloves in public to cover their claws for the safety of others. This was a mandate passed by the Draconian majority in the senate. Katet handed the guard his ID.

The Draconian on the left stared at the satchel that Katet was carrying.

"Should we search the satchel?" he asked the other guard.

"No," the other guard replied. "This fur comes here often. He is an envoy for the Sekhmetians' Foreign Relations Department. He was removed from the Military Research Division."

"They all look the same to me," the guard on the left said, baring his teeth. "Look how low he's fallen."

Katet's blood boiled. He wanted to rip the guard to pieces. The insults pushed him to the edge. But that would ruin the mission.

The guard on the right opened the door and stepped inside the office. Katet entered the room after the guard and *walked to the desk. Ambassador Crevan looked up to see Katet. Crevan stood up and motioned to him to sit.*

"Please sit. It's good that you came to see me off," Crevan said. "Even if it is on business."

"Yes, it is my friend. Here is the last group of documents to sign." Katet opened his satchel and retrieved some papers. He handed the paperwork to Crevan, who began signing the pages.

"The plant my wife gave you has grown large," Katet said.

A plant sat in a clear planter filled with water. The plant was about two-foot-tall with large lavender and light blue stripes running the length of the blooms. The pale green stalks had teardrop leaves. These stalks entered the water, and the roots clung to the sides of the planter.

"Would you be so kind to return the plant to her?" Crevan said. "That species is not allowed on my planet. It's too invasive and will take over the environment if allowed to."

"She will be disappointed, but she will understand," Katet answered. "Thank you."

"You're welcome," Crevan replied. "How has your meditations been progressing? Hopefully what I showed you helped immensely."

"Yes, it did, my friend," Katet said. "I now realize that my occupation was not my identity. When I first lost my position, I felt like I lost myself. Now I realize that what we do does not define who we are."

Katet gathered the papers and put them back into the satchel. He then took the plant from the top of the desk and walked towards the door.

The Draconian guard held his hand out to stop Katet from walking out the door.

Katet looked at him. "How can I help you?"

"Let me inspect what you're carrying,'"

Katet handed the guard his satchel, and the guard looked through the paperwork. The guard handed it back to Katet. He then inspected the plant and the vase and handed it back to Katet as well. The guard told Katet to carry on, and he walked out of the building and got into his car.

He started driving away towards his home. He checked his mirror often to be sure he's not being followed. He drove past his house towards the industrial park section of the city. When he got to his destination, he parked his vehicle along the side of the street. He then quickly glanced around and made sure he's not being followed. When he exited the car, he retrieved the satchel and the plant. He headed into what seems to be an abandoned warehouse. He walked towards the door on the other side of an otherwise empty room, entered the door, and went down the stairway leading to the basement area. He walked over to a shelf and reached behind it, and pressed a hidden button. The frame slid to the side and revealed a hidden room. He entered the room to find two Sekhmetians inside.

It was a large room with a metal desk with two people sitting at it, a male to the right and a female to the left. Past the desk, there was a large area with machinery and tools to fabricate machinery.

"Did you get it?" the male said.

"Yes, Ekon, I have it," Katet answered. He walked towards the desk, and as he passed a trash can, he dropped the satchel inside of it. "Isabis, your phony documents served us well."

Katet set the vase on the table. He tapped the rim of the vase, and it made a chime. He allowed the chime to ring to the end. He reached and grabbed the vase by the top and lifted it from the table. When he did this, the bottom of the vase deposited the Crystal Cube onto the table.

Ekon had been watching with great curiosity. "Katet, that's an interesting magic trick!"

"The vase is made from a crystal found on Planet Arcturus."

Katet told his companions he was going to go into his office to work with the Crystal Cube. Over the next few hours, Katet searched it to find a way to remove the Draconians from their planet. He found a weapon that used scalar technology to change or disrupt matter or energy, which could be used to destroy the Draconians.

Katet emerged from his office with good news. He explained to Ekon and Isabis what he had discovered. They immediately went to work constructing the scalar weapon. They all worked in shifts to not raise suspicions from their Draconian oppressors because there were patrols in this area twice a day.

For three months, the three of them worked on developing the device until they had perfected it. They ran emitters to the top of the warehouse that they were working in and disguised them the best way possible.

Before they could carry out their plan, a Draconian patrol with two officers spotted the disguised emitters and investigated the building. They watched Ekon walk down the stairs and followed him to the basement. They found the three Sekhmetians there with the device.

Ekon realized he was being followed and walked in a different direction down the hallway. One of the officers followed him, and Ekon quickly entered a nearby room. The officer followed him into it. Ekon attacked from behind the door, but the officer fired his weapon and hit him, which severed his right arm. Ekon grabbed his throat with his other hand and buried his claws deep within the Draconian's neck. The Draconian fired his weapon again, hitting Ekon in the chest, but Ekon held his grip on him. Ekon then fell to the floor and dragged the Draconian with him. Neither one of them survived the battle.

The second Draconian entered the room and opened fire on Katet and Isabis.

"Get down, Isabis!" Katet shouted.

But it was too late. She had already received a fatal energy blast to the chest.

Katet sprinted towards his enemy and pounced on him, knocking him to the floor. While Katet shredded him with his claws, the Draconian was able to fire one last shot into his stomach. Katet, in his last moment, fell to the ground and was able to crawl to the scalar weapon and activate it before succumbing to his injuries. Katet died covered with the blue blood of his enemy.

While the altercation was happening, random blaster fire had hit the scalar weapon, slightly altering its calibration before the device was activated. Despite this damage to the *device, it was still able to destroy the Draconians. They were disintegrated as the scalar weapon eradicated all Draconians from the planet and the surrounding heavens. A Draconian space station exploded at the same time.*

However, unbeknownst to the Sekhmetians, a rift in the space-time continuum has just occurred because of the scalar weapon's malfunction. This rift left Planet Sekhmet vulnerable to interdimensional invasion.

The rift drew the attention of an evil race from an alternate dimension called the Kemkaba people, also known as the Kemkabi. Now there was a problem that could potentially destroy the planet. They sent small groups of saboteurs to sow fear and hatred to use this negative energy to increase the size of the rift. Their ultimate goal was to pull the entire planet into their evil dimension.

The Kemkabi were humanoid beings filled with dark energy, with a matte texture to their skin. They were completely black, had white eyes, a broad nose, swept-back ears, and had no mouths. They could see perfectly in the dark. The males stood about six feet tall, the women about six inches shorter. They had three fingers with a thumb on each hand and had three toes on each foot with a large toe. They had crystalline hollow claws for sucking out their prey's energy and body fluids, thus killing them. Or worse, they could possess their victim and turn them into their acolyte and use them to inflict violence and trauma on others. These beings were called the Darkened.

The only way they could possess someone was if the person had been corrupted. If so, they would suck out their life force and body fluids, turning them into the Darkened. If the chosen victim was not corrupted, the Kemkabi could kill the victims but not possess their souls.

The Kemkabi could be killed, but they were stronger than humans, and it would require a powerful weapon of some kind to kill them. Only a well-trained and highly skilled warrior could successfully stand up to them. They were also impossible to reason with and had lost their ability to be self-governing.

They communicated through telepathy and could take shadow energy and materialize solid objects. They also could travel through and hide in shadows. They could move back and forth from the shadow realm into this dimension. They could also move from the shadow realm to the demonic realm and move back and forth. Their food sustenance was the shadow energy, and they could not go without it.

The Kemkabi came from an alternate reality that was utterly evil and desired to pull everything in creation into it. Once energy got sucked into these beings, it became a part of their group's soul. The entire soul was one being that absorbed all life into it, and every form the dark energy soul took was controlled by the one being. He was known, in human terms, as Satan/Lucifer, etc. The Kemkabi were hunters of dark energy for the Darkness. The more dark energy they consumed, the more powerful they became. They were a form of psychic vampires and were the embodiment of pure evil. They arrived from their alternative reality through the tear, and they were siphoning all the shadow and dark energy on Planet Sekhmet. The entire planet was being slowly pulled into their universe.

"On Planet Sekhmet, the average nighttime is sixteen hours, and the standard daytime is twelve hours. Now they've created an equal day to an equal night by siphoning the shadow energy of the nighttime. *Equinox* has now come to mean the movement on Planet Sekhmet to remove this parasitic entity feeding on the planet. This is the central issue Sekhmetians are currently facing. The authorities are warning Sekhmetians that a mandatory evacuation of Sekhmet may be necessary.

"Jayna, your job would be to stay ahead of their every move so that the authorities can stop them.

"I don't know how to do that!" I said.

"There's a teacher that can help you with that," John said.

"Are you sure we'll be safe?" I asked.

John answered, "The Sekhmetians assured us that it will be their highest priority to keep you and your family safe."

"Do you really think I can make that big a difference, John?"

"Yes," John said, "I do."

I turned to Mom and Dad and asked, "What do you think?"

Mom answered, "As long as we're safe, that's all that matters to me."

Dad then said, "Somebody needs to stop these evil beings."

At that age, I didn't fully understand what John had explained to us, but I knew if I didn't do something to stop the Kemkabi, I wouldn't be able to forget about the stories I had been told.

I took a deep breath and paused a moment. I felt a profound sense of longing to do what was right, but I had a strong sense of apprehension. This was not an easy decision to make, especially for an eight-year-old.

Dad asked, "What do you think, Jayna?"

"I'll do it."

"Are you sure?" Dad said.

"Yes," I answered.

"Okay, we'll move forward. I'll be in touch," John replied.

Moving On

The next day was Saturday, so Dad was home from work. Dad worked as a waiter in a restaurant in the business district of downtown New York City, and the restaurant was closed on the weekends. We loved it since it gave us all the weekends together. Mom and I were getting ready to go shopping for groceries and go about our usual Saturday routine when John arrived. We all sat down in the living room, and Mom then went into the kitchen to make him coffee. John waited until she returned to the living room before he began to speak.

"I have some news to share. I've been instructed to help you leave your home in Brooklyn and help the family relocate to Planet Sekhmet."

"How will we do this?" Dad asked.

"Marcello, first thing, a cover story has been created for you and your family to be able to leave your life here without creating any suspicion from family and friends. You are to tell everyone that you applied for a government position as a clerk and that you landed a job in Los Angeles. If anyone questions you, say that the position pays well and it was worth it for the family to move there. Then when you are done getting all your business in order and you are ready to leave, I will direct you on how to move to the next step."

"Which is?" Dad asked.

"I will escort you to the Cosmic Fountain and go with you to Planet Sekhmet. There will be a welcoming committee there to meet you and help you relocate."

"This is all happening very fast," Mom said.

"I won't have much time to spend with my friends before we leave," I said.

Dad said, "We have to figure out what we're taking, and what we're leaving behind."

It was done. The decision was made, and we proceeded to move forward. John helped my parents sell the house. This was a significant turning point for our family.

I was excited that I was moving to another planet but sad to leave the only home I'd ever known. I was sad to leave my friends too but I knew would be back to visit. I could tell that Mom was trying to hide how upset she was. There were times when she didn't know I was around, and I could feel how painful it was for her to leave our home. Dad seemed to have some anxiety, but he seemed a little less anxious about the move than Mom. The preparations moved forward.

When we were ready to leave, John picked us up in a town car. It didn't take long for everything we were taking with us to be loaded into the car. As we were driving away, I held Mom's hand. Mom and I cried as we left our home for the last time. I looked at Dad, and he looked sad, but he was looking out the window to hide his face from us. We were all apprehensive.

Mom turned to John. "Can you please tell us what's going on?"

"Natalie, this is a top-secret government program," John answered. "There is only so much we can discuss with you, but be assured you are in good hands."

John explained what the Cosmic Fountain looked like and what to expect when it was activated as we drove. We then went for a few hours and stopped to eat and refuel. We started going again and made it to Maryland before we took another break.

When we got to Ohio, John said, "It won't be long now."

It was late at night and very dark. John drove down a long gravel road through the country. The gravel road we were on entered a large tunnel that led into a cavern. We were not on a public road, and there were no other vehicles to be found. John had taken us to a location that was a secret government facility.

We drove deeper into the cavern. At one point, we passed large clear cylinders with giant humanoid bodies inside of them. Tubes were running from each cylinder connected to a large machine. I counted twenty. They looked otherworldly, and the entire experience seemed surreal.

Dad finally got the courage to ask John about the giants. "John, what are those giant bodies doing here?"

"They're ancient giants that are in stasis. Their race is called the Nephilim and they lived here on Planet Earth thousands of years ago."

"What is 'stasis'?" I asked.

"Stasis is when a person's body is suspended in time and not allowed to die. The idea is to reawaken the person at some future point," John said.

"The Nephilim are an ancient race of people who came to this planet thousands of years ago from Planet Malus in the Black Eye Galaxy," John continued. "This race of giants was given the name Nephilim. They are the descendants of the fallen angels. The Nephilim's physical bodies were enormous in comparison to ours; they stood around thirty feet tall. They were knowledgeable, and had excellent technological capabilities from their genetic memory passed on to them by their fallen angel ancestors. They created a culture that was all about raping and plundering other races from other worlds. Due to their great size and technological knowledge, they were very tough to fight. Many suffered through their atrocities until the Galactic Alliance had to come to put a stop to their plundering. They were such an abomination to so many that the Alliance decided to send the worst of them to Planet Earth, a beautiful and healing planet. The hope was that the Earth itself would help them heal the evil in their hearts, and they would eventually decide to plunder no more. They are the ancient giants that are mentioned in The Bible and other religious texts.

Dad said, "Then we need to make sure that they never become animated again."

"There's a plan to move them to another location," John said, "but it will take probably twenty years to be able to do so."

"Why doesn't the government just destroy them?" I asked.

John answered, "It's not that easy. Our government is trying to find some way to use them to its advantage. There are people with some crazy ideas in our government."

"You mean like people that think we need more nuclear bombs to blow up the planet hundreds of time?" Dad asked.

"Exactly!" John answered.

Dad asked, "What did these Nephilim do in the past?"

John answered, "When they came to Earth, they immediately organized themselves and formed communities. At that time, there were other humanoid races on Planet Earth as well that were inhabiting the planet. However, they were the size of humans today. They were not nearly as big or as strong as the Nephilim. The Nephilim, being a greedy and opportunistic race, managed to enslave the human population on Planet Earth."

"How did the humans deal with them?" Mom asked.

John replied, "The human slaves were suffering quite a bit and organized themselves for a rebellion. Well, they had their revolution, but it didn't go well for them. The rebels were all killed, and those that remained were the complacent and compliant ones. This victory led the Nephilim to become even more violent and more oppressive than they already were. Atrocities became the norm, and life on Planet Earth was unbearable for the surviving humans.

"The humans organized themselves again, this time in prayer, praying for the defeat of their oppressors. The humans yearned to be able to reclaim their freedom. Within a few years time, they received the answer to their prayers. The great flood that is mentioned in the Bible and other culture's legends took place. A small group of Nephilim fled to the Cosmic Fountain in Ohio and went back to Planet Malus. The rest of them were destroyed in the floods.

"Too bad it didn't get all of them," Dad said.

"The Nephilim waited on Planet Malus until the waters had receded. They sent a team of scientists with the original group that traveled through the Cosmic Fountain and created what you see here, a generator that has tubes going to each cylinder to maintain perfect temperature and oxygen levels to sustain the stasis. The machines are powered by magnetic generators. There is literally no end to the amount of power that it can make for free."

"Then why would we pay for electricity if it could be generated for free?" Dad asked.

"That's a really good question," John said. "The answer lies in Earth's ancient history. Thousands of years ago in the time of Atlantis, there was a battle between two groups of people. One group had the technology that created free electricity and were of the Light. The evil group used resources to create electricity so they could profit from it. This is the same technology we use today. The two groups fought bitterly and eventually the evil group won. This is why energy is not free."

This is so interesting, I thought. I looked at Mom and she looked dumbfounded.

"So why are the Nephilim here in stasis?" Dad asked.

"Another really good question," John said. "Eventually, the magnetic field of the Earth will be weakened enough that the generators will cease to function."

Dad asked, "What would cause that?"

John answered, "Nuclear testing has damaged the magnetosphere. Eventually, humans will create a technology that will damage it where the Nephilim will awaken from their stasis."

"How do you know this?" Dad asked.

John said, "We are always creating things and researching information that should be left alone."

"That's creepy!" I said.

"With rising political, economic, and environmental collapse, these dark forces will drive madness and mayhem all over the planet. They plan on starting the cycle all over again, and *this time* they plan on winning the battle for control over Planet Earth and its resources. That's why they have the glass cylinders near the Cosmic Fountain. When the Nephilim reawaken, one of them will go through the Cosmic Fountain to bring an army back to conquer the Earth. If they wait until World War III, when there is utter chaos on the planet in every imaginable way, combined with the lack of unity in Earth's populace, they stand a much better chance of taking over the planet and its resources."

"I have a question, John. How do we know all this information is true?" I asked.

"You're absolutely right!" he said. "How could we know? Well, we know from our contacts from other planets. They have proven themselves to be great allies and are always dependable. We have never gotten any misinformation from them that we can tell, so we assume they always give us accurate information. They are the Arcturians from Planet Arcturus that I mentioned to you earlier. More on them later."

There was dead silence, and we were in shock. This was not what we expected. John finally stopped the car. and we got out. "Let's get your luggage, we're here," he told us.

We looked around and only saw a large square with steps going down to some unknown destination.

"Where are we?" I asked John.

"We're at the Cosmic Fountain!"

We grabbed our luggage.

John turned to us and smiled and said, "Are you ready?"

We followed John, and he led us to the Cosmic Fountain.

There it was! He led us down the steps into the Cosmic Fountain's entrance. It looked exactly as he had described. There was a five-foot path that led to a round platform that was approximately eight feet in diameter. A five-foot water-like fluid surrounded it.

John led us onto the circular area of the device, and we knew what to expect. A many-hued prismatic energy came up from the fluid. It looked like a kaleidoscope of colors and shapes. In a few seconds, the figure of a woman formed within the energy.

"Destination please?" she said in a soft feminine voice.

"Planet Sekhmet," John said.

Instantly, the fountain's energy surrounded us, and I felt tingling all over my body. The experience only lasted about 30 seconds, but it felt longer.

We found ourselves at the bottom of a staircase as the fountain's energy gradually dissipated. At the top of the stairs was our destination planet, Planet Sekhmet.

"We're here, let's go!" John said.

We follow him up the stairs. I knew this was a moment I would never forget, the moment I first looked at Planet Sekhmet. We were on a hilltop in the countryside, and it looked a lot like Earth. Then, as I looked to the right, there were four Sekhmetians standing there waiting for our arrival. The lion people sure were sure an interesting sight for an eight-year-old!

Upon first look, I had to get used to their unusual appearance. After all, they had a human body with a lion's head. I was surprised, though, by how expressive their faces could be. Their features still had some human characteristics.

"The Sekhmetian women are very pretty!" Mom remarked.

Two male and two female officers greeted us. They were from the Sekhmetian military and wore a type of black uniform. They introduced themselves to us. Their names were Zamuel, Akiva, Tabanica, and Valora. They were very professional and courteous and seemed happy to see us. I felt welcomed by them, and my parents also seemed to respond positively to them.

They escorted us to a human settlement called Sirius. The housing development was very beautiful, and the homes were similar to those built on Planet Earth. Akiva explained this was done on purpose to help their Earth friends to feel more comfortable. He also explained how the use of magnetic generators powers the homes' utilities. All electricity was free on Planet Sekhmet. They also captured rainwater and used it for all household needs. Sewage was treated and then safely recycled back into the environment. This system did not create any pollution. The Sekhmetians had strict disciplines for environmental preservation so that the atmosphere felt pristine. The respect and reverence for the environment were intricately intertwined in their culture. They considered all-natural resources gifts from the Goddess. Planet Earth could sure learn from them!

Our home was a three-bedroom, seven-room house that had a basement. The home was beautiful on the inside, clean and efficient, and it was a comfortable place to move into. Wooden floors and cabinets, a modern kitchen, and even a skylight over the dining area made the house very attractive. We were all pleasantly surprised because the furniture was rustic. All beddings, towels, soaps, everything that we needed were provided to us as well. A beautiful flowery smell permeated the house. The Sekhmetians went to a great deal of trouble to make us as welcome and comfortable as possible.

Mom and I liked the soap they provided. The soap came in round bars, and they had a beautiful floral scent that left your skin feeling silky smooth.

These soap bars would make great Christmas gifts, I thought, *but how would I explain where I got them?*

We unpacked our bags and made ourselves comfortable. What a lovely home! The sense of excitement and anticipation began to overwhelm me. How extraordinary was all of this, and what did the Sekhmetians have planned for me? Who would I be working with, and would our work be successful?

Yashi

During the next day, we heard a knock on our door. When I rushed to the door to see who it could be, I found our Sekhmetian Representative on our front step. It was her job to see to our needs and concerns. This beautiful Sekhmetian woman was called Xantha. What was striking about her beauty was the fur color on her head. It was a beautiful light shade of golden blonde, a lighter shade than the other Sekhmetians. She wore it well, and it gave her a distinct and unusual look. She was a kind and gracious woman who made us feel loved and cared for.

"Good morning, how is everything?" she asked.

"We're fine, Xantha," Mom said. "We were just finishing our breakfast."

Xantha was invited into the house, and we all sat down on the couches. She turned to my parents. "We have an instructor for Jayna stopping by later on this afternoon for their first meeting. Her name is Yashi and she is one of our most revered teachers. She's from Planet Arcturus. The curriculum here is more advanced than on Earth. She's going to tutor Jayna until she's ready to begin school here in Sekhmet. She's also going to help her to develop her other abilities as well."

Xantha told my parents that there would be a neighborhood meeting tomorrow, and we were invited to attend. She discussed how this was normal for new arrivals on Sirius. She stayed a little longer and then left. She left us a pamphlet with her contact information and reminded us she was only a phone call away. After Xantha went, it seemed like an eternity until Yashi showed up.

She arrived at around 4:00 pm, and my father answered the knock at the door.

"Welcome Yashi. Please come in," Dad said.

"It's a pleasure to meet you!" Mom added.

When Yashi walked through the door, her presence was divine indeed. She was a great beauty and had a gentle and loving demeanor. She literally could calm others without saying a word. She only needed to spend time with them. Her presence was so comforting, and I was immediately happy with her.

"Hello, Jayna," she said, smiling.

"Hello, Yashi, it's nice to meet you," I replied.

She wore a diamond necklace and headband with a diamond in the center. Ordinary women did not wear these kind of precious stone adornments. She was as poised as a queen, and her platinum blonde hair was styled with soft curls, which accentuated her beauty. She was about 6' tall, slender, and had blue skin like all of the Arcturians. She wore a purple flowing gown.

Yashi stayed for a couple of hours and discussed the upcoming school year's curriculum. She also talked about the spiritual issues we were to address in the future.

"Jayna," she said. "Do you know what prayer and meditation are?"

"Well," I said, "I know I say prayers to God, so that must be talking to God. But I don't know what meditation is."

"That's okay," she said. "You are right. Prayers are *talking* to God, and meditation is *listening* to God. We want to be sure we are listening too!"

Being eight years old, she was slowly introducing me to the role that was destined for me and all the preparatory work that was required for me to succeed in my soul's mission. She made it clear that I was going to be strictly disciplined and there was a great deal of schoolwork ahead of me. Be that as it may, I was still so excited and couldn't wait to begin.

"Yashi, I'm so happy to be here working with you!" I said.

"Jayna," Yashi said with a smile, "your enthusiasm for the Light is one of the reasons why you were selected for the role you've been given. Also, Father God chose you and your soulmate to lead as warriors in this upcoming spiritual battle. Both of you will strictly follow the Light's direction."

"How do you know about my soulmate?" I asked.

Yashi answered, "I have gifts as well. One of my abilities is can see other people's soulmates. Now that I am close to you, I can have a more accurate reading,

"Your soulmate's name will be Landry, and he's due to be born in 1970. You will be twelve years older than him. Father God has decided what your roles will be in this spiritual war, and you both will be given the right conditions to meet. The two of you will be warriors in a critical time in history. This is in your soul contract.

"A soul contract?" I asked.

Yashi answered, "This is an agreement that a soul makes with the Creator before being born.

"There's much to say about this subject, too much to go into at this time. However, we will be discussing this subject again when you are older. Now it is important for you and your parents to go through a period of adjustment, and later we may use the time for such in-depth discussions."

"Yashi," I asked, "can you tell me about yourself? Are you married? Do you have children?"

"Certainly, Jayna," Yashi answered. "Your curiosity is normal. I was born on Planet Arcturus in the year 1539, which would make me 480 years old in Earth years. On Arcturus, we generally live to be about 1,000 years old. Due to various factors, we don't age the same way your race does. We have a different genetic makeup. And we don't have the same environmental pollution that plagues Planet Earth. Plus, we have far greater technology that allows us to live out a much longer lifespan."

"You don't look like you're ancient!"

"What kind of school did you go to?"

"I went to what you would call a 'seminary' and was trained in the spiritual arts and sciences."

"I never heard of spiritual sciences before."

"That's one of the more important things I'm going to be teaching you."

Were you ever married?"

"Yes," she said. "I married a man named Rahmi Onan when I was in my twenties. We had two children, and then four grandchildren, and then ten great grandchildren and so on. At this time, we have a total of 623 decedents, and we're still together after all these years!"

"That's a long time to be with somebody. Do you see your husband often?"

"We see each other a few times a month," she answered. "We are both busy with our jobs, but we always make time to be alone. We're very fond of each other and cherish our time together."

"What does he do?"

"Rahmi is an Arcturian ambassador on Planet Alcyone, which is located in the Pleiades star cluster."

"That's so incredible!" I said.

"Yes, he is indeed blessed. God gave him a great gift for diplomacy, and he does well in his position."

"When I get older, I want to travel among the stars!" I said.

"Jayna, would you like to do some travelling tomorrow?"

My eyes widened with curiosity. "What do you mean?"

"Well, we have a guided tour scheduled for tomorrow. We always welcome our newcomers with a tour of Sirius.

At lunchtime, we'll stop at a Pizzeria. And yes, we do have pizza on Planet Sekhmet. We found that pizza is very popular among Americans and it helps to make them feel at home. Then, after the tour, we all go out to a restaurant to have dinner. We even have Sekhmetian chefs that can cook American, Italian, Chinese, Japanese, and Greek food. Our staff enjoys serving guests from Planet Earth."

"Great! I'm looking forward to it," I said.

"Alright, Jayna, I'll leave you on that note," she said. "I'll be back next week to begin working with you. Have fun tomorrow!"

"I will," I said. "A tour on another planet is something I could hardly imagine!"

Incredible joy ran through me. It felt like this was the right place for me. Yashi was one of the greatest blessings I've ever received.

Tour of Sekhmet

The next day, the welcoming committee at The Cosmic Fountain came to pick us up. They were in a dark blue vehicle that closely resembled a bus, and Tabanica came up to our door to escort us into the bus. We all exchanged greetings and pleasantries as our tour began.

The tour was no less than extraordinary. The Sekhmetians created a city that was metropolitan-looking with an artistic flair. There were businesses with colorful storefronts, beautiful homes made of wood and stone, and lovely gardens. If I didn't know I was on Planet Sekhmet, the city could have passed for a town in the USA. So far, we just stayed in the city of Sirius, but my curiosity was peaked. What do the cities and towns of Planet Sekhmet look like? Is the architecture the same, or do they have their own style? How about their businesses? Do they have storefronts like we do? I didn't want to interrupt the tour, so I decided to wait until the right moment to ask.

We spent the day driving around touring the city, and we stopped at a pizzeria for lunch.

Good pizza, I thought. *Pizza is one of my favorite foods.*

When we were done touring, we were taken to a restaurant called the Diner, and our dinner was unforgettable. The food was delicious. We ordered Chinese food. It was very authentic, and we couldn't tell the difference between their food and ours.

The best part of the experience, however, wasn't the food. We met other residents from Planet Earth there, and we began to make friends. Such interesting people! There were a group of musicians there that night that told us they were going to put on a concert the following week. They were a '60s rock 'n' roll band, with the name *The Psychedelic Sun.* They all wore psychedelic tie-dye outfits and looked the part of '60s rockers with loud clothes and scraggly hair.

How amazing, I thought. *Rock 'n' roll on Planet Sekhmet!*

There were five of them. The lead singer's name was Jimmy, and his bandmates' names were Mike, Tony, Bill, and Tommy. We asked them to pull their table close to ours so we could talk to them. They were very friendly and accepted our invitation.

"So, fellas," Dad said, "please tell us about yourselves! We're interested in your story."

"Sure," Jimmy said. "We'd love to share."

"Sure, sure," the other fellas said.

"We're all children of Sirius' older generation," Jimmy said as he leaned back in his chair. "Our parents were all chosen to participate in this program due to their great musical talent and arrived on Planet Sekhmet in the early part of the 1940s. Back then, we were all toddlers.

"In the late 1950s, we all got together and decided we wanted to form our own rock 'n' roll band. We were particularly interested in the growing counterculture movement in the United States and Britain in the early 1960s. We decided to experiment with music and came up with what would later be considered a new sound. We wrote the song *The Cosmic Circus* and the song made its way back to Planet Earth through intermediary channels. It became a smash hit single in 1962. Other rock bands were inspired to write similar types of music. The song originated a new genre of music called 'psychedelic music.' It became the rave among teens and young adults."

"I remember it, that's a really cool song!"

Tony played the drumbeat of the song on the table, and Jimmy sang the chorus. Dad and Mom started talking to them about the music that was being created on Sekhmet. The band then asked them about the music scene on Earth. They spoke for the next hour and a half. We all had a wonderful time.

We made a date to meet again in a couple of weeks to see a concert and then go to dinner afterward. We got the information for the show, and Mom and Dad looked very happy. This gave us something fun to look forward to.

On the car ride home, however, Dad and Mom weren't saying much.

"Why is everyone so quiet?" I asked.

Mom answered, "That experience reminded me of being around the table with family."

"Tonight," Dad added, "reminded me of working with the guys in the restaurant. I wonder how they're doing."

There was sadness in their voices. It seemed that the reminiscing we did at dinner reminded them of home. I thought about my friends on the block and also felt a little homesick.

"Brooklyn is still really fresh in my mind," Mom said.

Dad said, "It hasn't been that long since we left. It's going to take some time to get used to being here."

When the time came, we went to the concert and out to dinner at an Italian restaurant owned by Sekhmetians. We all had a good time. Sirius was starting to feel more like home. There was a strong sense of community in this settlement, which helped us to feel accepted. Everyone was beginning to feel like family.

Dad asked Mom, "What did you think about the food, honey?"

"It's okay," Mom answered.

"Exactly. It's okay, but not really good," Dad said.

"Dad," I said, "why don't you and Mom open up your own restaurant? You both love to cook and we could all get together in the restaurant and have fun like we did tonight. What do you say?"

"Jayna," he said, "owning a restaurant is a lot of work. Your mother and I would have to decide if that's how we want to spend our time."

"You saw how much fun we all had tonight. Would you consider it?"

"Jayna," Mom said, "you have a good idea. Why don't you let your Father and I decide if we want to take on the responsibility of owning a restaurant?"

"Okay," I said.

After about a week, my parents decided to go forward and open up an Italian cuisine restaurant. Dad's cooking was excellent, and Mom could hold her own. I felt confident the community would love and support their business. They decided to call the restaurant *The Italian Bistro*.

We all went to work to create our Italian restaurant with a homey feel. It was fun for us to work out all the details and present it to our new community. The project also brought us into contact with many of the city's people and, as time went on, we made more and more friends.

So far, our experience on Planet Sekhmet was a joyful one, with the only downside being us leaving our family and friends behind. The Sekhmetians allowed us to go through the Cosmic Fountain back to Ohio from time to time to visit with family and keep up the illusion of our supposed move to LA. Our visits also kept our family from searching for us or drawing any attention to our disappearance. No one we knew on Planet Earth was any the wiser to our true mission. Quite a feat indeed.

Once we made the transition to our new situation, life here was joyful and exciting. We made many new and exciting friends. All of us were glad to have the chance to see life on another planet, and better grasp of the true history of Planet Earth. The truth had been kept from the Earth's population on purpose due to the spiritual darkness overtaking their planet. If only they knew the truth!

My work was just beginning.

The Work

Yashi took an apartment on the same street that we lived on so that she could be close by to tutor me. The following week, we began our study. We worked in the living room, which slowly transformed into our work-study room. The space was light and airy, and we sat comfortably on the couches to resume my studies. We used the coffee table for our books.

While being well educated, Yashi was also a kind and patient teacher. The first year of my studies began with all the subjects an eight-year-old would study, but we moved quickly through the material. Yashi was very meticulous and wanted to be sure I could perform well academically. She made sure I knew all the subject material and left no stone unturned. At the end of every workweek, she spent the last day of the week covering only religious and spiritual topics.

There was also the issue of my psychic ability. Every day for one hour, I was taught to sit still and pray and meditate. It was called my "quiet time." Afterward, Yashi would test me with ten cards of different geometric symbols. I was asked to tell her what card she had chosen. If one of my answers were wrong, she never scolded me. But only when I could successfully answer all ten cards correctly would we move on to other questions regarding the Kemkaba people and their next move.

These sessions did prove helpful. I was able to use my psychic ability to tell the Sekhmetians where the Kemkabi would strike next. They were targeting different people in government agencies and the military. We were able to stop any further infiltration. So far, our mission was successful. The Kemkabi were being held back. However, the bigger problem was stopping them from pulling the planet into the rift from the already generated negativity, which was ever increasing.

After I progressed, I had started concentrating on the Kemkabi to see their next move. I saw a Sekhmetian military officer carrying a briefcase from one of their military installations. I could see that he had some of the characteristics of the Darkened. I also could see his uniform and make out his name tag as well. He was using a device to hide his actual appearance. A few moments later, he met with a human Darkened and said, "The device is ready. You can take it to the movie theatre."

I followed the man's path to the movie theatre. I watched him enter it and sit down in the back as the movie played. He placed the briefcase on the floor, opened it up, and activated some kind of device. This device emitted an energy that I hadn't seen before. Moments later, I understood what the device was designed to do.

Shortly after, I heard a man say, "Why don't you move your big head out of the way!" to the person sitting in front of him. Another person responded, "Why don't you just shut your mouth and watch the movie!" Then, people start arguing and cursing at each other. A brawl ensued, and chaos erupted across the movie theatre. This weapon was worse than a bomb. It caused people to become hateful and violent, which could lead to becoming Darkened.

I came out of my trance and was able to tell Yashi what I had seen, and Yashi had relayed the information back to the Sekhmetian military so that they could keep the officer under surveillance and stop the attack.

Every time we stopped one of the Kemkabi's plans, they weren't able to use the dark energy to further their agenda. We were able to keep the night and day hours on the planet equal, so the Kemkabi didn't get any further. They were trying to create mayhem any way they could and were primarily successful in further corrupting the already corrupted Sekhmetians. The spiritual darkness on the planet was still increasing, albeit a little bit slower. The ongoing battle was still tricky.

Yashi and the Sekhmetians were doing everything they could to make this experience as pleasant as possible for my parents and me. They felt this was important for the overall success of this project.

Yashi and I worked hard and, after six months, I was able to enter the elementary school in Sirius. The first year of my stay on Planet Sekhmet was full of school, spiritual study, and playtime with other Planet Earth children. The Sekhmetians were very careful not to do anything that would stunt my natural development. Making friends and learning social skills were part of their program. The other children were very intelligent and friendly, and I slowly began to bond with them. They were kind to me and accepted me as their friend. Their warm welcome and appreciation were critical to my successful adjustment to the new environment.

Initially, I did miss my old school friends from Brooklyn, but I gradually began to adjust to the new situation. The Sekhmetians were very sensitive to my emotional and educational needs. Their culture was designed to help children grow to their fullest potential. Healthy childhood friendships were an integral part of emotional development and maturity in a growing child. Children are raised to believe harmony with one's environment was a key element to a happy and successful life.

One of the children, Cecilia, became my best friend. We would go on walks together, played games together, and told each other our secrets. She had blonde hair and blue eyes and was a beautiful child. But she was very mischievous. She would hide other kids' books from them and play pranks on them as well. She was disciplined a few times for her behavior, but despite being a nuisance at times, Cecilia was always there for me.

One day at lunch, Cecilia asked, "Do you want to come over my house after school?" My Dad just got the new season of 'Bewitched' and 'My Favorite Martian' on the LaserDisc recordings."

'My Favorite Martian' is funny," I said, "but if people only knew the truth, they would lose their minds!"

Cecilia answered, "They're not as cool as we are. We live on an alien planet and they don't even know we're here!"

"There are plenty of cool people back on Earth," I said, "But just because they don't know what we know, doesn't make us any better than them." I felt sorry for Cecilia because she didn't have somebody to teach her how not to be judgmental.

"Whatever," she said.

"I can't come over after school because I have to go home and do my training with Yashi," I said.

"Don't you have enough training by now?" Cecilia asked. "What do you do?"

I answered, "I practice meditation, I work on my precognitive abilities, and I train to use my telekinetic abilities."

"That doesn't sound very exciting. What else do you do?"

"Yashi teaches lessons on spiritual matters," I answered, "so that I can control my anger and not be so judgmental."

"Why don't we go play on the swing set?" Cecilia asked. "Because that's about as much fun as I think you are going to have today!"

Cecelia didn't understand that I enjoyed the time I spent with Yashi because I learned important things.

We pushed each other on the swing set. I like playing with Cecilia even though we different. She was still my best friend.

The Work

Life was pleasant, and I enjoyed my routine. Yashi explained I was being prepared for my life's work. She was brought into the project to mentor me, and help me develop special abilities. Her main focus with me was divine connection. We talked about things like telekinesis, spiritual healing, pyrokinesis, and divination. She emphasized that all spiritual gifts result from divine connection and are to be respected as such. For instance, if someone were to develop special abilities for the sake of fame and fortune, they would create heavy karma, and ultimately destroy their life. All spiritual gifts are to be used properly; there was a severe warning on this subject. Father God heavily disciplined those who misused such powers. Yashi made it clear that if I ever misused my gifts, she would no longer work with me, and would remove me from the project. I assured her it would never happen. I gave my solemn word, and I intended to keep it. I made a promise to her and myself; I would never sell out! Never!

I was grateful for all that Yashi taught me. I wanted to have the same peaceful presence that she projected. Always calm, always positive, and never nervous or upset. What a challenge to be like her! She was a great role model for me, and I would always be better for knowing her. I prayed every night God would help me develop my skills and progress to the next level of development. I strived to do my best in all the exercises that she gave me.

Over the next four years, my training intensified and my abilities improved drastically. A new device was about to be introduced to me by Yashi that changed the way I saw everything.

Make Light of It

When I was twelve years old, Yashi spoke to my parents about putting me on a vegetarian diet. She said not eating meat would help me in my work. My parents said that wouldn't be a problem, so I was weaned off of it to help me in my next phase of development.

One day Yashi came to the house. We went to the living room, and she said, "I have brought something with me that I think you're capable of working with."

She retrieved a three-inch by three-inch crystal cube from her bag.

"What's that?" I asked.

"It's called the Crystal Cube," she answered.

"Where did it come from?"

"It came from Arcturus. It's a device made from a very special type of crystal from my home world."

Yashi then presented the Cube to me, and I took it from her. Holding the Cube, I could see there were geometric patterns on its surface. As I focused on them, they began to emanate a light blue glow. Yashi said concentrate, and reach out with your mind. I tried to follow her instructions, but it was more difficult than I thought it would be.

"Relax," Yashi said, "and allow the connection to take place."

The more I tried, the more difficult it became. I started to get aggravated.

Yashi said, "You must let go and be in the moment. Don't try to anticipate what will happen. Allow the energy of the Cube and your energy to form a pathway.

I concentrated on the Cube again, mentally reached out to it, and did not force the connection. I was in the state of "being," and that's when the link happened,

The Cube's glow became brighter, and I could now feel the power flowing between myself and it. I thought, who created this? I then heard in my mind the name *Vayu*.

"Vayu created the Cube. It told me!" I said to Yashi.

"It can do much more," she answered. "Why don't you observe him when he made the Cube?"

As soon as I thought it, I saw a man in my mind that I knew was Vayu. He was cutting a large piece of crystal with a tool. He worked proficiently and, an hour later, the Cube had been cut to size. He then started carving the geometric symbols on its surface. I saw energy flowing from him through the tools he was using into the Cube. After he was done carving, he placed the Cube on top of a machine. He then walked over to a computer and typed a command, and information started downloading into the Cube. It began to glow with the same blue energy as the information was being transferred into it.

He walked back to the Cube and held his hand over as it received more information. The energy transferred from Vayu into the Cube, and it slowly floated into the air and hovered underneath his outstretched hand.

I heard Yashi's voice, so I pulled my attention back from the Cube to hear what she was saying.

"So how was the experience Jayna?" Yashi asked.

"It was like I was there," I answered. "I'm sorry I was there so long; you must have been waiting here for hours!"

Yashi answered, "No, it was mere moments. Time moves at a different pace when you are linked with the Cube."

"He was able to make the Cube float!" I said.

Yashi said, "I know you can do that too."

"I would have to concentrate," I said, "to lift the Cube, and use its powers as well. I don't think I could do both at the same time."

"Don't worry," Yashi said, "if you experience difficulty. It's not about succeeding or failing, it's about connection."

I said, "Alright."

I reached out with my mental energy to cause the Cube to float in the air. I concentrated on making the Cube hover. I then tried to link my mind to it, but the Cube started to slowly drop to the floor. A moment later, I was able to succeed in creating a link between us, and by doing so, this intensified my telekinetic ability. It became easy for the energy to flow through my mental pathways. The Cube raised back up into the air.

"I'm doing it!"

"You're doing great!"

"What else can the Cube do?"

Flashes of knowledge entered my mind. The Cube could be used to enhance my psychic ability to see the past, present, and future. It showed me Vayu healing somebody with the Cube.

The Cube almost seems to have an intelligence of its own. As soon as a question entered my mind, the answer seemed to already be there. I sensed that the Cube held a vast amount of information like a universal library.

I heard Yashi's voice say, "I think that's enough for the day; you should rest."

Yashi put her hand under the Cube, and I allowed it to fall into her hand as I severed the link to it.

***

As time went by, I kept practicing, and I eventually mastered my abilities. In the early years of my training, Yashi specifically focused on developing my character. Honesty, integrity, kindness, respect, harmony, selflessness, and truth-seeking were the key qualities that she worked to instill in me. She was as no-nonsense as she was kind and, at times, did show her stern side. She warned about selfishness and prideful behavior and the disciplines given when one is prone to such behavior. When I was fourteen, we had a rather tough conversation about the subject.

"Yashi, how do you discipline bad behavior in children?" I asked.

"Why do you ask?"

"Just curious."

"I'm glad you asked me this question," Yashi said. "I've been waiting to address this with you. You have been very well behaved so far and have not needed discipline, but you can also be rebellious and hot tempered if you feel someone is trying to control and dominate you. It's not too hard to bring out the worst in you."

"Why do you say that? I asked her.

"You were born with an indomitable will. This is an issue to be addressed."

"Yes, please continue…"

"Do you remember you told me about the time your mother scolded you for playing with the light switches when you were seven years old? You told me you were very angry and upset that your mother wouldn't allow you to do what you wanted. Do you remember?"

"Yes."

"To ignore her authority over you, when she left the room, you went back to the light switches and kept turning them on and off. You were not going to let her stop you from doing what you wanted to do. This is a critical issue in your life. Your indomitable will surfaces if anyone tries to control you.

"Your mother did not understand this about you, and felt that she was doing her job properly as a parent. She felt it was her right to scold you. She is the parent and you are the child. In her mind, that means you are subordinate to her and her will. In her blindness, she could not see that you would only become rebellious from her scolding, and you would continue your behavior even worse than before. This is something for you to understand. The Creator gave you an indomitable will for a reason, but if you are not handled properly, you could become angry and rebellious and behave badly. But on the other hand, if you have improper behavior, it will be a poor reflection of you and not on others. Do you see?"

I realized what she was saying. I pondered it intensely for a moment, and then answered her. It's not easy to take responsibility for your bad behavior.

"Yes, I do understand," I answered. "But I do have a question."

"Yes?"

"So, the Creator give me an indomitable will, but why is my indomitable will so important?" I asked.

"The Creator sent you to be a warrior for the Light. You will have to deal with very difficult and evil people in your life, and you will have to be steadfast against their power. You are naturally confident in your abilities, that is your divine gift. However, you must mature and not be angry and rebellious. I have been particularly careful not to be bossy or domineering with you, because if I were, you would surely rebel. This quality in you could be very positive if used properly, or very negative if you cannot learn to handle difficult and arrogant people. You will naturally rebel to any kind of controlling behavior. But, on the other hand, you must learn to be patient and tolerant of others' weaknesses. This will come in time, it's a natural part of the maturation process. I'm trying to help you understand the gifts you possess or the Darkness will wreak havoc through you. They want you to become angry and lose your temper to bring out the darkness in you. This will help them to easily manipulate you. The spirit of evil is always looking for expression in this dimension. If you succumb to anger and impatience, you will indeed be used by the Darkness to bring about discord in your environment. That's why I was called in to work with you. You potentially could go negative yourself if you get too angry. The Arcturians are not prone to anger, and are a very patient people."

"Okay," I said. "But then how do you discipline children on Planet Sekhmet?"

"Now," she said, "I will address your question. I wanted to first bring up this subject to you so you will completely understand my job with you. My mission is to help you develop to your fullest potential, but with that, there is always a possibility of things not going as planned. You must understand this dynamic about your-self. It could be positive in the right situation, or it could be potentially harmful.

"The Sekhmetians are careful to administer discipline that is neither too lenient nor too harsh, and the it depends on the infraction. Disobedient children are not permitted to have playtime or entertainment time for a week. If the child is dishonest in any way, they are immediately taken to a counselor for therapy. The issue is, why do they feel it is necessary to speak a non-truth? We work to find out their hidden fear and resolve it. If they do anything harmful to another child, then they are given a spanking. We are only strict when necessary.

"We are very vigilant here in Sirius when it comes to raising children; we teach them to be honest and honorable. But, be that as it may, in recent times, the city of Sirius has had a problem with a growing number of its citizens being corrupted. And, of course, you are well aware of the situation with the Darkened. This is the very reason we brought you here to Sirius. We have long-term plans to use you as a comedic entertainer when you're older. This will inhibit their ability to draw negative energy from the planet's population.

"Jayna, remember when you won that talent contest as a young child for being funny?

"Yes," I replied.

"It's no coincidence that you were given comedic talent by the Goddess. She works through you so that you can make others laugh. You've never had to work at comedy because She was doing all the work. You simply allow yourself to be a conduit for the Divine. When you get older, you can use your comedic talent to make people laugh again. This can help to alleviate a great deal of spiritual darkness. *We are going to prepare you for your work, which is 'to make light of it!'* We did not tell this to you at first so as not to overwhelm you, but it was always the plan for you to be a public figure since you are so naturally funny. That laughter dispels the Darkness and the shadow energy that they feed off. This is another way you can disrupt the Kemkabi. When you are ready, we'll bring you to our public TV station. You'll have a comedy show where you will use your natural ability to make the whole planet laugh. That has been the plan all along. This can help defeat the Kemkabi as never before."

"There's great work ahead of me," I said. I was happy to think I was going to be able to make people laugh again.

"Yes," Yashi answered.

***

Time went by quickly, and before I knew it, it was time for high school. Sirius High School was the next step for me, and, in many ways, it was very similar to the high schools back on Earth. The Sekhmetians saw to it that our educational experience would closely resemble our culture as much as possible. The only real difference was the advanced curriculum offered. The Sekhmetian culture was more academically advanced than even the most prestigious schools on Earth. Plus, Sirius High School offered courses in Intergalactic Sociology, which taught students about various races throughout the universe. The school also did have all the activities that go along with high school, sports teams, hobby clubs, and social activities such as group dinners and outings.

Throughout my high school years, I did manage to maintain my friendship with Cecelia. We did our homework together on many nights. She outgrew her mischievousness and did not get into trouble any longer.

I had to learn many of the lessons via the computer, so my typing skills were very good and I learned how to work in various computer software programs. There was a lot of schoolwork given me, as Yashi said this was part of my curriculum. I wondered if Arcturian children were raised the same way. For such an advanced culture, there must be an enormous amount of information to be learned over the course of an education. I wondered what life was like on Planet Arcturus?

The Light and The Dark

Yashi and I were working together the following day, and I asked her about Arcturus.

"Yashi, can you tell me about the spiritual side of life on Arcturus?"

"Certainly," she responded. "Arcturus is an old planet; it's about 7 billion years old. It orbits the brightest star in the Bootes constellation. But, most importantly, we are a race of beings that are spiritually-oriented. We are all of the Light and are close to being angels. Because of our collective vibrational frequency, only light energy souls enter into fetuses. The light energy repulses the dark energy souls, so there is never a case where one slips through. Our culture has advanced to this point. There is no spiritual darkness on our planet. We've been successful in banishing shadow energy. The Darkness cannot work through us simply because we will not tolerate spiritual darkness in any form. That is the only way the Darkness can find an entry into someone's physical being.

"Children are raised with love and proper discipline, neither too little nor too much. We take raising children to be our greatest privilege, and teach them they are the embodiment of the Creator's light energy, Mother/Father God. Our joy is service, and our life experience is a pleasant one. No poverty or war exists on our planet, and we overcame disease a very long time ago. Ours is an ancient culture. Through all the millions and billions of years of evolution on Planet Arcturus, we have worked out every imaginable issue of conflict that could exist. We simply refuse to fight or argue about anything. If there is disagreement, we always find an amicable solution to the problem and never harbor angry or hateful feelings towards each other.

"The situation I'm describing sounds similar to the culture that the original Sekhmetians wanted to create. The major difference, however, is the ferocity of the Sekhmetians, being half lion. They are great warriors of the Light indeed. The Arcturians are not used by Father God, the same way the Sekhmetians are. We do not wage war; we heal and negotiate. We are a different people. We are known for being able to dissipate anger."

"The Arcturians are similar to healing angels, I'd say."

"Correct," Yashi answered.

"Yashi, how about the people from Earth?" I asked. "What would you say about them? Would you call them angels or demons, or both?

"Both."

"Why would you say that?"

"Jayna," she replied, "the answer to that question is quite complicated and has a number of several dimensions to it. The best way for you to understand the answer to your question is to learn about Planet Earth's history. It's all about spiritual warfare. It would be best if you saw how people can be motivated by negative emotions, especially greed.

"After your eighteenth birthday, we're going to give you an assignment where you will see first-hand what greed can do to people. We're going to send you to work at one of the major banks in New York City. There is much corruption there, and you will learn about spiritual warfare through your job."

"At a bank?" I asked. This didn't make sense to me.

Yashi nodded and said, "We want you to see first-hand what the Darkness does to steal money and siphon energy from the populace. Your assignment is to learn as much as you can about the banking industry, and relate it to spiritual warfare. You will have the education of a lifetime!"

"How interesting!" I said. "That's not a connection I would have made by myself. But now that you mention it, I can see there would be great opportunity for the Darkness to work through its minions in this field."

"Correct, you will see for yourself," Yashi said with a knowing look.

I had a distinct feeling this was going to be an incredible experience. It was more than I expected to see people willing to destroy another's life for money.

Spiritual Warfare

The next four years went by quickly. A heavy school and work schedule occupied most of my time. Yashi was there for me every step of the way.

On my eighteenth birthday, Yashi came over to my house and had dinner with our family. When we were done, we went to the living room couch and sat down as we always did when we were working. I knew she would be sending me to New York City to work in the bank as she had previously mentioned.

"Jayna," she said, "has anyone ever taught you about the history of Planet Earth?"

"Yes, we went over that subject in the Catholic school I was enrolled in on Earth. They taught us about Adam and Eve. And I remember the nun told us civilization was approximately 6,000 years old."

"Did you ever consider that you were given misinformation?" she asked. I noticed she was looking closely at me to see my reaction.

"No, Yashi. I simply accepted what was taught to me and never questioned its truthfulness. Was that a mistake?"

"Yes and no. Both. Yes, because the time frame they gave you was incorrect, and no because you could not challenge authority at such a young age. Not to worry, this is easy to correct. We will have to discuss the true history of Planet Earth. It is not what you were taught. We have volumes of books here on Planet Sekhmet on this subject, but we will give you the general overview."

"Okay," I said. "I've come to realize all is not as it seems."

"That is correct," Yashi said. She looked at me with a proud smile and continued, "A small percentage of people on Planet Earth realize that there is great propaganda regarding Earth's true history. It's hard to make the transition to the truth once someone has been led astray in their early years. That's why it's so important that we teach you at a young age so that you can avoid falling into that pitfall. Many are stubborn about what they think they know and still more cannot handle the truth.

If they were to be told the truth about Planet Earth's true history, they would have to go into denial or they would act very hostile. For instance, if someone from my race would present themselves to a person from Planet Earth and they were not ready to handle it, their mind would tell them they were imagining it. If the situation were forced on them, they would become fearful, angry, or even possibly violent. This behavior would indicate their inability to process the information. This is a major reason why the Arcturians have not publicly revealed themselves to the people of Planet Earth. If we did, it could cause great shock and trauma for those who are not ready to receive this revelation. We could not do so without causing great harm."

"I understand," I said. "I can relate to the shock. When John first told us about the Cosmic Fountain, I felt overwhelmed."

"Yes," she said.

"The people from Planet Earth must be made ready to handle the truth. How do you prepare the people for the eventual revealing of the Arcturians to the public?" I asked her.

"There are many who are writing science fiction stories, TV programs and movies. There is a small group of people in Hollywood who are in communication with some of our people. They are channeling accurate information to them about advanced technology. The rule of thumb is if you see it in the movies, then the device already exists! There is still so much information that Earth has not embraced. Your home planet has had as many advances in the last century because there are a number of extraterrestrial races that have been working with the governments of the world, and trading information for raw materials."

"Interesting," I said.

"Gold and silver, which are real money back on Planet Earth, are also used for trade. Both metals are great conductors of electricity."

"Yashi," I asked, "what do you mean gold and silver are real money. Back on Planet Earth, we use dollar bills and coins for money. Is that not real money?"

"Yes and no," she answered. "Gold and silver are mentioned in the United States' constitution as money, so in that sense, the coins that have silver in them are real money. The paper bills that are used as money are actually not money, but 'legal tender.' This is the game the Dark ones play to cheat the people."

"How do they get cheated? I don't understand!" I told her as I started to feel a sense of uneasiness. Was she telling me, collectively speaking, we are all being made fools of by them?

"Please let me explain how they manage to fool the majority of people on Planet Earth. Their monetary system is a faulty one. If the people only realized how they were being cheated, they would rise up against their oppressors, and Planet Earth would free itself from its parasitic infection.

"It will take many of these experiences in your life's work for you to understand precisely how insidious the Darkness can be. It uses many different ploys throughout someone's life to manipulate them into giving away their financial sovereignty and freedom. You will be able to see this first-hand. Working in a bank will show you how people are taken advantage of daily.

"With that being said, I have plans to go over with you. As promised, I've made arrangements for you to start a new job at one of the six largest banks on Planet Earth on Monday, September 6th. John will give you the rest of the details at a later date.

"Before we are ready to leave for New York City, however, I'm going to be showing you how to give updates to the Sekhmetian military regarding the Kemkabi, starting this upcoming Monday, August 23rd. We have until Tuesday, August 31st, to work together. That gives us more than a week to work on developing a new skill for you. We are going to work on teaching you astral projection. You will learn how to send your astral body anywhere in the universe. Once you learn this skill, you can literally astrally project to Sirius and give the Sekhmetian authorities updates. We cannot fall behind on tracking the Kemkabi while you are away. We must continue the updates, or the Kemkabi will undoubtedly succeed in furthering their plans.

This sounded like it might be challenging. I felt a sense of apprehension. Yashi picked up on my fear and said, "I think you're perplexed, Jayna, but you are more than capable of accomplishing this feat.

I had become accustomed to Yashi knowing exactly how I felt. Her empathic abilities made it easy for me to work with her because she helped me overcome my anxieties.

She continued, "We will finish our training by Tuesday night so that you will have time to pack and get ready for your trip on Wednesday. On Thursday morning, September 2nd, I'll take you to the Cosmic Fountain, and John will meet you there in Ohio and drive you to your new apartment.

"We found one for you in Brooklyn Heights because we knew you would love the area. You can commute easily to your job in midtown Manhattan from there, and you'll be surrounded by the beautiful buildings and architecture that you so love about Brooklyn. We can also send your mother with you to Brooklyn to help you settle into the apartment.

"When you get to the bank, there will be someone from the Light to share sensitive information with you. She will explain all the inner workings that you need to become familiar with. The Darkness does not want people to find out how their game is played. If they feel someone could potentially expose them, they will indeed terminate them. Not to worry, however, John and his team will be watching over you and your future friend, and will provide back-up if necessary."

"Okay, Yashi," I said, "this sounds good. I will be ready for you Monday morning."

"Wonderful, Jayna," she answered. "I'll see you then."

***

Yashi arrived promptly at 9:00 am, and we got right to work. We had more than a week to practice and, after few days of trying to astral project unsuccessfully, I finally had my first out-of-body experience.

Yashi and I were sitting across from each other, and I was using the techniques she had shown me. I was doing my best to break free from my physical form. I realized I felt a little thirsty, so I stood up to get a drink of water. I walked over to the counter to get a glass, and when I tried to pick it up, my hand went through it! I was so surprised. I turned around, and I could see my body sitting on the couch. I saw Yashi open her eyes and looked at where my astral form was standing.

"Very good, Jayna," Yashi said. "Now, if you can think of a place, you can move there!"

I was pleased. It reminded me of some happy times I had with Cecilia at school. In an instant, I was standing in the schoolyard. I could see the swing set and where we played hopscotch. I thought I'd better get back to Yashi and I was there.

I walked over to my body and re-entered it. For a brief moment, I felt every cell in my body moving. It was an intense experience.

Once I got the hang of it, astral projection was easy to do. I practiced until it was second nature to me. Yashi then taught me how to use my energy to allow others to see and hear me. Before wrapping it up, we did a test run, and I was able to successfully send an update to the military officer in charge of the Kemkabi situation on Sirius, Lieutenant Jagannath.

With one day left, I got my suitcases out and started packing. Mom helped me figure out what outfits to take and what not to take. I obviously would need the right wardrobe to work in a bank, so we got some money together for me to go shopping for new work clothes. We went downtown, and Mom helped me pick out new outfits, and we got all the last-minute details taken care of.

Thursday morning arrived, and Yashi drove Mom and me to the Cosmic Fountain. The trip through the Sekhmetian countryside was beautiful, with its rolling hills and flat plains. The trees were similar to the ones on Earth, but some did have beautiful multi-colored blooms that we had never seen before.

We went through the Fountain, and when we arrived in Ohio, John met us there and drove us to my new apartment in Brooklyn. It was in a brownstone building on Clinton Street and had four large sunny rooms with a full kitchen. Mom and I spent the next two days shopping to buy the necessary furniture and accessories I would need in the apartment. We purchased colorful curtains and rugs, and new furniture as well. When we were done, the apartment looked beautiful, and I was happy to be there.

Mom stayed with me until John arrived on Sunday. When he left, he took Mom with him and drove her back to the Cosmic Fountain. He left a package of documents with me that gave me further information regarding my new assignment.

The bank's name was The New Yorker's Bank. It had many branches all over New York City, and other branches all over the world. I was going to work as an administrative assistant to an investment banker, Rodney Brackman, handling his phone calls, travel arrangements, and typing. He was very brilliant at his job and serviced the bank's wealthiest clients. He invested their money and made both the client and the bank great profits. His former assistant retired, and he needed someone to fill her position.

Yashi had gone through government contacts to land this job for me. Rodney Brackman was a high roller and, due to his great success, he was sought after by many investors. He was in his fifties, had salt and pepper black hair, stood about 5'10" tall, and had an olive-tone skin with brown eyes. He looked good for his age; he wore it well. He had a beautiful office in midtown Manhattan overlooking the skyline and had pictures of his wife, children, and grandchildren on his desk. They were a handsome family indeed. Various diplomas were hanging on the wall. I wondered about his disposition. Was he a stressed-out executive with drug and or alcohol addictions, or was he a brilliant, well-balanced individual with a happy and successful life? Time would tell.

As the days passed, it turned out Rodney was a pleasure to work with. He was very professional and personable and was always in good spirits. I could see why he was so popular with his clients. He was charismatic and inspired confidence.

I felt grateful that this opportunity had been given to me. I liked the other people in the office as well. As it turned out, the job I was given was a busy one and time passed quickly. Many people called throughout the day, and there was much work to be done.

The first three months went by quickly, and the job was pleasant. I met many interesting people and enjoyed my new position.

When the holidays came around, I asked for the week off between Christmas and New Year's. Rodney didn't have a problem with it; he said he would hire a temp for the week. So, I was able to go back to Sirius for a Christmas vacation. When the time arrived, I called John and asked him to drive me to the Cosmic Fountain.

Portal to Transformation

My parents picked me up at the Cosmic Fountain and drove me home. They had a holiday party planned at the restaurant, and I arrived just in time. It was so good to be back. I felt very much at home in Sirius. I now had my home in two cities. Each felt familiar and comfortable to me.

I contacted Yashi and asked her to come over to my parents' house. When she arrived, we caught up on everything that was going on and on our work with keeping up with the Kemkabi.

For the next few days, we focused heavily on the Kemkabi. We had made great strides in holding them back; however, they were fighting back hard.

We had to go to the authorities several times to report future attacks on the Sekhmetian citizens. As always, they created fear and havoc and it was always one thing after the next. It was a relief to be in Yashi's presence again, especially after being apart for so long. The next thing I knew, words were tumbling out of my mouth.

"Yashi," I said. "Do you ever feel like your life's work is unbearable at times?"

"No, never," she said. "But I do understand why you would feel that way. The Kemkabi are so evil and so determined to pull us into their universe, they'll stop at nothing. Maybe what you need is to have development in a different part of your life to balance out your work. You have worked very hard for years. Maybe it's time you find yourself a love. You are of age now."

"Well, since you mentioned it," I said. "I do feel ready to start dating. It would be great to have someone to share fun with. I do have friends, but a 'special friend' would be nice."

"Jayna," Yashi said, "you don't know it, but you just touched on a subject that I've waiting to talk to you about. Here is an opportune moment for this discussion."

Oh God, I thought, *this will be good!*

"What's that, Yashi?" I asked.

"Jayna, it's called 'the special relationship.' Humans are very fond of them."

"What's wrong with that?"

"On Arcturus," she said, "we've learned not to engage in this type of thinking. Yeshua also spoke about this subject. It's a very important spiritual issue to address in one's life."

"Okay," I said, "but why?"

"Because, Jayna, love is not special."

"But a romantic relationship is special, isn't it?"

"Jayna," she replied, "this is a major pitfall that one can fall into. Love is love, no matter how it expresses itself. For instance, you love your parents, love your friends, love your pets, or even animals. Is the love that you feel for all of these beings any different? The only difference is the *expression* of love. Indeed, we do not express love the same way to everyone, because it is not appropriate to do so. However, the essence of love is always the same in each and every relationship."

"Well, what if you do make your romantic relationship special in your life? What would be the harm in that?"

"The answer to your question lies in your expectation of the relationship. If this relationship is indeed 'special,' do you give the other person special powers to make you happy? Furthermore, are you happy because of them, or are you satisfied with or without them? Are you making that person more important than other people in your life? Does your happiness depend on them? Are you codependent? What happens if that person leaves you? Can you still be happy?

"These are important issues to be addressed. They are major life lessons and usually not learned quickly. It's easy to fall into this trap, especially when one falls in love. They feel as if the presence of their beloved has suddenly transformed their life and they experience bliss. Isn't that a central theme of your music culture? So many are singing and dancing to the joy of finding love and romance. But my question to you is this: will that be your ultimate form of happiness?"

"Uh, I'm not sure," I said. "I never thought of it in that way. I've always dreamed of finding my true love."

"Is your love for others not true?" she asked.

"Yes, Yashi," I said. "Of course, it is. It's just not 'special.'"

"And how is that 'special' love different?"

"Well," I said. "It makes one feel like they are walking on air!"

"And is that why the love is 'special?'"

"I would say so!"

"I'm glad you admitted it, Jayna. You don't realize what you just said."

"I don't understand, Yashi," I said.

"I know, Jayna. You fell into a trap that so many falls into without realizing it. All love comes from the Creator. The Creator's love for us is as true and genuine as any love could be. There is no more perfect love than this. It is *universal love*. No one of us is more loved than the other. We all are equally important."

"I understand that," I said.

"Good!" Yashi said. "Now here's where it gets interesting. Do you know the difference between *like* and *love*?"

"Yes," I said.

"Good," she answered. "Now we are getting to the heart of the matter. We may *love* everyone, but not necessarily *like* everyone. Love never changes. It's the same in every relationship, only the expression changes. But *like* is completely subjective. We *like* only those who please us. Furthermore, *like* can change quickly if someone says or does something distasteful to us. We literally can *like* someone one day and *not* the next. But *love*? *Love* is eternal, like the Creator. It has no beginning, no end, and is eternally boundless.

"Love is free like the air. Does God give air to some to breathe and not to others? Or is air available equally to all saints *and* sinners? Can we hold on to the air and say,

'This air is mine and I'm saving it for the special people in my life.' Could we achieve such a feat? Of course not. Air is given to all with no favoritism. Love is the same. Only in *selfishness* do we favor those who we like. To love all is *unselfish* as is true love."

"So, what you are saying," I said, "is that the only true love is an *unselfish* love, which means there can be no favoritism. If we are selfish and love the ones we favor, then we have 'special relationships' and are missing the point entirely concerning love."

"Exactly!" she said.

"There's much to say about this subject. Many spiritual teachers and traditions have addressed it. It is the ego's attempt to trick us into believing that we shouldn't love those who 'don't deserve it.' First, who can say what someone 'deserves?' This is a sign of ignorance. Again, here is the ego and its antics. No matter how grievous someone's errors may be, all are deserving of love. The Creator's love is perfect.

"We all are unconsciously desiring something. Somewhere deep within each of us, there is a desire to be loved perfectly, but who can love perfectly except a divine being? Furthermore, it takes quite a bit to transform the carnal self into the spiritual self. On Arcturus, our race has transcended this carnal self, but on Earth, it just isn't so. Your race is still mostly unconscious. There are a few who are awake, but this will change as time goes on. More and more people will be waking up on Earth in the years to come. The Light reveals itself more and more, and the Darkness will begin to lose power and fade out. This is the mission of each one of us. Those of us of the Light aspire to embody the spirit of love or be an expression of the Creator, be it male or female."

"Okay, Yashi," I said. "Then what you are saying is that it's okay to have a boyfriend, just don't fall into the trap of a 'special relationship.' Be sure to love all equally. Correct?"

"Correct," she said.

"Got it," I answered. "Let's see if I can find a young man that feels the same way!"

"Jayna," she said. "It's time to think about dating. Have you given it any thought?"

Yashi now is addressing a choice I will have to make, I thought. *She's talking about having a boyfriend! Oh, Lord!*

"Yes, Yashi, I have," I answered. "There are some really cute guys around, and I wouldn't mind going on a date with them!"

"Jayna, have you considered any other desirable quality in a man other than 'cute?'" she asked.

"Like what?"

"Like character," she said, "compatibility, mutual interests, and compatible religious beliefs."

"Ugh.....yeah," I answered. "Do you think I would only date someone for their looks?"

"Just checking," she answered. "Young girls can be silly and even foolish with respect to young men. That's why we encourage dating at a later age to prevent teenagers from getting lost in immature foolishness."

"You've got a good point there, Yashi."

I took to heart everything she said. I knew she was right. We humans seemed to have an inborn tendency to make our love relationship "special," so not doing that did seem to be challenging. I prayed that night to be guided to someone who would be a suitable choice for me to begin a relationship with.

When my vacation time was almost up, I got my things together and made arrangements to have John pick me up at the Cosmic Fountain. When I said goodbye to Yashi, I asked her to pray that I find someone to have a relationship with. She agreed and hugged me before we parted.

John drove me to my apartment in Brooklyn and we had a pleasant ride back. I unpacked and got ready for the next day's work.

It was good to be back. I enjoyed my routine and my new life in New York. I decided to join a local gym near work and started working out three nights a week.

I also joined a vegetarian club based in Manhattan. It was comprised of a group of people that met on a regular basis to eat out together at all the many vegetarian restaurants in the city. I started meeting with them once a week and enjoyed all of our culinary experiences together. They were fascinating people there, all of them were very talented and successful. It reminded me of Sirius in a way, and I felt blessed to be a part of this group. I was the youngest member, but there were other young members as well.

One night, I noticed a young man who was about 5'6" and had black hair with hazel eyes. He was slim and was very handsome. His name was Conrad Ackerman, and he was a computer programmer at an investment bank in midtown Manhattan, just a few blocks from where I worked. He looked to be in his mid-twenties, and he was sitting across from me at our dinner table. He introduced himself to me, and we began talking. He was very charming, intelligent, and funny. I liked him very much.

I noticed the next time we went out to dinner that he sat down next to me. This time he walked me to the train station when we were done eating and asked me for my phone number. I gave it to him, smiled, and walked away. I couldn't stop thinking of him the whole way home. He was very likable.

When I got home, I went through my usual routine, but I received a late-night call. It was Conrad! He called to tell me how much he enjoyed talking to me and invited me to meet him for dinner next Friday night.

"Jayna," Conrad said, "how would you like to try that new Japanese restaurant that everyone was raving about at dinner?"

"I'd love to, Conrad!" I said. "What time would you like to meet?"

"How about 6:00?" he asked. "That would give me time to work late and finish up a project I'm working on. Does that work for you?"

"Yes."

"There're some great art galleries in that neighborhood. After dinner, if you'd like, we could take a walk and check them out."

"Sure!"

"Great," he said. "See you then."

"Goodnight, Conrad," I said.

"Goodnight Jayna," he answered back.

When we got off the phone, I had a strange feeling. It felt like a premonition. I got a distinct feeling that he and I were going to be together. I could almost feel it. Some part of me was excited, but another part of me was apprehensive. *Time will tell,* I thought.

Our first date went well. Dinner was delicious, and the restaurant was charming. We walked around the neighborhood and visited the art galleries. We had a great time, and Conrad rode the subway with me home and walked me to the door. He gently leaned over and gave me a little kiss on the lips. I had butterflies in my stomach, and I smiled at him. I turned around and put the key in the door and went upstairs.

Conrad called me when he got home. He told me he had a wonderful time and asked if we could meet next week and go out again. I was thrilled he asked me back out and agreed to go out with him again. We started to see each other regularly. We got along very well, so we decided to go to boyfriend/girlfriend status after five months.

Being with somebody in New York City was wonderful! There was so much to do. All the restaurants, shows, museums, stores, and art galleries were never ending! Conrad and I saw each other two to three times a week and grew closer and closer over time. We finally got to the point where a sexual attraction had developed and was becoming unbearable. One night, he came to my apartment and stayed over, and that was the first time we made love. It was beautiful, and I had completely fallen in love with him. We began staying together every weekend, and for the first year we were together, we had a harmonious relationship. We never argued and our bond deepened over time.

However, about a year into the relationship, we began fighting. It turned out Conrad was domineering, and I was not well suited to be with a domineering man. I was too fiery for him.

One night at dinner, Conrad asked me, "Jayna, what street did you walk up to come to my apartment?"

I answered, "I walked up from First Avenue. Why?"

"Didn't I tell warn you about that street? It's dangerous!" There was an angry tone in his voice, and he was scolding me. I felt like he was treating me like an infant.

"I'll walk up any street I want to!" I snapped at him.

Shortly after this, he stopped returning my phone calls, and he wouldn't answer his door when I went over to his apartment. It was obvious our relationship was over. Even though I knew it was for the best, it still hurt.

Just when I thought I was getting back to normal, I had an unexpected encounter with him. Conrad decided to start dating someone else, and I bumped into them at one of the vegetarian dinners. It was very awkward. I left early and went home and cried my eyes out. It hurt so much to see him with someone else. I was so heartbroken! My very first heartbreak. I felt like I could not stand the emotional pain, and wanted to drown my sorrow. The only consolation I had was that I saw the pain in Conrad's eyes, and I could see it hurt him too to see me.

All I wanted to do was go home to Sirius and see Mom, Dad, and Yashi. It was so hard for me to go to work when I was so distraught. I wasn't able to do my astral projection work either. I was too upset.

At work, Rodney could see how upset I was, even though I tried to hide it. I finally broke down and asked for a week off. He agreed. I called John, and when I was ready, he came and picked me up and drove me to the Cosmic Fountain."

When I arrived in Sirius, Mom and Dad were waiting for me at the Cosmic Fountain. They were supportive, but I needed to talk to Yashi. The pain was more than I could bear.

Mending the Heart

The next day, Yashi came over to our house, and I hugged her when she came in.

"Yashi, I'm so glad to see you!" I said, and then I burst into tears. "I can't stop crying!"

"Jayna," she said, "come here." She put her arms around me and walked me over to the couch. She held me in her arms as I sobbed. "You're experiencing the pain of separation right now. This is a necessary part of your development. Here, let me give you some of the homeopathic remedy for grief that I brought with me today. It's called Ignatia. It will help you to feel better. Jayna, take this please."

She handed me the dropper bottle of Ignatia and said, "Here, take four drops of this."

I did as she instructed, and I immediately felt the emotional pain of my broken heart lessen as the remedy took effect. The pain was still there, but its sharp edge vanished. The remaining pain was uncomfortable but not unbearable.

"What is a homeopathic remedy, Yashi?" I asked in between sobs.

"To answer your question, *Homeo* means same, and *pathos* means suffering. So, the same energy that causes you suffering is the same energy that will heal you. This is called the law of similars.

"Homeopathy is energy medicine that works on your energy body, not on your physical one. The physical body comes from its energy field and not the other way around. Both physical and emotional suffering originates in the person's energy field first as an energetic dysfunction. Over time, the energetic dysfunction will eventually manifest in the physical body as suffering. To correctly address an illness or emotional pain in the body is to work out the energetic dysfunction in the energy field first and then letting the body heal.

"I brought Ignatia with me, which is a homeopathic remedy for grief. Homeopathy can also help to work out emotional pain as well. It will work on your energy field and help you to process your pain. Not to worry. As overwhelming as may seem, this is a normal part of your life process – loss and grief. You don't realize it right now, but you are in the midst of a potential transcendent experience."

"What!" I said.

"Jayna," she said, "Please sit down. Let's talk. Now is as good as any other time to discuss this subject. You are experiencing loss and grief right now, and it is indeed painful. You probably feel you don't know how much of this you can stand and you want to find relief for your pain, but you don't know how, correct?"

"Correct," I answered. She piqued my interest, and my crying was starting to subside.

"This process is part of the spiritual maturation process," she said. "When we are in terrible emotional pain, if we let ourselves feel the pain to the fullest without running away from it through addictions or hedonistic behavior, we are given a portal through which we can travel through towards our ultimate freedom.

"For example, if we are heartbroken about the death of a dear friend, we will experience grief. If we let ourselves feel the pain to the fullest, even if we feel we will die if we do, the experience itself becomes a gateway of sorts. If we are willing to stay in pain and accept it completely, the acceptance triggers a transcendent experience. Our egos are purged through the pain. When we have completely allowed the pain and suffering of the situation without judging it, the ego vanishes, and so does the pain. And we are set free! That pain can no longer get a firm grip on us and we have a transcendent moment.

"Jayna, do you see the opportunity here? It's of the utmost importance that you understand the lesson here. If you don't process your pain correctly and bury it, you will create an addiction cycle.

"When in overwhelming emotional pain, the typical reaction is to find whatever means necessary to stop the pain. This is the most critical moment in this process. If one turns to any addictive behavior, such as drinking, drugs, smoking, or sexual behavior, to self-medicate and numb the pain, then addiction is born. Once this happens, the pattern is set in the brain. Whenever one feels overwhelmed emotionally, there will be a knee-jerk reaction. The individual will turn to an addiction as an avoidance strategy.

"For instance, how many broken-hearted people have turned to alcohol to numb their emotional pain? This is an old story. Does alcohol solve the problem? Does it make the situation any better? Or does the alcohol create an even bigger problem than the one it is addressing?

"In every loss, there lies the seed of spiritual healing. That is if we use the situation correctly. Ultimately, there can be no loss if we focus on our divine nature and not our physical one. The animal self experiences loss. The divine self is perfect, whole, and complete and requires nothing to sustain itself. It merely experiences the joy of the moment, regardless of circumstances.

"For example, a man loses his job and feels depressed because he is concerned about sustaining his financial obligations for his family. At that moment, he emotionally feels crushed and carries in his heart a heavy emotional burden. In this situation, he has two choices. He can allow himself to feel all the negative emotions that one could feel in this situation, such as fear, anxiety, loss, humiliation. He can also turn to an addiction to drown his pain and create a second problem to add to the first one. Suppose he chooses to let himself work through all the negative emotions that one could feel in such a situation and works through them in their entirety. In that case, he will feel the emotional relief from the release of the pain. He can only obtain this once he has stopped running away from the pain.

"What's most important to remember is that pain is our friend. It knocks us down to teach us, not punish us.

This teaching is paramount in Arcturian culture. If we experience pain, it draws our attention to wherever the pain originates. If it is physical pain, we will investigate what is causing the discomfort and follow through with treatment. If it is emotional pain, it is there to show us our attachment. All emotional pain comes from the ego; only the ego can hurt.

"This process was designed by The Creator when we got trapped in a three-dimensional reality. Once we are willing to confront the ego and its hold on us, it can no longer grip us, and therefore, we no longer experience pain."

"Exactly!" Yashi said. "Life in a three-dimensional world is designed to have ups and downs, gains and losses. The wheel of fortunate turns continuously, and we are given opportunities to work out our karma through the ups and downs of life. The ups are joyous and make our lives pleasurable. The downs, however, are not so easy to get through and cause us considerable pain. But herein lies the opportunity for us.

"By allowing ourselves to experience pain to the point when we feel overwhelmed by it and feel as if it can kill us, we are allowing the life process to purge our ego. That's the key. The ego is purged with the pain of loss, which comes from attachments. The moment our pain stops, we are set free from ego! And, if we practice our spiritual disciplines every day, one day the ego will be ready to die entirely, which gives birth to the soul self, or the authentic self. It is this self that is connected to the Divine. Once this happens, we experience a union with the divine self. In the Bible verse John 3:3 NIV, Yeshua says, 'Very truly I tell you, no one can see the kingdom of God unless they are born again.' This is the death and rebirth he was alluding to. When the ego dies, that which separates us from the mind of God dissolves, and we directly experience The Divine.

How many people run away from this work? Your world is filled with people fighting addictions. The various cultures on your planet do not adequately teach their people how to handle life losses. Losses are to be expected. Each of us will experience the pain of loss due to death unless we die as infants. In that case, the infant provides the opportunity for the others in his/her family to suffer loss. Most of us survive infancy, which means we will lose loved ones throughout our lives, and we will experience pain, grief, and sorrow. This is the life process. Those of us that 'get it' realize that their loved ones have moved on to live in another dimension."

"Yashi," I asked, "Do Arcturians suffer grief when they lose their loved ones?"

"Jayna," she answered, "We have billions of years of evolution in our culture. We honor our deceased, but we don't suffer grief and loss as deeply as those in your culture. Our race transcended ego a long time ago. We have a process that we go through when someone dies.

We all gather around the deceased body, much like you do, and honor them and their lives. However, we do not suffer so deeply at their departing. We focus more on the spiritual lessons of their lives and their return to Spirit. We see the bigger picture.

We do not fall into an addiction cycle as many do on your planet. We are well aware of the pitfalls of such behavior."

"Such as?" I asked.

"Jayna," she said, "People on Planet Earth have been intoxicating themselves for eons of time. The real issue is why do they do this when there are apparent severe consequences for doing so. Many lives have ended because of alcohol and drug overdoses. Intoxicants poison the body, so why would someone want to do this to themselves?

One possibility is a person is suffering from unconscious guilt, and they want to destroy themselves. Drugs and alcohol will do the job and do it well.

Another possibility is they enjoy being intoxicated and the physical pleasure they derive from it. If they do this enough, the intoxication becomes an addiction. Once the habit has taken hold of the body, it is difficult to overcome, although not impossible. Pleasure-seeking behavior can begin this process and, for many, it does not end well.

Intoxication can also be a learned behavior. Suppose a child witnesses his parents or family members becoming intoxicated. In that case, that child may very well copy the behavior one day. The child believes that being drunk is just part of life and is expected of them. Many celebrations use alcohol as a tribute to success and achievement. Alcohol is also used to celebrate weddings.

Liquors can also be used as a coping mechanism. When people are stressed, they drink to relax. When they are emotionally upset, they drink to cope with overwhelming emotions they cannot process. When people are in grief, some turn to intoxicants to help them to cope with the stress and pain of their loss. Intoxicants are used quite often for self-medication."

"Yashi," I asked, "What is a better way to relax and cope with stress?"

"Jayna," she said, "This question can be answered in many ways. There are herbs one can take that will relax you without being toxic to the body. Also, walking in nature, bathing, pleasurable work such as hobby work, etc., can help relax a person. And always remember, a divine connection will relax you, which is my recommendation.

"I knew you would say that!" I said.

"Are you feeling better?"

"Yes," I answered, "but I am tired. I think I'd like to call it a night."

"Okay, Jayna," she said, "just let me know when you're ready. We can't let the Kemkabi get a break from us. The situation is too serious."

"Yes," I said. "We'll go back to work shortly. I'll call you. Thank you for coming over. You mean so much to me Yashi!"

I threw my arms around her and gave her a big hug. She was always a comfort to me. How dear she was to me!

Cash Mirage

When the week was over, I felt better and was ready to return to work. John picked me up at the Cosmic Fountain. I went back to Brooklyn and my old routine, but this time without Conrad. I didn't want to date for a while as I needed time to heal. This whole experience left me devastated, and I did not want to get into another relationship until I felt ready to do so.

I focused on my job and my spiritual work. I yearned for my soulmate, but I knew he was still years away. He would be the love of my life someday, but not just yet. The time just wasn't right.

As the days went by, little by little, I was starting to feel better. I began praying for successful completion of my assignment at the bank.

Yashi had me work here to learn about spiritual warfare, but I still could not see the connection. That was about to change. One of my friends at the bank was going to help me connect the dots. Her name was Lorraine Geller. She stood about 5'6" tall and was slim, had straight brown hair and green eyes. She was a pretty woman and was always well dressed.

Lorraine was head of the Trading Floor at the bank. Due to her great talent and determination, she worked her way up to her department's top position. She was well known for her astute financial advice and her intuition on trading stocks. She worked with Rodney on some of his clients' investments and came to his office almost daily. I would process the investment paperwork for Rodney and hand them off to Lorraine.

One day Lorraine commented on how proficient I was at my job. Then slowly, we began to build a rapport. One day she asked me to join her for lunch, and we met in the cafeteria. Little did I know at the time that she was going to be the one who helped me to see the connection between banking and spiritual warfare. Eventually, she turned into a source of information for me.

Her husband, Todd Geller, was in his early fifties. He was tall, slim, and balding. He was British. He was an executive in the bank as well but worked in another building. He was the executive director of the Mortgage Department and had multiple managers and numerous staff. He had been recruited from the London office to work in New York. He was very familiar with how the global financial system worked. Lorraine was privy to knowledge and information that an ordinary person would not be. She knew a great deal about the banking industry and the global financial system.

At first, our relationship was a casual friendship. We started meeting for lunch in the company cafeteria daily and began to build a friendship. She was in her late forties and was my senior by over twenty years. But we hit it off, and she began sharing with me what I could not learn in a classroom.

As it turns out, the banking industry was filled with fraud in many ways. There was much to learn about the financial system, and I learned the various dirty tricks that were played in this industry. My next job would be to relate them to spiritual warfare.

As the months went by, Lorraine began to trust me more and more. One day while we were eating lunch, she shared a somber and unfortunate story with me. As it turns out, her husband's colleague, a banker from the

Miami office, was about to go to the press about all that the banking industry does not want the average person to know.

He was found hanging from a rope tied to the light fixture in his office right before he was about to do so. His death was officially called a "suicide." His family knew better but could not do anything about it. This was a strong message that they had better not speak out against all the corruption in this industry.

Lorraine was upset when she shared this story with me. Her husband was also upset and worried about what would happen to him if he dared step over the line. I could understand their concern. At the same time, I couldn't stand knowing that the Darkness could continue to do as they pleased without some kind of public outrage.

"Lorraine," I asked, "I've given this a lot of thought. I would love to know what the banking industry is trying to keep from the public. Could you please help me understand?"

I knew I was putting her on the spot, but Yashi did say I was to learn about spiritual warfare while I was here, so I decided to ask anyway.

"Jayna," Lorraine answered, "this is a very sensitive subject. You know that, right?"

"I know. I promise to never say that you told me any of this."

"Yes," she said. "This is certainly an issue. It must never come out that I shared this with you. This could put not only my life on the line, but my family's as well. This corruption is so widespread. It wouldn't take much for someone to overhear us and report me to the top brass. Losing my job would only be the beginning."

"I completely understand," I said. "You have my solemn word I will never divulge my source."

"Okay," she said. "How about we meet after work and go to dinner? That way we can be sure no one at the job can overhear us."

When I got to the restaurant, it was crowded as usual. Since it was the middle of the week, there wasn't a line outside to get in. I sat down at a table for two by the window and waited for Lorraine. I enjoyed this restaurant for several reasons. The simple wooden tables and down to Earth décor gave the restaurant a homey feel. The food was delicious and reasonably priced, and the service was excellent. There wasn't anything I didn't like about Angelica's, and I hoped Lorraine would like it as well.

She arrived promptly at 7:00, and we placed our order shortly after that. I waited until the food arrived before asking her to continue our conversation.

"So, Lorraine," I asked, "are you feeling like sharing tonight?"

"Well," she said, "this isn't easy to talk about, but I will share with you what I can. I certainly don't know everything there is to know about all the corruption, but I do know a good bit."

"Sounds good to me."

"Are you ready for this?" Lorraine asked. "This is quite intense!"

"Shoot!"

"First, I have to go over a little bit of American history. Back in 1913, by an act of Congress, a privately owned company became the central bank of the United States. This meant that they could issue currency and loan it to the United States Treasury. Now remember, in the Constitution, Article 1 Section 10, it clearly states that gold and silver are money. After 1913, however, this private company was able to issue paper money as a promissory note and the money must be paid back to the private company with interest. Are you still with me?"

"Yes," I answered.

"Okay. Here's where it gets complicated. First, they create money out of thin air on a ledger sheet or on a computer. The money does not actually exist, but they pretend that it does. This private company, by the way, has fooled the American people into thinking that it's a government agency, but it is not. Since 1913, this company has been allowed to lend the Treasury billions of dollars at a time. Now remember, the Treasury must pay the money back to them *with interest* for something that never existed in the first place. Furthermore, all income taxes in the United States are paid to the Treasury who, in turn, pay back the loan to this private company with interest. This is probably one of the greatest scams of our time."

"Lorraine, that's infuriating!" I said.

"Jayna, it gets worse," she replied. "This is how the current economic situation works in our country and other countries as well. Those that are running the planet right now have invented a clever game to siphon the wealth from the people. They teach this system of economics in schools, and brainwash students into believing that their system is correct, lawful, and successful. In fact, their system is none of those things. The whole premise of their system is based on one fact: they use paper currency backed by nothing. This is called 'fiat' currency. "There are fiat currencies used all over the world. The powers that be use this system to manipulate the people into believing their worthless currency is viable. The only currency that is worth something is a *hard asset* backed currency. A hard asset is an asset that is tangible, like gold, silver, and commodities.

"If a paper currency is used to represent a hard asset, then the paper currency can work because it is a currency backed with an honest and tangible asset. That asset has worth, so in turn, the paper currency has worth, but only because of what it represents. Paper money has no inherent value. It is simply easier to trade with paper money than tangible assets.

"The fiat money cycle runs its course by eventually creating inflation. Inflation is created by excessive money printing. The more money is printed, the less value the money has over time. To keep up social services such as Public Assistance and all the various government handout programs, they keep printing more and more money. Also, when the too-big-to-fail banks need bailout money, they keep printing more money. As a result of too much money printing, it will take more money to buy goods and services due to inflation. Because of excessive money printing, the dollar loses its value on the world stage of currencies.

"There is another factor as well. All the energy that is being used for heating, industry and transportation comes from the oil that the planet produces. The powers that be made the United States dollar the world's reserve currency. This means that all trade for oil must be done in dollars, which increases the dollar's value. Also, all international trade is to be done in US dollars as well. The dollar right now is the premiere currency on the planet, but the time will come when the dollar will crash because it must.

"It is impossible to maintain a healthy financial system with never-ending money printing that does not represent any tangible assets. When inflation runs its course, the dollar will be worth less and less and eventually become worthless. No country on Earth will want to trade in a currency that has no value. As the value of the dollar goes to zero, all international trade in dollars will stop, and all American asset prices will go to pennies on the dollar.

"When this happens, the ruling elite use their money to buy up hard assets such as buildings, railroads, and airports. This is how they maintain financial power over the populace. The rich get richer and the poor get poorer.

"This cycle repeats itself over and over. The private company gets wealthier, and the Treasury must keep making payments to it to keep the illusion of prosperity going. That is until the currency collapses, then it will be a free-for-all.

"If all the money that people put into banks is based on fraud and if one day the value of the United States' dollar collapses, the only assets people would have left would be hard assets. If the dollar's value crashed on the world market, people would panic, which would cause bank runs. Everyone would run to their bank to take their money out so that they wouldn't lose their life savings in a bank failure."

"What would be the problem if everyone ran to the bank to withdraw their money?" I asked. "It's their money, isn't it? Why couldn't everyone take their money out of the bank?"

"Jayna," she replied, "there's still a part of this situation you don't understand. There is something called 'fractional banking.' This means a bank only is required to keep one-tenth of their deposits in the bank at any one time. They are allowed to lend out ninety percent of their deposits to make money. If there is a panic and a bank run, the bank's cash deposits could be wiped out since only ten percent of the bank's deposits are ever in the bank at any one time. The bank would not have the rest of the customers' money to give back.

"That was what happened after the 1929 stock market crash. The market collapsed, which eventually led to bank runs. Not everyone, however, was able to get their life savings out in time. Many people went bankrupt. So many people who had made countless sacrifices just to have money in life savings lost everything. They became destitute and died paupers."

"So how does that relate to our current situation?" I asked.

"Well, the cycle is playing itself out again. Fiat money can still work for many years to come, but at some point in the future, it will start its cyclical decline. The powers that be are using this corrupt and unconstitutional financial system to steal money from the people. Everyone in the US is paying back, through their taxes, money loaned to the Treasury that never existed in the first place. Furthermore, they are paying the loan back with interest. These corrupt people are parasites!"

"So, is this the information that your husband's colleague was planning on sharing?" I asked.

"Yes," she answered. "And there's more. There's much to be said about insider trading, laundering drug money, and placing bankers in top positions at the central bank."

"That's a mouthful!" I said. "How about we take one point at a time?"

"Okay, no problem," Lorraine said. "Insider trading? That goes on all the time. If you are in 'the club,' you are privy to this information. There are well connected people who make money all the time from insider trading. This is a fact of life in the banking world."

"Are there ever indictments for insider trading?" I asked.

"Yes," she answered, "but they are the exception rather than the rule. It goes on every day."

"And laundering drug money?"

"Oh, that goes on all the time too."

"What?" I asked. "Are you kidding me?"

"No, Jayna. I'm not. This is one of their open secrets. Actually, in the basement of the building we work in, the top brass in the banking world meet to distribute the cash they launder from drug money. It's an unbelievable situation. The corruption that exists in this industry cannot be overstated."

"That's shocking!" I said.

"Indeed."

"You mentioned bankers being placed at top positions at the central bank," I continued. "Does that happen so that they are in an opportune position to create profits for the bankers?"

"You got it!" she said.

"How is it possible that the bankers can get away with so much?" I asked. This was starting to infuriate me!

"It's a corrupt system to begin with," she said. "And, if you add in the corruption of all the other people that are involved in creating this situation, it's staggering. Not to mention the regulatory authorities. They're corrupt too."

"So, corruption and spiritual darkness are taking over the planet?" I asked.

"I'd say most definitely yes," she answered.

"I appreciate you sharing this with me, Lorraine. I am going to pray about it."

"That's just what we need, Jayna," Lorraine said. "We need spiritual light to dispel this darkness."

"Agreed," I answered.

With that, we finished our dinner and left. I needed time to process all this information. I went back to my apartment and prayed and meditated. I finally felt a sense of relief after doing so. Our conversation left me feeling deeply worried about the state of affairs on this planet. Also, there were questions I wanted to ask Yashi.

Mortgages and Misers

As I worked in the office, I was more aware of what may be going on around me. I noticed Rodney had meetings with a manager and an appraiser from the Mortgage Department, which seemed very odd. He usually worked with investors, and they didn't usually buy real estate from him. What was this about?

I noticed Rodney started locking the door to his office when he wasn't around, and he had never done this before. It made my job more difficult because I needed to put files and papers that he needed to sign on his desk. When he was working on the computer, he always would turn the monitor so I couldn't see it when I was in the room. There were too many things that looked suspicious to me, so I decided to use the Crystal Cube to see what was going on.

The next day around lunchtime, Rodney had another meeting with the manager from the mortgage department. As their meeting started, I knocked on the door.

"Can I help you?" Rodney said.

I opened the door and stuck my head in. "I have an errand to run. Do you mind if I take my lunch early?"

"Sure, Jayna," he answered. "That would be fine."

"Great, thank you."

I grabbed my purse, and left the office and headed across the street to a local chapel. When I got there, the chapel was empty. I sat down and pulled out the Cube, and concentrated on the room where Rodney's meeting took place. I could see the two men sitting in the office. I was able to shift my view so to see the computer screen and see the account information.

"Are you able to get the money we need to set everything up by tomorrow?" the mortgage manager asked Rodney.

"Mitch, I can use the Heinemann account," Rodney answered. "I'm working with that account right now and it has $150,000 in it."

"Yeah, that'll do. We can easily triple that. We can get Richard to reappraise it the day after tomorrow, early in the morning. In the afternoon, I'll work on the loan."

I listened for a few more moments and gathered as much information as I could. Apparently, Rodney was embezzling money from the accounts he managed. Rodney, Mitch, and Richard have some type of scheme going.

I needed to get this information to Lorraine. I had to find a way to lead her to the data so this criminal activity could be dealt with.

I called Lorraine and left a message. Later that afternoon, she returned my call. We agreed to have dinner at Tavern on the Green. This restaurant was lovely, and the food was superb.

I told Lorraine that Rodney was having meetings with mortgage department people and asked her if she knew what was going on.

"Well," she said, "I don't know anything about the mortgage department, but there's been issues with a number of large accounts. The bank auditors came in and found that there's been money moved from segregated accounts with no explanation. Then, the money would be returned within a couple of weeks."

"Doesn't 'segregated account' mean that it's illegal to take money out of the account?" I asked.

"Yes," she answered.

"Lorraine," I asked, "is there any way to find out where that money went to?"

"Yes," she said, "but it wouldn't be easy. It is possible to follow the paper trail. That is, if the paper trail doesn't lead to a dead end. The money could be transferred to a numbered Swiss account. There would be no way to find out who the account belongs to. Furthermore, because of strict privacy banking laws in Switzerland, there's no way to monitor the activity of any given account. The only way it's possible to investigate suspicious banking activity in that country is by a court order."

"Lorraine," I said, "I heard the Heinemann account being mentioned."

"The Heinemann account?" Lorraine said. "They have accounts in banks all over New York. I think they're living in Spain this time of year. If someone was going to manipulate that account, this would be a good time to do it. Rodney has access to all of his accounts and if he's meeting with mortgage department people, that's a red flag."

"What do you mean?" I asked.

"Sounds like someone has their hand in the cookie jar. I'll take this information and see what I can find out. I also have to talk to Todd and see if he knows anything as well."

"You both should be careful because we don't know what kind of people Rodney makes deals with."

"We should be okay. I don't think it's that bad."

"Lorraine," I said, "if Rodney is embezzling a great deal of money, there's no knowing what he would do to cover his tracks."

"Why do you say that?" she asked. "Are you psychic or something?"

"Maybe. You can never tell," I said. "But most importantly, this situation could be very dangerous."

"I don't think it's possible that anyone could tie Todd and me to this situation," she said.

"I hope you're right."

We then finished our meal and called it a night.

A week went by, and I finally received a call from Lorraine. We decided to meet again for dinner. This time we met in Brooklyn Heights at a Mediterranean restaurant that I liked. I ordered my favorite dish, Tabbouleh Salad.

Lorraine arrived late and looked upset. She didn't order anything, so I asked what was wrong.

She explained that Todd had told her that the bank auditors were auditing his department, and there were issues with loans. It appeared that there were large numbers of defaulting loans.

"That many loans defaulting isn't normal, is it?" I asked.

"No," she answered, "it isn't. I think what's happening is Rodney, with Mitch and Richard from the Mortgage Department, are committing loan fraud. Rodney takes money out of one of his client's account, buys real estate with it, and then has the property appraised at a higher value by Richard. Then Mitch sets up a loan with the higher price to be purchased with a shell company and the funds go to Rodney. Rodney then returns the money he appropriated from his client's account. The loan is defaulted on by the shell company and Rodney splits the profits with Mitch and Richard."

"That's really complicated," I said.

"If it wasn't so complicated, it would be easy to follow the paper trail and wouldn't be so hard to prosecute them when they're caught. That's probably why they are not worried about the auditors. There's only one issue Todd mentioned to one of the auditors. They should check the Heinemann account."

"And then what happened?"

"The auditor asked where he got his information. Todd told him that it was confidential."

"I hope no one overhead the conversation with Todd and the auditor."

"I'm sure everything will be fine."

I noticed Lorraine hadn't ordered anything and looked nervous. "Lorraine, are you going to order anything?"

"No," she said. "I don't feel like eating at the moment. I would rather just go home. I'm sorry."

"I completely understand," I said. "No problem. Please call me if you need anything."

"Thank you, Jayna," she said. "I will."

With that, Lorraine got up and left. She clearly was upset.

I had an uneasy feeling about all of this and went home and used the Cube. I started viewing for Todd over the next coming few days. I was able to see a newspaper article stating that he had fallen in front of an oncoming subway train at the Port Authority Station in New York City. I concentrated on the date and time of the incident. According to the article, the accident took place sometime around 6:00 pm that day.

When I looked into the Cube, I was peering down on the event as it unfolded. I saw a man wearing a hoodie pulled up over his head and a scarf around his face so he could not be easily identified. He moved slowly through the crowd. He placed his hand on the small of Todd's back and pushed him in front of the train. He then disappeared into the crowd in the confusion.

This repulsed me and it made me sick to my stomach to see someone so callously take another person's life. I then searched the Cube to see if Lorraine was in danger as well. She had taken time off after Todd's death and was killed in a car crash. She crashed into a guard rail and went over a ravine, and her car caught on fire. I didn't even have to look in the Cube to know that somebody ran her off the road. This was disturbing, even though I knew I could keep this from happening.

If I stopped Todd's death, that would prevent Lorraine's death as well because there would be no funeral. So, I had to get to work and fast. If I warned them, then the assassin would be able to change his plans and kill them at a different time and place. What I needed to do was stop Todd's assassination at the train station. Todd and Lorraine would still be in danger; however, this would eliminate the immediate threat.

So, I devised a plan to deal with Todd's attacker at the train station. It was time for me to meditate and go to bed.

The next day, I arrived at work and looked for Lorraine to pick up her documents like any other day. But today, her assistant Mary came to pick them up.

"Where's Lorraine?" I asked.

"I'm not sure," Mary said, "but I did hear that she's having meetings with some of the top brass today."

"Is everything okay?"

"I don't know. That's above my pay grade."

A little bit later, Rodney came out of his office. How are you doing today, Jayna? Has Lorraine stopped by yet?"

"No, Mary picked up the documents today," I said.

"Hmmm. That's strange." He bent down and said in a soft tone, "I heard she's in some trouble."

"What do you mean?" I asked.

"I heard they found an account in her name with a large sum of money in it."

"That sounds serious!" I said.

"Yes, yes it is serious," he said, smirking. "By the way, is my golf date with Mr. Zimmerman still on the schedule?"

"Let me check," I answered. "Yes, it is. Would you like me to call and confirm?"

"No, that won't be necessary," Todd said.

"You know, Jayna, I know you're friends with Lorraine, but you might want to be careful hanging around those kinds of people because you might end up having the same problems they do," he said as he walked back into his office.

Was that a veiled threat? It was becoming clear Rodney bit off too big a piece of cheese in the mousetrap.

Within a few minutes, Rodney exited the office carrying his favorite golf club that he always practiced with in his office.

"I should be back sometime after lunch," he said.

"Have a good game, Rodney!" I said as he left.

"I will," Rodney said. "I have my angles covered."

A few hours later, I saw Lorraine walking down the hallway towards the elevator. She made eye contact with me and gave me a wink. She went into the elevator, probably going to her floor to work. I filed papers and worked on the computer for the rest of the day.

Rodney returned shortly after lunch and was smiling. He had a file tucked under his arm.

"Did you have a good game?" I asked.

"Of course," he said. "And I landed the Zimmerman account."

"Congratulations," I said. "That's awesome!"

"Here's the file that I need you to start working on." He laid the file on the desk and went in his office.

I worked on the Zimmerman file for the rest of the afternoon until it was time to go home. Before I went home, I knocked on Rodney's door to let him know I completed the file.

"I'll see you tomorrow, Rodney," I said.

The next day, I brought with me a change of clothes with a hoodie. When the workday ended, I changed my clothes in the bathroom and headed for the Port Authority train station. I got there in about a half-hour or so and found a place to sit down near where the attack would occur.

I made myself comfortable and held the Cube inside my pocket. Within half-hour, I saw Todd make his way to the front of the platform to enter the train when it arrived. As the train entered the station, I saw the assassin walk behind Todd and get into position to push him. As he approached him, I used my telekinetic ability to move Todd quickly to the right. This caused the killer to trip on Todd's left foot. The assassin lost his balance and fell off the platform in front of the train. Todd looked utterly bewildered and people starting screaming and the chaos ensued.

I was glad that I could save Todd, however, this didn't feel like a triumph. I didn't want anybody to die from this, but there was no other alternative. This was the only outcome where they would be safe. My heart was heavy and felt like a lead weight. A great sadness came over me.

I walked away from the scene and headed home. I arrived at my apartment in Brooklyn Heights and went through the motions of my regular evening routine. I prayed for help with my overwhelming sense of grief.

I checked the Cube to see if there were any upcoming plans that the Darkness had for Todd and Lorraine. There were none as of yet. I breathed a sigh of relief and then prayed that they would be kept safe.

***

The next day, I went to work, and I didn't see Lorraine. I was worried about her. With so much going on, she more than likely was distraught. I wanted to reach out to her but decided to wait until I saw her at work.

The following day Lorraine came by Rodney's office. Rodney hadn't come to work yet. In the meantime, Lorraine asked to meet me for lunch. We agreed to meet at 1:00 pm.

When I got to the cafeteria, Lorraine was already there. She was in a somber mood, and I could see the strain on her face.

I smiled at her. "Hey. Are you okay? What's on your mind?"

"You heard what happened to Todd yesterday?" Lorraine asked.

"Yes. Everyone is talking about it. Is he okay?"

"He's shaken up, but he's okay. He told me something strange happened. He said he felt a hand on his back and it pushed him towards the tracks of the oncoming train. But something moved him aside and a man fell onto the tracks. He thinks the man was trying to kill him, but failed. He said it must have been his guardian angel protecting him."

"That's an amazing story," I said.

"And it's strange that Rodney hasn't shown up for work yet. But he does have meetings with clients and potential clients early in the morning on occasion."

I then bent over to whisper to her. "Lorraine, can we meet for dinner? I would like to be able to talk freely. I'm not comfortable talking here about this."

"Sure," she said. "How about we meet at 7:00 tonight at Tavern on the Green?"

"Great," I said. "I'll be there."

Trouble On The Green

We finished our lunch and went back to our jobs. I could feel her anxiety. After work, I went to the chapel to meditate and pray before I had to leave to meet her.

It was not easy for me to shake the sense of anxiety that I felt. Rodney was suspicious of me, I'm sure, and there's no telling what he and his partners would do.

When it came time to leave, I took the train to the west side and began walking to the restaurant. I looked up the street and noticed Lorraine was briskly walking ahead of me. I ran to catch up to her, and we walked the rest of the way to the restaurant together.

Right before we got there, a man sprang up from behind some bushes that lined the sidewalk leading to the restaurant. He stood about ten feet away from us.

He pulled a gun from his jacket pocket and aimed it at Lorraine.

"Here, take my money," Lorraine said to the attacker in a shaky voice.

"I'll get that after both of you are dead!" the man said.

With that, I motioned with my left hand to use my telekinetic ability to pull the pistol from his grasp. It flew to the left and landed in one of the bushes. I reached out with my right hand and used my energy to hurl him over the bushes. His body flailed as he moved through the air, and he hit a tree with a dull thud. He slid down and collapsed face down on the ground. Lorraine stood by, shocked.

I stepped behind the bushes towards the man lying on the ground. He wasn't moving, so I rolled him over to look at him. He didn't look familiar to me.

I checked his neck for a pulse; he was still alive, but I wasn't sure how badly he was hurt. I stood up and turned around to look at Lorraine, and she hadn't moved from the spot where she was standing. I walked over to her.

"Are you okay?" I asked.

"I just had a man try to kill me," she said, "And he flew through the air without anybody touching him. He smashed into a tree and is he dead?"

"He's still alive," I said, "But he may have some broken bones."

"And you ask me if I'm okay?" Lorraine said.

She pauses and says, "I believe so, but I don't want to go to dinner."

"Can you walk over and look at the man's face?" I asked.

"Are you a magician or something, Jayna?" Lorraine asked.

"Okay, I'll go take a look."

"No," I said, "I'm not a magician. I have psychic abilities."

"Yes, Jayna," she said, "I've seen this guy before. Is this how you found out about what Rodney was doing?"

"Alright," I said, "I can see that you're disoriented. I'll explain it to you. I have psychic abilities and can predict outcomes of things that haven't happened yet. My abilities include precognition, astral projection, and telekinesis. That's how I found out what Rodney was doing. I also used my abilities to protect Todd, as well as using them to save us tonight."

Lorraine's voice was trembling. "I see," she said. "I think I would like to just home go now."

"You're still in danger," I said. "These people won't stop until you and Todd are no longer in their way."

"Todd and I are going to testify against Rodney. We already told the district attorney that we would. But now, I'm really concerned because I saw the guy on the ground and another man talking to Rodney outside the building a few days ago."

"Then that means Rodney might have a number of people working for him. We're not safe, Lorraine. I need to contact someone who can help us. Let's go into the restaurant so I can make a phone call."

"Jayna," Lorraine said, "we should tell the people in the restaurant that there's a guy passed out under their tree."

"Yes," I said, "and then they'll call the police. That's a good idea!"

We entered the restaurant, and I asked if I could use their phone. They let me use the phone at the front desk, and I was able to reach John. I told him there was an incident. He said he would arrive shortly. As I was on the phone, I heard Lorraine saying a man passed out under the tree. I listened to the greeter say that they would look into it.

We had to wait our turn to be seated. Within a few minutes, we were escorted to the next available table. We sat down and looked at the menu and pretended to be interested in it. We ordered an appetizer first and slowly began to eat our food.

Within an hour, the greeter came to our table with John behind her.

"The other member of your party has arrived," she said.

John then sat down at the table. I introduced Lorraine to him and, in the meantime, the greeter asked him if he wanted to see a menu. He politely refused.

"I have a vehicle waiting outside," John said. "I noticed when I came in that the police were outside and an ambulance was removing the man from the restaurant's property."

"John," Lorraine said, "Jayna told me you can keep my husband and me safe."

"Yes, I can," John answered. "I work for a government agency and Jayna is a part of a government program. There's much to explain and we can discuss it further. There's a car outside that can take you and Jayna to a safe house."

"Safe house?" Lorraine asked. "What about my husband?"

"Can you call him so we can pick him up and take him with us?" John asked.

"Yes," Lorraine said. "He's working late tonight. I'll call him on the way out."

We left the restaurant after Lorraine made her phone call. She told Todd we would pick him up at work.

When we arrived at the bank, Todd was waiting in the lobby for us and speaking with the bank security guard.

"Hello dear," Todd said to Lorraine. "Who is this?"

"This is Jayna. She works for Rodney."

"Hello Todd," I said. "It's a pleasure to meet you."

"Likewise," he said. "Lorraine's spoken very highly of you."

"There's a car waiting out front for us," I said.

We walked out of the bank's lobby and entered the car.

"Who's the gentleman in the car?" Todd asked.

"That's John," I said. "He'll be driving us to our destination."

I got into the front seat while Todd and Lorraine went into the back seat.

"Hello, Todd," John said. "I will be taking you to a safe location. I'm a government agent and I'm here to help you."

"Well," Todd said, "what's going on?"

Lorraine's hands were shaking, and her voice trembled as she said, "Todd, there was an attempt on my life tonight."

"What? Are you okay? What happened?" Todd asked.

"Jayna was able to deal with the threat," Lorraine said. "She then called John for assistance."

"Then she must be some kind of highly trained agent herself," Todd said.

"We should be at our destination within a few minutes," John said. "We can talk more there."

"I'm glad she's on our side," Todd said to Lorraine. "To bring Rodney to justice."

"Yes, she is," Lorraine said. "She's a very resourceful and, uhm, gifted young woman."

"I believe we are in danger," I said

Lorraine explained to Todd who John was and what had happened back at the restaurant. Todd was clearly upset.

We arrived in front of a building on the Upper West Side. It was a three-story brownstone and was very attractive. John took us inside, and there were already three agents there. Two of them looked familiar to me, but the third agent seemed to be new to this assignment. John told the agents to watch outside for any suspicious activity. Two agents went upstairs to look out the windows on both floors, and the third agent walked to the front door to keep watch.

"I don't think we were followed," John said to the agent by the door.

The agent nodded and continued his watch.

"There's a table in the dining room that we can sit at," John said as we followed him to the back of the house.

We sat down and waited for John to begin speaking. He placed the papers on the table.

"My name is Agent Tinkerman and, for me to explain more of the situation, I will have to ask you sign a non-disclosure first. Please read the document thoroughly and, if you'd like, sign it and we can proceed."

"Isn't that a bit excessive?" Todd asked.

"No, sir, it's not," John answered. "At this point, it is standard operating procedure."

"Very well, then," Todd said.

He and Lorraine looked over the document and signed it. John then put the paperwork in a folder.

"Alright, now that's out of the way," John said. "Now I can get started."

John explained to them about the secret off-world program that involved Planet Sekhmet and mentioned that I was an integral part of it. He told them all about the human settlement in the city of Sirius and the agreement that our government had with them.

"Do you really expect us to believe this?" Todd asked.

Lorraine spoke up and said, "After what I saw Jayna do tonight, I totally believe it."

"What do you mean?" Todd asked.

"I saw Jayna pick a man up that was ten feet away from us with an invisible force and hurl him about twenty feet up against a tree."

"So, Jayna," Todd said, "if this is true, I would like you to show me this trick."

"It's not some parlor trick, Todd," I answered.

"Well," he said, "Can you show me?"

"Are you sure you want me to do this Todd?" I asked.

"Yes," he answered.

"Okay."

There was a bowl of fake fruit on the table. I started lifting the fruit into the air. The orange was the first piece of fruit to hover over the bowl. Then I lifted the apple to orbit around the orange.

"That's interesting!" Todd said.

"Todd," I said, "please pick up that pen and hold onto it as tight as you can."

"I don't know if I believe this or not," Todd said. "There could be wires moving the fruit around."

"Oh, stop it dear!" Lorraine said.

"Got a tight hold of it?" I asked.

"Yes," he said.

I concentrated on the pen and pulled it from his hand. It flew through the orange, but I stopped it before it hit the wall behind me.

Todd was speechless. He didn't know what to think. The fruit pieces returned to the bowl and, the pen floated back across the table to hover in front of Todd.

"Here's your pen back," I said to Todd.

"Oh, my goodness!" Todd said. "This is all really happening!"

"There's a lot of more interesting things to see than this," I said.

A strange tone emanated from John's location. He reached inside of his jacket and retrieved a device from his inner pocket. It looked like a communication device from a popular TV show, a sort of folding telephone. He answered the call.

"Hello, this is John speaking," John said. "What do you have for me?"

The person on the other end of the line spoke with John for about five minutes and then ended the phone call.

"What kind of phone was that?" Todd asked. "I've never seen one like that before."

"It's called a mobile phone," John said. "It's completely wireless. It's something our agency uses. This is some of the technology we have acquired from Planet Sekhmet. The call I just received was about the man who attacked Lorraine and Jayna in the park. He is part of a criminal organization. He's an enforcer for a big crime syndicate."

"Did you find out about the guy who tried to kill Todd?" I asked John.

"We couldn't identify the body, but we believe he's another member of the criminal organization as well."

"It was you, Jayna," Todd said, "Who saved me. Now it all makes sense."

"You got me," I said with a smile.

"So, you're my guardian angel!" Todd said.

"Yup," I said, "I just don't have a halo."

"Todd and Lorraine," John said, "you both need to go into some type of protective custody or witness relocation program. There are multiple options for you, but the safest one would be for both of you to go to the human settlement called Sirius on Planet Sekhmet. You could stay there indefinitely with virtually no risk and you wouldn't have to give up your identities."

"Can we think about it and get back to you?" Todd asked.

"Sure," John answered. "You can stay here if you'd like until you make your decision. I have to caution you though, if you leave here, you will be in great danger. If there's any grocery items you would like, please make a list for me. Also, there are multiple bedrooms upstairs, you can pick any one that you like. And please let me know if there's anything else we can help you with."

The following day Todd and Lorraine decided they would go to Sekhmet until a day before the trial date. John assured them he would contact the bank to tell them they were in protective custody, and he would see to it that their home would be taken care of until they returned.

I decided not to go back to the bank; it might be dangerous. I asked John to speak to the program manager and tell him that I was not going back to the job at the bank. He said he would relay the message. I also asked him if he would take care of vacating my apartment in Brooklyn. He agreed to do so as well.

John then drove us to an airfield where a small private plane flew us to Ohio. We went through the tunnel that led to the underground caverns, which held the large humanoid giants in suspended animation. Lorraine was disturbed at the sight of these enormous people.

Todd and Lorraine were struggling to stay calm in the extraordinary situation they now found themselves in. Todd thought we would take some kind of alien spacecraft to Sekhmet, but we told him we would be traveling there much faster by the Cosmic Fountain. We explained to him what it was, and he seemed intrigued.

We reached the Fountain, and we stood at the top of the stairs for a moment.

"Have a safe trip. This is as far as I go," John said.

"How does this work?" Todd asked.

"Just follow me down the stairs, and you'll see momentarily," I said.

"This doesn't look technologically advanced," Lorraine said. "It just looks like a stone platform with some liquid around it."

"Then you should find this next part interesting," I said.

They followed me down the steps into the middle of the platform. A moment later, the Manjin appeared.

"Destination please?" the Manjin asked.

"Planet Sekhmet," I answered.

With that, the prismatic energy rose up from the liquid, and transporting to our destination had started.

"These lights are beautiful!" Lorraine said.

"And amazing!" Todd said.

Within thirty seconds, the energy subsided, and we arrived at Planet Sekhmet.

"What happens now?" Todd asked.

The World of Deception

We walked up the stairs. Yashi was waiting for us at the Cosmic Fountain to drive us back to Sirius. It was good to see her again. She was beautiful as always.

"Hello," she said, "I've been waiting for your return."

"Todd and Lorraine," I said, "this is my mentor, Yashi."

Todd and Lorraine looked dumbfounded. They both paused a moment before they said hello.

"We're going to take you to an apartment that's been provided for you," Yashi said. "After you settle in, Jayna can take you shopping to buy clothes and supplies."

"Yashi," Todd said, "are you a Sekhmetian?"

"No, Todd," Yashi answered. "I'm from another star system, Planet Arcturus."

"We would like to talk to you about that," Todd said.

"Why, of course," Yashi answered. "But we need to get you settled in first."

Yashi drove us to the apartment where Todd and Lorraine would be staying. Todd commented that Sekhmet didn't look that much different than Earth, but he said he noticed he felt weaker here. I explained to them the difference in gravity.

"The apartment is already furnished and has food in the pantry and the refrigerator," Yashi said. "You only need to shop for clothes and personal items."

Yashi parked the car in front of the apartment building. Everyone exited the vehicle, and Yashi walked up to the man standing outside.

"Greetings," Yashi said, "we're here to get the keys to the apartment."

"Hello, my name is Joe," he said." I'm the apartment manager."

Yashi then motioned for the rest of us to come closer.

"Let me introduce you to your new tenants," she said. "Todd and Lorraine Geller." She then motioned to me and said, "And this is Jayna."

Joe handed a set of keys to Todd and said, "So where are you from?"

"We're from New York City," Lorraine answered. "Where are you from, Joe?"

"I'm from Nebraska," he said.

"How did you get here?" Lorraine asked.

"My parents and I came here when I was young," Joe said. "They were farmers. My dad was good at cross-breeding different plants to increase the yields produced to make the plants a lot hardier. He just had a knack for it. I think he could grow potatoes in concrete."

"He sounds very gifted," I said. "That's good knowledge to have."

"You should see some of the stuff he grows here now!" Joe said. "The plants that he's created now feeds this entire city."

"That's impressive," Todd said. "People on Earth know the importance of farmers."

"Yes," Joe said, "They sure do."

Joe motioned to us to follow him to the back of the building. "I'll take you to your apartment and we can talk on the way."

We all followed him, and Joe told us about the apartment. It was a spacious four-room apartment with lots of closet space. He showed it to us and then left. Yashi left shortly afterward, and I took Todd and Lorraine downtown to do some shopping.

We went to the mall and went to my friend Cecilia's clothing shop. It was great to catch up with her; we hadn't seen each other for a while. She and I spoke while Todd and Lorraine shopped. Cecilia and I agreed to go to dinner together sometime soon. When Todd and Lorraine were finished shopping for clothes, we left her store and went to other shops to get necessities.

***

Later that afternoon, we went back to the apartment. Todd and Lorraine said they were tired and they would like to rest. I figured it was hard for them because their bodies had not adjusted to the gravity yet. Also, they had just gone through a traumatic event. I told them that they could call me at my parents' house if they needed anything. I gave them the number that they could reach me. We said our goodbyes, and I headed home.

I called Yashi when I got home and asked to meet her tomorrow. She agreed.

When Yashi arrived in the morning, I greeted her, and we decided to sit in the backyard to catch up.

"Yashi," I said, "I've got so much to tell you!"

"Okay," she said, "I'm listening."

I told her about all of what Lorraine had shared with me, and Yashi listened intently. It was good to be able to share this with her. The information was heavy on my heart and I knew Yashi could understand it in a way most people could not.

"Yashi," I said, "I have some questions I wanted to ask you."

"Yes?" she asked.

"Well, after listening to Lorraine's explanation of the financial system of our country, I thought about it in spiritual terms."

"And?"

"If you look at the situation from an energetic point of view, money is simply a form of energy. Correct?"

"Correct."

"If this is true, by creating money out of thin air and loaning it to the Treasury, energetically speaking, this process does not take up much energy at all. Now, once it is paid back with money earned through hard work, which does take a great deal of energy, this process becomes the way the Darkness can sap energy from the populace without them realizing what is happening to them. As you said, they are a parasitic infection within creation."

"Yes," she said, "this process is vampiric. They are sucking the life force out of people to enrich themselves.

They are profiting from the people's hard work with little to no effort of their own. This is one of the ways they sap people's energy."

"They always seem to be siphoning off some type of energy. Is that in their nature?" I asked.

"Yes, Jayna," she answered. "It is. They always are looking to fill their energetic needs. Since they disconnected from the Creator, they don't tap into the infinite energy of the Light. They need a constant source of energy or they will become weak and powerless. This is why the Kemkabi is constantly consuming dark and/or shadow energy. They especially like to feed on the darkness within one's soul.

"How hideous!" I said. "Is there any way to reason with them?"

"No," Yashi responded, "the Kemkabi cannot be reasoned with. But people can turn from their evil path and reconnect with the Light. It depends on the person and where they're at in their life process at that particular moment. Many have come back from the Darkness; however, we still lose so many more to them in comparison. Corrupted souls are given a chance to correct themselves, but they become absorbed into the Dark One if they fail to do so. All dark energy souls are extensions of one dark soul, the one we call Satan. Once a soul is absorbed into the dark energy, it loses its autonomy and has no will of its own. It will simply become another tentacle of an enormous being that is selfish, vain, and devoid of compassion. Very sad indeed.

"Deception is only possible in a physical dimension. In Spirit, it is impossible to deceive. The Darkness cannot hide in the spirit world, but in a physical world, it deceives constantly. In fact, the Darkness laughs at its deceptions."

"How does that make sense?" I asked. "Didn't God create the universe and all of us in it?"

"Jayna," she answered, "the answer to your question is complicated. The story of creation is not what you were led to believe."

"I'm not sure what you mean, Yashi," I said.

"Jayna," she said, "to explain this, it's important to understand that the creation story that you've been told is not entirely correct. Furthermore, it is not in its proper context. The creation story simply states that God created the heavens and the Earth, but there is more to it than that. The correction of the teachings of Yeshua has not come out yet, but a book is in the works. The name of the book will be *A Course in Miracles,* and it will come out in 1979. It will be given to a scribe by the name of Helen

Schucman. We can, however, go over the fundamental basics with you."

"Sure," I said. "This is fascinating."

"Okay," she responded. "In the beginning, there was only the Creator, Father/Mother God. The Creator desired companionship, so He/She decided to create a companion. That is when our soul was born."

"*Our* soul?" I asked.

"Yes, Jayna," she said. "*Our* soul. Simply put, the only two souls that existed in the universe were the Creator and its companion, which is, collectively speaking, all of us."

"But, Yashi," I asked. "How could this make sense? There are so many of us."

"The companion soul was playing and decided to create a three-dimensional reality where thought created physical form. It made many worlds and universes. It delighted in them. The physical universe was a three-dimensional light show, constantly changing like a movie playing through a movie projector. But remember, all different parts of the creation were still part of one being. It just was experiencing itself in a new and playful way.

"Then, the different parts of the companion's creation began to separate from the whole and started to become selfish. Gradually, these different parts were becoming more and more separated from the companion soul, and then something huge happened."

"Yes?" I asked.

"The companion soul forgot to laugh at the thought of being separate from the Creator, its parent. In a moment of fear, it shattered into many pieces, just like a piece of glass. At that moment, all of the individual parts of our collective soul were born. Father/Mother God had to step in. There was a problem that had to be handled.

"A three-dimensional universe had been created, and the child of God had splintered into many fragments. How does God now fix this problem? God decided to create ego-mind. In this mind, every fragmented soul part would believe it was a separate and autonomous entity. This ego-mind was powered with dark energy.

"Each soul, in its sense of separation, would feel miserable and seek out relief from its lack of joy. As each fragment fell deeper and deeper into physical pleasures, it felt more and more unhappy. And, the more pleasure one experienced, the more one wanted. As a soul gets pulled into a carnal existence, they retreat further and further away from their true home in the spiritual realm with their Creator. Whether they know it or not, every soul yearns to go back home and be with Father/Mother God.

All selfish and pleasure-seeking behavior always leads to a *disconnection* with Spirit. Conversely, all spiritual-based behavior always leads to a *connection* with Spirit.

"Now here's Planet Earth's great legacy. As all of this was going on billions of years ago, the original fragmented pieces of the one soul created Planet Earth and all of its natural wonders. It was a magical time on Earth. Fragmented parts of the soul could manifest in many beautiful forms and pop in and out of this dimension. Lovely forms were created, such as trees, flowers, butterflies, fairies, flying horses. However, some of the soul's fearful fragments felt ashamed and guilty for leaving the spirit dimension and playing in a physical one. So, in their madness, they began manifesting in the world as ugly and violent life forms, and all kinds of monstrosities were created.

"The great battle that is depicted in the Bible began. The souls that were of the Light were trying to free the souls that got trapped in matter. The Darkness had been born. All life in a physical dimension is based on spiritual warfare. Furthermore, Satan, who led the rebellion against God, was wholly absorbed into the dark energy. He was the first dark energy soul. Then, as the battle raged on, as each fragmented part of the group soul rebelled with the him, they too were absorbed.

"Soon, there were legions of souls that were willing to go 'dark' in rebellion. Satan was given leadership of the entire group's soul, and each fragmented part lost its autonomy. Now the Dark One could control every one of them. Or in other words, after a soul gets absorbed and becomes a dark energy soul, the person becomes a reflection of this evil group's soul. For example, if a person chooses to give their soul to the Darkness through a black magick ritual, first the contract that the participant has requested must be agreed to by Satan. Once he approved the contract, the magick goes through, and their soul gets absorbed into the group dark energy soul. The person's individual soul is lost until they can recover it by coming back to the Light. They are no longer the person they once were; they are now the Dark One, *appearing* as this new person. All the 'dark' souls in the universe are different manifestations of the same dark soul. Do you understand?"

"Yes," I answered. "But Yashi, how about the rest of us?"

"Good question, Jayna," she replied. "The rest of us are light energy souls, which are all connected to the Creator. In effect, there are only two souls in the physical universe that are interacting with each other, the many manifestations of the light energy soul and the many manifestations of the dark energy soul.

"There is an essential dynamic for you to understand in this spiritual warfare. Remember when I told you the dark energy souls disconnect themselves from the Light?"

"Yes," I answered.

"Since the Darkness has disconnected themselves from the Creator, they then have no energy source. They are addicted to negative energy since they have no energy source to replenish themselves. So, they must constantly be absorbing negative energy from fighting, hatred, anger, fear, and violence. This is why the Darkness is always creating wars and conflicts to replenish their energy reserves. If they cannot 'feed' from a source, they lose their energy and cannot function. They must be able to absorb negative energy from someplace. This is the reasons why they are so prone to anger and violence, which is literally in their nature. They must feed off the psychic energy it produces so they can recharge their energetic battery. Otherwise, they will grow weak, become sick, and die.

"The light energy souls, on the other hand, have a constant source of energy since they never disconnected from the Creator. It is not necessary for them to 'feed.' They simply live their lives.

"The constant battle between them is what is commonly called the battle between good and evil. Evil is always trying to inspire anger and hatred to feed and they are always trying to trap unsuspecting souls in matter, thus being absorbed into the Dark One. Misery loves company."

"The soul, or the One as it is sometimes referred to, became trapped in its own creation. The more the fragmented soul forgot their roots, the more deeply immersed they are in this physical dimension's illusion. Before you know it, millions of individuals became more and more carnal. In their physical form, they lost themselves in the illusion of life. They forgot all physical manifestations of life were just frozen light beams. They realized that we're subject to physical universe's laws, such as karma and reincarnation, but they decided this was a fun game. Whatever sensual pleasure they could experience while in physical form was worth the karma it would produce. They decided to go full steam ahead and create as much pleasure as possible in their spiritual ignorance. This led to pleasure-seeking behavior, which is known as hedonism. The problem with this is once you feed the carnal self with pleasure, the sensual self will want more and more.

"There is an old Cherokee teaching about two wolves. One represents the carnal nature of humans, the other represents the divine side. The wolves compete for food. Whichever wolf wins the battle for food will grow big and strong, and the other wolf will become skinny and frail.

"If a person is spiritually oriented and lives a life of principles and virtue, they will feed the wolf representing the divine side of human nature. That wolf will grow big and strong, and the other wolf will starve to death. If the reverse is true, then the carnal side of a person will become big and strong, and the divine side will starve to death. This is the inherent battle of the flesh versus the spirit that is discussed in many religions of Planet Earth. It all comes from the basic issue of whether we use. of lives to further trap ourselves in hedonistic pleasures, or if we choose to use our lives as an opportunity to serve the Divine.

"All paths, regardless of the religion, have two basic choices. Do we use our lives to indulge our own personal pleasures, or do we use our lives as an opportunity to serve the Light? The Darkness is all about life in a physical dimension and gratifying our pleasures. The Light teaches love, honor, and service to the Divine. The Darkness will provide the pleasures of life, the Light will give opportunities to free ourselves from this trap.

"Those who succumb to worldly wealth and status, as well as physical pleasures, are drained into the anti-matter energy self or ego-mind. Here is the fundamental conflict of Spirit versus matter. It's all about each individual's level of awareness. Are they firmly grounded in the belief of the union of all life, or do they believe they are a separate and autonomous being from the group soul?

"If a soul chooses the dark path, they indeed will fool themselves into believing that they are somehow 'special,' and not part of the group soul. Furthermore, they do think it is possible to bring harm to another without bringing harm to themselves. Here is their delusion of grandeur. In their minds, they possess the power to judge, vilify, condemn, and execute punishment to another. One well-known fact among the psychiatrists of your world is that humans project their fears. This issue plays out quite dramatically in terms of human behavior. The Dark ones are always projecting their fears and the ego-mind will always see things darkly and unjustly judge."

"What is the best way to overcome the ego-mind's tendency toward spiritual darkness and judgment?" I asked.

"The proper way to overcome the darkness of the ego-mind is to bring light into through meditation and prayer.

The mind is creative by nature but is inherently dark. If you connect to the Divine daily, this will bring light into our thoughts. Beautiful creations can be imagined, such as artwork, writing, music, and architecture. However, if no light is brought into the mind, it will create ugliness, such as evil speech, gossip, and even violent and criminal behavior. This is why there is no substitute for daily spiritual practice. There are many ways to do this, and each person must find their way. Some simply need to walk in nature to feel their connection to the Divine. Others will pray and meditate daily. Still, others will require some ritual or ceremony. In the end, there is no right or wrong way, just whatever works for an individual."

"I've felt connected to the Divine in all the ways you mentioned at one time or another," I said.

"Coming to Sirius has been an excellent path of development for you," Yashi said.

"Yes, it has," I said.

"I'll be back tomorrow so we can continue," Yashi said. She walked to the door, and I followed her, hugged her, and said good night.

After Yashi left, I sat down to meditate and felt a deep sense of spiritual connection. She always had such a profound effect on me.

I had a profound meditation which was a blissful experience for me.

When I opened my eyes, I saw a flicker of light for a split second. It looked like the multi-colored energy that the Cosmic Fountain surrounds you with. I looked again, and it was gone. What was this about?

I stared at the spot where the flicker of colorful energy appeared for a couple of minutes and, suddenly, a Manjin appeared. Now she was in complete focus, and I could see her.

"What's your name?" I asked her.

"Aviya," she answered.

"What brings you here tonight, Aviya?" I asked.

"Here?" she asked. "I realize you experience a 'here' at this moment, but in my experience, I simply am. You were just able to see me tonight. I reside in another dimension, one that does not have the same rules as yours. The Manjins exist outside of space and time. We are always 'here' as you say, you simply cannot see us. Tonight, however, you had a different experience."

"That's so interesting," I answered. "Could you please explain further?"

"Certainly," she said. "All of life is one large being. All the various beings are simply vibrating at different frequencies. Tonight, your meditation brought you closer to your divine self, and for a split second, you saw into another dimension. When you focused on what you had seen, you caused your perception of me to change into a separate being. In the fifth dimension, we are all part of one being, much like waves being part of an ocean. Your focus allowed you to see me as your mind understands life in this dimension. When we are done speaking, I will seem to disappear to you, but I will be in the fifth dimension as I always am. Only your perception of me will change."

With that, she smiled and disappeared.

After speaking with the Manjin, I had a different view of life in this dimension. My path was starting to come into focus.

Under Construction

It was good to be back in Sirius. New York City was an incredible place to be, but Sirius is now my home. The Darkness did not have as strong a hold on Sirius as they did in New York City.

I was so glad this ordeal was over. Taking on the Darkness was challenging, to say the least, and it was good to have a chance to recuperate. Mom and Dad were watching me closely to be sure I was okay. Yashi checked on me periodically. For the moment, it was good to rest and relax.

Lorraine and Todd were getting adjusted to their new environment, and they seemed happy to be in Sirius. We had a dinner for them at my parents' restaurant, and they made many new friends.

When the time came for Rodney's trial, they went back to New York City to testify. The testimony of Lorraine and Todd cemented the guilty verdict from the jury. They tried to stay in New York, but they received multiple threats from anonymous sources. While they were in protective custody, the bank offered them a lucrative severance package. They decided to accept it and take up permanent residence on Sekhmet. The bank in Sirius was happy to provide them with employment. As a result of this, Lorraine, Todd, and I all became close friends.

At this point, I was at crossroads and had to decide what my next step should be. I prayed and meditated daily and asked the Holy Spirit to give me an answer that I could understand.

One night in a dream, I saw Lucille Ball. She looked stunningly beautiful. She wore a gown and was wearing a diamond crown on her head. Her face was beautiful and radiant, and she clearly was being presented to me in the dream as a queen.

"Lucy," I said in the dream, "it's you…it's so good to see you!"

She smiled at me.

"Lucy, you've made the whole world laugh!" I said.

"Jayna," Lucille answered, "you can do comedy work as well. Remember, I am always with you."

With that, I woke up.

I prayed for guidance on interpreting the dream and while I was meditating that night, the correct interpretation of the dream came to me.

The Lucy I saw in the dream with her queenly appearance and demeanor was a symbol of the Goddess in one of her incarnations as Lucille Ball. The Goddess was telling me in the dream that I could do comedy work, remembering She was always with me.

I felt deeply that I should pursue comedy and acting. I called Yashi and asked to meet with her. I told her about the dream and asked if it was possible to put together a comedy show in Sirius. I felt this was the correct time to do so. As Yashi had told me in earlier years, this was the plan for me all along.

Yashi smiled and said it could be done. Tomorrow she would go to the TV station downtown and talk to the director. If she got his approval, she would then speak to the program manager in Sirius to ask permission for me to appear in a public comedy show. She said she would get back to me when she had an answer.

Yashi got in touch with me about three days later.

"Jayna," Yashi said, "We have decided that this is a good time for you to begin your public comedy show. It will help you move forward and also bring great laughter to Planet Sekhmet. We can start meeting with the TV people in Sirius and start working on your show. We plan on televising you, not only in Sirius, but all over the planet. It is the Goddess Herself that wants to work through you. She desires to express Herself as a comedienne, and you are Her pick.

"Comedy will help to dispel the spiritual darkness that is trying to overtake Planet Sekhmet at this time. As the light of laughter fills the airwaves, the dark shadow energy can't get a grip on the energy of the people of Planet Sekhmet because light dispels darkness. Laughter energy is like an invisible force field that will protect those in its surroundings without ever having to use any sophisticated technology to stop the dark energy's force. You were given the gift of comedy for this very reason. Your family could not understand your greater mission. To them, you were just a funny child. They brought you to a talent show to test your natural skill as a comedienne. You won the competition without any effort whatsoever; you simply spoke to the audience in a way that you found funny. The key here is that the Goddess did all the work; you just went along for the ride. You were a vessel for the Goddess, expressing herself through a child. You cannot even remember all the laughter you inspired. Your family had parties and invited everyone to your comedy shows. It was the Goddess who made them laugh, not you.

"Now it is time to bring down the house again, but this time on Planet Sekhmet. You are old enough now to understand the bigger picture. Your mission now is to use comedy to help push back the influence of the Kemkabi and keep them from doing any more damage to the planet's inhabitants than what they've already done.

We purposely waited until after your first heartbreak to bring this opportunity to you. If we had put you in front of the public earlier, you would have gone through the experience anyway, and you would have had a hard time continuing your work on the show until you recovered. Heartbreak was inevitable; you are destined to be with Landry. We did not try to stop you from going through the experience so you would learn from it and grow stronger because of it.

"Now a new mission is given to you. The comedy program will do you more good than you know. If you could see the energetic battle taking place, you would be thrilled that you could do so much to stop the Kemkabi."

"When can I start?" I asked.

"I'll call a meeting," Yashi said, "and let you know the details. I'll get back to you tomorrow."

"I can't wait, Yashi, this is incredible!" I said.

"I know," she said. "This is a wonderful project for you."

The next day Yashi came by and picked me up. We walked downtown to the TV station. There was a team of people waiting for us when we got there, six people in total. Four men and two women. The men's names were Clarence, Sheldon, Alex, and Troy. The two women's names were Joy and Heather. They introduced themselves to me, and we all went into a meeting room with a long oblong-shaped wooden table. We sat down, and Yashi led the discussion. I remained silent.

Yashi finally spoke to me and gave me a chance to speak. "Jayna, what kind of show would you like to do?"

"Well," I answered, "I would like to perform in a comedic sitcom, one that is similar to the ones on Planet Earth. It would be fun to create a storyline where we could bring out the humor in human behavior and give people a laugh!"

"Good choice, Jayna," Troy said. "I like it. What would you suggest for a storyline?"

"How about a story," I answered, "about a couple who are mismatched and married with two children. They love each other, but cannot get along. Because of the children, they stay together and their incompatible relationship creates humor."

"Jayna, we could have our writers create such a story for you," Clarence said. "Yashi tells us you are prepared to commit to working in a show. You know, there will be long hours and a great deal of work. Acting isn't as easy as it looks. Actors go home exhausted after a day's work. It only *looks* easy."

"Yes," I answered. "I am prepared to do whatever it takes to make this show work. I love to make people laugh; it's always brought me great joy. If I could do this again, that would be awesome. I would be honored if you would consider me for this position."

"Very well," Joy said. "We'll work out the details and get back to you."

"It was great meeting all of you," I said.

They all said goodbye to us. Yashi and I left and headed home. This was the beginning of a new chapter in my life. Imagine having your own TV show! The more it sank in, the more I realized how great a responsibility I have been given, and the more determined I became to do a good job. As Yashi taught me, this wasn't about me; this was about letting the Goddess do Her work *through* me.

Within a month, I got a call, and it was time to go back to the TV station and start getting ready for the production. The name of the show would be *Sirius Family Fun.* The show would be filmed in a TV studio in front of a live audience. They wanted the laughter to be authentic. The crew was busy setting up the stage and props.

It seemed surreal. How could this be happening to me? I was given my own show on another planet! In a million years, I could not have imagined such a thing.

I remembered my early years well; lots of fun with family and friends. Putting on shows seemed so natural; I couldn't imagine life any other way. But now, I had to make an adjustment that I did not have to make as a youngster. This show had a script. I never used a script as a child. I simply said what I thought was funny. Now, this was a completely different ball game. What I did as a child could not be carried over into this situation. I had to learn lines and be able to act successfully.

All of a sudden, I felt a wave of panic hit me. What if I don't remember my lines? What if the audience doesn't find me funny? What if I bomb out and no one wants to see the show? I didn't feel the same sense of confidence I felt as a child. I never had to work to make people laugh.

But as Troy reminded me, acting was hard work. There was a job to do and not much room for error. An actor must be very disciplined to do the job well. I turned to Yashi for help.

I called her and said, "Yashi, I need to talk to you!"

"Yes?" she answered.

"Could you please come over?"

"Okay, I'll be there within the hour."

When Yashi arrived, I met her at the door. We sat down on the living room couch like we always do.

"What's wrong, Jayna?" she asked.

"Ugh, all of a sudden, I feel apprehension. I've never worked in front of a camera before and now I have to remember lines! I'm not sure I can do this successfully. Do you have any advice for me?"

"Jayna," she said, "I was waiting for this. I knew your apprehension would hit you suddenly. I didn't bring any of this up to you so you could feel your fears on your own with no help from me.

"You are correct. You are not ready to work in front of a camera just yet. You're not frightened by being in front of an audience, you've been in front of audiences countless times. You have no stage fright. But acting in front of a camera is different than stage acting.

Furthermore, you have to follow a script and also follow your cues. It takes more work than you realize to do this kind of show. We let this happen for you so you would get in touch with a human sense of fear and insecurity. But not to worry, we are all here for you. This has already been addressed behind the scenes. We found an acting coach and mentor for you, and her name is Rebecca. You'll meet her tomorrow.

"At this point in your life, you're ready to learn discipline. As a child, your gift was natural. As you say, no work was involved. But now, there is a great deal of work to be done to perform in this kind of show. The only way you can succeed at this job is to buckle down and learn how to act and not rely on your inborn comedic talent to carry you through the show. You must learn to act and act well, but also learn to work well with other actors. You all take cues from each other; you all need to work as a team. If one fails, you all fail. That's how this kind of job functions. It's a team effort. The show's success depends upon the abilities of the team to work together cohesively, much like a sports team. The only way to succeed is that each of you must do your part to create success for the overall team. To do so, each of you must not only consider your own job, but take into consideration your fellow teammates' jobs as well.

"The success of a show such as this also has several factors to it. The writers must write good scripts, and the director must give good direction. The actors must act well and give and receive their cues successfully. The stagehands must do a good job, and the business office must be efficient. Do you see all that it takes to create a show? Much more than what meets the eye. It's the *synergy* of the group that will determine its success.

"Every member of this production is of the Light. We are all light energy souls. The Goddess wants this show out since it's our best defense against the Kemkabi. The laughter will keep those demons at bay. Their dark shadow energy can't work through the light produced by a peal of humor-filled laughter.

"If people were to create a burst of haughty, arrogant laughter, that kind of laughter would create dark shadow energy. This behavior is not of the Light. Those who participate in such behavior increase the dark shadow energy of their surroundings, and also, this dark, murky energy stays with them in their energy field.

"Dark energy souls all engage in gossip and conceited laughter. In their arrogance, they strive to create the illusion of superiority to feel good about themselves. However, to do so implies a superior position. Have you ever met a humble demon?"

"No, Yashi, never," I said. "Have you?"

"No, and I never will," she answered. "How about we call it a day? There are some things I'd like to do before the day's over. Can you be here first thing in the morning and be ready to start at 8:30 am? Rebecca will be here as well, and the two of you can get acquainted with each other."

"Yes," I answered, "I can be here at 8:30. I'll see you first thing in the morning."

The next day we all met just as planned. Rebecca was very beautiful and personable. She was light-skinned with curly blonde hair and brown eyes, and we hit it off instantly. I knew I would succeed with her as my trainer. It just *felt* right. We got right to work.

I was given a month to train before we began taping the show. The other actors were fun to work with, and the whole crew got along. This was a fantastic experience already, even before we started production. I felt deeply blessed.

When it came time for the show to begin, I felt adequately prepared. I wasn't nervous. Rebecca knew her job well. and I learned quite a bit from her. She was an excellent coach, and Yashi said I was doing well with her too.

Sirius Family Fun

The show began in September. The whole crew was excited, and we got off to a flying start. The first show was a hit; we got rave reviews! I was exhilarated!

The show continued to do well for the first few episodes. The public loved it, and we were all elated that our work was well received. After about a month, the show's director, Mark Snyder, got a phone call from the authorities in Sirius. A gentleman from Planet Earth was a new arrival; he and his wife were just settling in. The gentleman was a brilliant engineer with several successful skyscraper projects. He was recruited to a program, which brought him to this planet in an exchange program to learn advanced Sekhmetian engineering technology to take back to Planet Earth. He was married to a celebrity actress. Their names were Bradly Pressler and Emma Evans, and Emma was seeking a job opportunity as an actress. They asked Mark if he would consider creating a part for Emma on our show.

Mark called a meeting, and we all discussed the possibility of adding a new character to the show to accommodate her. After a lengthy discussion, we decided to give her and the new character a try. Mark got in touch with the couple, and they immediately came down to the studio. They both seemed happy and excited.

"It's such a pleasure to meet you all," Emma said.

"And thank you for allowing us this opportunity," Bradly added.

"We're happy to have you both with us. We're all looking forward to working together," Mark said. "Can you be here first thing in the morning, about 8:30?"

"Mark," Emma asked, "when will the car come to pick me up?"

"Emma," Mark answered, "We don't have a car to come to pick you up; you'll have to drive here."

"I can arrange to have someone bring you here in the morning," Bradley said to his wife. "This is not a problem."

"Jayna," Emma asked, "do you have a driver?"

"I walk to work," I answered. "It's only a fifteen-minute walk."

"So, you do your daily exercise when you walk to the set," Emma said. "You leave your car at home?"

"I don't own a car," I answered.

"Oh," she said, "isn't that's interesting." She paused. "Well, don't you worry about people following you to the studio?"

"No," I answered. "People here on this planet normally let you have your privacy. Celebrity here is much different than on Earth. There are no fan clubs or people constantly hounding you for an autograph. And when you go to a restaurant or event, you don't have to worry about being mobbed."

"Well, how are you supposed to build your stardom to get the better parts?" Emma asked.

"We consider the writers the stars of the show," I said. "We believe the message is more important than the person saying it."

"Without actors to speak the lines, there would be no show," Emma said. She then turns and walks away. "I will see everyone in the morning," she said over her shoulder.

"Emma," I said, "it was great talking to you. I'll see you then."

I breathed a sigh of relief as I walked away. Emma's behavior was petulant and confrontational, and I needed time to unwind from a long and challenging day.

As I left the building and started to walk home, Yashi drove up. I got in the car, and she drove me home.

"So Jayna," Yashi said, "how was your day?"

"Well," I answered, "it was interesting. There's a new actress named Emma and she is going to debut her new character on this upcoming episode. She's going to start working tomorrow. She was a celebrity actress on Planet Earth and was a big star in Hollywood. She doesn't realize that celebrity is different on Sekhmet than it is on Earth. Actors are not considered special here like they are on Earth. They're simply well-known."

"Narcissism," Yashi said, "is not uncommon in show business because of all the attention the celebrity receives. Narcissistic personality disorder can develop. The person believes themselves to be bigger than what they actually are and become insensitive to others' needs. They cannot handle criticism and have a grandiose sense of entitlement."

"You're right about that!" I answered.

"You'll be able to see in the next few days if she suffers from that disorder or not," Yashi said.

The following day, I arrived at 8:30, but Emma had not arrived yet. We proceeded to go through the lines and work with Wardrobe to get ready for the upcoming episode. The show was normally scheduled to air at 3:00 pm, and if Emma did not arrive soon, it would put the show behind schedule.

At 9:30 am, Emma arrived. "I'm here. We can start now!"

"We've already started and are working with Wardrobe," Mark said.

"Then where's my dressing room?" Emma asked.

Mark grinned. "Right this way." He walked to a door on the left-hand side of the set and opened it. "It's at the end of the hallway."

She opened the door and, to her surprise, the other female show members and I were in the dressing room.

Emma scowled. "Is this my dressing room?"

I smiled. "It's everyone's dressing room, Emma."

Pam, one of the Wardrobe people, stepped up and said, "Emma, this is your dress."

"I can't change in front of everyone," Emma said.

"You can go behind the screen and change there, Emma," Pam answered.

Emma grabbed the dress and stomped towards the screen. "How am I supposed to work in these conditions?" she said in a low tone.

Emma changed behind the screen and stepped out. The dress was very nice. It was emerald green with a fitted top, had a black patent leather belt with a silver buckle, and a full pleated calf-length skirt.

"This dress doesn't show off my figure," Emma said.

"I think you look beautiful in your dress," Pam said.

"I so value your opinion, Pam!" Emma said sarcastically. "I could use a drink, though."

"We don't serve alcohol on the set," I said.

"What?" Emma said. "I wish my manager was here to straighten this all up for me. He always knew everything I should do back home."

"So, is drinking on set part of what he would recommend you to do?" I asked.

"It's just to take the edge off," Emma answered.

"I don't think there's much of an edge here, Emma," I said.

There was a knock at the door.

"It's time for dress rehearsal," Mark called out.

We all left and went to the set. I noticed that Emma's hand was trembling. She was a professional actress, so

I didn't think it was nerves, but rehearsal went well nonetheless. Emma's performance was okay, but she did seem a little off.

We broke for lunch. Pam, the hairdresser and the makeup artist, asked Emma and me to join them.

Emma looked at me and whispered, "Do we eat with them?"

"Yes, we do it all the time!"

"Why don't we go to The Italian Bistro?" Pam said.

"Sounds good to me," I said. "How about it, Emma? Do you like Italian food?"

"Do they have wine there?" Emma asked.

"Of course they do. It's an Italian restaurant," I said.

"Then we should definitely go," Emma said.

We went to the restaurant, and we had a lovely meal. Emma enjoyed the food and said it was a nice restaurant to have in such an inadequate town.

Emma had multiple glasses of wine, but she still seemed to carry on and act normally. She obviously could handle her alcohol.

We finished the meal and went back to the set. The episode went fine. Emma seemed to be more agreeable after our lunch. Although, she made one mistake on a line, I was able to improvise and recover the scene. The studio audience enjoyed the performance, and we would see how the people that tuned in to the show enjoyed it. So far, so good.

I saw Emma talking to Mark before she left. I didn't get to say goodbye to her.

I then went to Mark's office after changing clothes to see what he thought about tonight's episode.

I knocked on the door. "Come in."

I opened the door and walked in. "How did you like the show?"

"I think it went fine," he said. "But Emma said you made a mistake on your line. But I know that's not what happened. Emma made a mistake and tried to blame it on you. Is there anything I need to know?"

"Well, I saw her hand shaking today before we went to lunch," I answered. "She also drank a bottle of wine by herself, and it didn't seem to affect her very much."

"Oh," Mark said, "so she might be a lush?"

"What's that?" I asked.

"An alcoholic," Mark answered.

"But she's a Hollywood actress. She has money, fame, and celebrity friends."

"Yes," Mark says, "but that doesn't mean she's happy. A lot of those celebrities have miserable lives. They congregate with each other to show off their wealth and the influence they have with other important people so that they can feel good about themselves."

"What do you mean by 'important people?'" I asked.

"Politicians, other famous actors, sports celebrities, journalists, doctors, people like that," Mark answered.

"Oh, okay," I said.

"I'll keep an eye on Emma," Mark said. "Hopefully, she won't cause any more issues."

"Thanks, Mark," I said. I got up to leave. "Have a good evening."

I made a note to myself that I need to ask Yashi more about this. She was going to stop by my house tonight.

After she arrived, I fixed her some tea, and we went into the living room.

"Yashi, it seems the Darkness could easily ensnare celebrities," I said.

"Yes, this could potentially happen," she answered. "There are many dimensions to this issue. You were blessed by being taken away from the entertainment business on Planet Earth. Although it may seem desirable from the outside looking in, those who achieve celebrity status are trapped by their own creation. The only exceptions are the ones that are sent by the Light. Your childhood hero, Lucille Ball, was one such person. She was an incarnation of the Goddess as well. It was the Goddess who was funny; Lucille was her priestess. The Goddess worked through her and made the whole world laugh. Lucille was very beautiful and talented indeed, but it was the Goddess that the people saw all along.

"There were a few from the Light that were sent into the business, but most were not sent by the Light. The Darkness sent so many to work in the entertainment industry, to settle its soul contracts. Many souls went into the contracts with them for the sake of fame and fortune. The Goddess allowed them to succeed in the business only because their success would trap them. Many rich and famous people are not as happy with their fame as they would like their fans to believe. In these circles, drugs and alcohol are prevalent. If fame and fortune could make a person happy, would they need drugs and alcohol?

"The rich and famous are always on guard for people that are trying to take advantage of them and their success. Many try to ride on their coattails and want to use them any way they possibly can. Some people want to be friends with them just so their celebrity status will make *them* look good. For this reason, they stay within the same circles of successful people so that they are not prey to predators of such nature. The many people star-struck people appear foolish to them. They also have to spend a great deal of money on security so that their family members don't get kidnapped. If you add in losing privacy and getting mobbed, does that sound like a desirable lifestyle?

"From the outside, it looks very glamorous. The celebrity is followed by cameras and fans, and are often times seen getting in and out of limousines, and meeting with other celebrities and even politicians. But is their lifestyle desirable? So many think so. All the people that are not as wealthy, not as good-looking, or as fortunate seem to have a less successful life. This is not true, however. That's part of the spiritual maturation process. When one is confident in themselves and their abilities, there is no need to 'show them.' How many go into show business to become a 'star?' And, even if they succeed, does success make them any different than they were before they began?

"If a person needs to show how important they are, this is a sign of fear. The dysfunction is called 'the need for outer validation.' They literally cannot feel good about themselves and their lives because they have a deep-rooted insecurity. Show business is full of people that are trying to compensate for a feeling of inadequacy. They foolishly believe that a celebrity lifestyle will compensate for their insecurity. Unfortunately for them, this is not the case. Celebrity could never properly address their fears."

"What would properly address such fears?" I asked.

"Divine connection," she answered. "We all have a deep sense of fear because we are separated from our beloved Creator, Mother/Father God. When we connect to the Lord, we feel safe, whole, and complete. There is no substitute for God. Even connection with another soul could not completely replace our need for divine communion. That's why so many of romantic fantasies are just that – fantasies. Even though we feel a high at the beginning of a relationship, this will eventually fade as life goes on. The only real endless joy comes from our own personal divine connection. No one can do this for us; we must do it for ourselves.

"Those who desire celebrity are running away from their deepest fear, insecurity."

"Emma mentioned her manager was giving her advice. Are managers really that important? I don't have one," I said.

"The Darkness," she answered, "first pulls people into the trap of celebrity. Once they have them in their grip and their success is assured, these dark powers keep a hold on them to make sure they follow orders by the Dark minions, or they will instantly lose their fame. There are multiple issues here. First, they are given a handler, which means this person gives them directives. This person shows up as a manager, a publicist, or somebody else close to them. They must obey them unconditionally or lose their career. That person can tell them what to wear, who they can date, what to eat, who they can have a relationship with, and how they must appear in public. They'll also make up a storyline for them concerning their private life. They can be married or involved with multiple partners. The handler is always in charge, and the celebrity loses control over their own lives. Many news reports of celebrity sightings and dates were staged to create stories for each celebrity that was decided upon by their handler.

"Also, as a person's celebrity status grows, generally speaking, so does their ego. Suppose a person has an excellent celebrity status and is called a 'superstar.' This new level of celebrity elevates them to a superior position than others, and they more than likely will develop some form of egomania.

"The Darkness loves this because the bigger someone's ego is, the easier they are to control. And remember, the ego is nothing more than dark energy that is contained in all of us until we purge it out of our system. That's what transformational work does. Those that do not do transformational work will have to deal with a big ego. If not purged, then life itself will send them situations that will purge their egos. In other words, they encounter humiliating problems until they learn humility. If someone does the work on their own, these situations need not manifest in their life. The bigger someone's ego is, the stronger the Darkness becomes. The smaller someone's ego is, the weaker the Darkness becomes.

"With the increase of celebrity status glorification on Planet Earth, the divine connection becomes weaker and weaker. In your world, most people don't understand the dynamics of spiritual warfare. They are raised to believe it's a great privilege to be rich and famous but disregard its pitfalls. Most of your planet has not understood this basic spiritual lesson. Endless joy can only be found through divine connection. Being a celebrity is just another face of addiction. The person becomes addicted to an image of themselves that is not true to life, and then they use that to compensate for a feeling of insecurity. Little do they know that they lose more than they gain by succumbing to its lure.

"Celebrity puffs up the ego by granting 'special' status to them since the rest of us are not celebrities. We cannot be considered as belonging in the same class as they are. Only a very mature person or a very developed soul can successfully handle celebrity status and, even then, it's still a challenging situation for them. Humans have an inborn tendency to inflate the ego. You were blessed to be taken away from all of this. By the time we bring you to celebrity status, you will completely understand all of its pitfalls and be sure not to fall into them. This is true for your soulmate as well. The two of you have to overcome your egos and shadow self for your mission to succeed. If you both are determined and diligent, you indeed will succeed. It's within your grasp."

"Remember, spiritual darkness or evil, whatever you would like to call it, is always looking to manifest in our dimension."

"How about drugs?" I asked. "Don't they contribute to the Darkness?

Yashi answered, "Intoxicants are very big in your culture. An intoxicated person will undoubtedly give way for the dark energy to overwhelm them. The person can become possessed through intoxication. If a person is hateful or corrupt, that also gives an evil soul an opportunity to work through them and they can become possessed. For the prideful, evil spirits will also look for a way to get into you. The best way to stay out of any possession is to stay away from all intoxicants and prideful, hateful, or corrupt behavior. If you manifest any of these qualities, the Goddess allows evil spirits to enter you and find expression. If light dispels darkness, then the light of spiritual attributes will dispel their darkness as well. Virtue will always win the spiritual battle against devilry."

"My planet needs these lessons," I said. "It needs spiritual elevation."

"Indeed," Yashi answered. "That is exactly what Planet Earth needs right now. All the spiritual darkness would not exist if the major part of the population would spiritually wake up. There is an unimaginable amount of corruption, hedonism, misinformation, and toxicity on every level that is consuming the planet as we speak. We must first address the Kemkabi here on Planet Sekhmet and, once that pursuit is successful, we can move on to Planet Earth."

Falling Star

After Yashi left that night, I got ready for the next day's work. The whole Emma situation was very challenging, and I prayed that night that we could successfully resolve the situation with her. Her behavior had become a problem for everyone on the show.

A few days went by, and Emma seemed to do better. She wasn't quite as mean-spirited with people on the set, and all seemed to be going well until one day, she came to work angry. She had shown up late as per usual, and we had already been to Wardrobe. We were ready for our dress rehearsal.

"Is everything okay?" I asked her.

"Oh, I'm just fantastic!" she said sarcastically. "I need to speak with Mark."

I noticed she was carrying a few envelopes in her hand as she stormed towards Mark's office. She didn't knock. She pulled the door open, stormed inside, and slammed it behind her.

I heard Emma shouting, and Mark answers her, but I couldn't make out what they were saying. This went on for several minutes. Then the door flung open, and Emma walked towards the dressing room.

I could see Mark standing in the doorway holding the letters. It was apparent he was furious. I walked over to talk to him.

"Not right now, Jayna," he said. "Excuse me, I have to make a phone call."

Emma had made her way to the set and was ready for rehearsal. We started rehearsing, but something happened that threw everything off. Emma began to take my lines and forced me to ad-lib a couple of times. Finally, I had enough.

"That's not how the script is written," I said. "Why are you doing this?"

"I should be the star of the show," she answered. "I'm a famous actress and I have a lot more experience than you do. My husband brought me to this place where everything I had accomplished doesn't mean anything."

Tears ran down her face. "I have to put up with a mediocre part on a mediocre show and I work with a bunch of novices who aren't qualified for Wardrobe, who seem to think some young woman can do half the job that I can. The fans are sending me letters, 'You're so great on Jayna's show!' Your fans are ignorant. They don't know what a good show would look like. But I can tell you it's definitely not this."

She sank to the floor and sobbed as she started talking to herself under her breath. I heard voices coming from the door of the set. I recognized one of the voices belonging to Bradly, Emma's husband, and Mark. Bradly stepped through the door and walked over to Emma. He reached down and lifted her to her feet. He put his arm around her, almost carrying her.

"Come on," he said to Emma.

They walked out, escorting her off the set.

"I'm sorry about that everyone," Mark said as he stepped forward. "I've talked to the writers, and they are going to be changing the script. We'll probably have to work through lunch."

"That's fine with me," I said.

"I think Emma's ego finally got to her and she just had a meltdown," he said.

"And," I said, "she's finally realized the fame she has doesn't mean anything."

"You're probably right, but we need to get to work now."

We worked through lunch and were able to adjust the new script successfully. The show went well that night, and the rest of the week went well too. But we did start receiving letters asking what happened to Emma's character. The letters kept coming for several weeks. I finally got in touch with Emma's husband. I asked him if it would be okay to come by their house, drop off the letters, and speak to Emma. He agreed, and I stopped by on the weekend.

When I got to their house, Bradly opened the door. "Jayna," he said, "welcome. Come on in."

I stepped inside, and Bradly led me to their backyard's flower bed. Emma was outside tending to the garden. She looked well.

"Hello Emma," I said. "This is a beautiful garden! Did you do this all yourself?

"Yes, Jayna," she answered. "I have a lot of time to do things I've always wanted to do. I'm no longer being pulled in different directions. My husband helped me design the garden. There are so many varieties of flowers on this planet that we don't have on Earth, and I've discovered that I'm good at gardening."

"Well," I said, "the landscaping here is absolutely beautiful and all the stone work is amazing."

"I see things a lot differently now that I've stopped drinking," Emma said. "It's been a good three months.

My husband said he'd had enough of my antics. All of our issues came to the forefront. He would no longer tolerate my actions. He told me one of the reasons he brought us here was to work on our relationship. We both were always too busy to have time to be together. Since I left the show, we started spending a lot of time together ,which helped heal our relationship. When we were on Earth, we were pulled in opposite directions. It's not like that here."

"I'm glad to hear things are going well for you," I said. I walked over with the large sack of mail and set it down next to Emma. "By the way, I have a bag full of fan mail for you."

"Thank you for bringing them," Emma said. She started to look through the letters. I noticed her expression changed as she started reading them. She looked deeply touched. She read a few notes and then looked up at me. "As much as it's touching to see appreciation of my work,

I don't want that life anymore, but I'll be happy to answer the letters anyway."

"I'm sure your fans would be grateful to hear from you," I said.

"Jayna, would you like a cup of tea?" Emma wanted to change the subject.

"Sure," I answered.

With that, Emma went back into the house and returned a few minutes later with a serving tray and tea. She motioned for me to follow her, and I did. She led me to a patio table, and we sat down.

"Emma, I noticed you don't want to talk about your fans. What's really bothering you?"

"My fans have no idea who I really am," she said. "They also don't know what it costs to be a superstar. One of the reasons I started drinking was to deal with the pressures that were put on me. The other reason was I couldn't handle what was done to me, trying to break up my marriage with Brad."

"What was done to you?" I asked. "You're still with Bradly, so you must love him."

"Yes," she answered, "I love him, but my manager wanted me to leave him and marry another movie star. He said it would be better for both of our careers and it would make our fans think it was some whirlwind romance. So, I told him there was no way I would do this. He told me that I had no choice. One night, there was a huge party, but my husband had to work late so he couldn't be there."

A tear runs down Emma's cheek as she gathered the strength to tell her story.

"I went to the party by myself," she continued. "And my manager was talking to the actor that he wanted me to be with. He told us to get better acquainted. So, we talked for a while, talking about movie roles and working with certain directors. Other actors would come up and make small talk with us like we always do at parties so that the press can see us together and think we're some big happy family.

"A few hours went by. My manager brought me a drink. It must have been drugged and I started to feel woozy. I said I needed some air, but he said I just needed to lay down. I was taken to one of the bedrooms in the mansion and I passed out. They then took revealing pictures of me in bed with the other actor. My manger showed me these pictures later and he told me that I was going to do what he told me to do. If I didn't, he would show those pictures to my husband and that he'd also make sure I would never work in another film again."

"That's one of the most despicable things I've ever heard," I said.

"This business is full of ugly stories like that. It's good you never got involved in any of this."

"How did you keep from marrying this other actor?"

"He ended up having an accident on the set of a film," she said. "He was in a scene in a barn and an oil lamp fell over and started a fire. He had burns over half of his body. He could no longer be a leading man. Shortly after this, Brad was approached for this program in Sirius. I figured it was the best way to escape that situation because the manager still has all those photos. Acting and being on the show here still brings back those memories even though it's not the same here."

"You've been through a lot," I said. "Were you able to tell Bradley about this?"

"After I had the breakdown at rehearsal," she said, "he brought me home and we had a really long conversation. I was able to tell him everything. He was really hurt, but he was able to put that aside and help me deal with all of the pain that I was in. I told him I didn't want that life anymore and he totally supports me in that decision. And now our relationship is getting better. I am not afraid of what my former manager might try to do."

"You know, that's quite a story," I said. "You've overcome a great deal. That's a great love story."

"My life is back on track. I feel at peace now," she said. "The love story is truly what people want, but so few actually have it. If it weren't for me being on your show, I don't think it would have happened quite like this. Thank you, Jayna."

I was amazed at what she had said. I didn't know quite what to say. "Your welcome," I said. "I notice that you look really vibrant since you've stopped drinking."

Emma smiled. "That's not the only reason."

"What do you mean," I asked.

"I'm pregnant!" Emma said. "I'm three weeks along."

"Congratulations," I said. "Are you going to have the baby here or on Earth?"

"We're going to have the baby here," she answered. "I think this could be a good environment for our family. Brad can go back and forth to Earth to maintain his business and work on projects to pass on what he's learned here. He's also writing a book on architecture and engineering so that should create more income to keep his business afloat."

We talked for a bit longer, but it was starting to get late in the afternoon, and I needed to get back to the set.

Emma and I walked to the door.

"Jayna, you can come back anytime you want," she said. "I enjoy your company."

"I would like that," I said.

"The show is actually really good," she said. "And the people you work with are top notch. Please tell them I'm sorry." She opened the door for me.

"Why don't we get together and go out to the Italian restaurant sometime?" I asked.

"Sure," she said. "They have good food there."

"Yeah, I know," I said. "It's my parent's place."

"Really?" she said. "I had no clue. But no wine for me."

"It's a deal," I answered.

Tough Work

For the next six months, I focused mainly on our TV show. The team worked very hard to make it a success. I didn't have much time for dating. Work was so demanding, but I did find time to go on a few dates. I found the men interesting but could not give the possibility of a relationship any real consideration due to my heavy work schedule.

Time flew by and, before I knew it, the show's first season was over. It was February of 1981 and I had a three-month break before the next season began.

It felt so good to have a break. Life was so hectic making a TV show. Now I could concentrate on my spiritual studies again. The Kemkabi had been pushed back. The number of Darkened entities had dropped by 25%. The strategy was working. However, due to the show's break, the number could start climbing again in no time.

Yashi and I met at her apartment this time. I loved being there. This was the apartment of someone close to nature but also had an artistic flair. This environment was both beautiful and relaxing.

I had the Crystal Cube with me because we were going to practice my pyrokinetic skills. Her couch was comfortable, and I felt at home.

She had me focus my attention on bringing forth fire, and she held my hands over the Cube. The Cube added power and energy to whatever I was doing, and once I was able to bring forth fire, the Cube would make the fire even bigger and more powerful.

I have been trying to focus my energy on producing fire for over half an hour; nothing was happening.

"Yashi," I asked, "something is wrong. I can't seem to tune in."

"Jayna," she said, "just relax and let it happen. And, if nothing happens, we'll try again some other time. Don't worry."

I tried for another fifteen minutes, but still no results.

"Yashi," I said, "I must be blocked somewhere. Nothing is happening. Can we try another time?"

"Certainly," she said, "there's no rush. We can explore what could be causing your blockage. Any thoughts on it?"

"No," I said. "I can't think of a thing."

"Alright, let's call it a day. We'll try some other time."

"Okay, Yashi. I'll see you tomorrow."

With that, I grabbed my belongings and left.

This issue stayed in my mind for quite some time. What was wrong? Why couldn't I tune into my natural spiritual gift and manifest it? I was starting to doubt myself, and I was even beginning to doubt Yashi. How do I know I am pyrokinetic in the first place? What if she is mistaken and all of this is a waste of time? If Yashi can't help me, who could?

Maybe I need to take a vacation? Should I go through the Cosmic Fountain and go back to Brooklyn to visit family and friends? Would that possibly trigger a past event in my childhood that I can't even remember? I prayed for an answer to my dilemma. Divine connection was always the answer, but what could be blocking me?

Thoughts of uncertainty kept going round and round in my head. Was I afraid of success? Was I afraid of my own power? Was I holding on to some trauma that I hadn't resolved yet? What was the problem?

Spread My Wings

My first decision was to move out of my parent's home and be on my own. Housing in the area was available, and it seemed to be the right thing to do.

I asked Yashi to go to the authorities overseeing my program and ask for permission to move out. I was twenty-three years old now, old enough to fend for myself. The TV program did provide an income, so it helped me to feel more like an adult.

Yashi got approval for me to get my own place and agreed to help me. We met Kensley, the landlord, with multiple rental listings through the city's website. As soon as I met him, I had an uncomfortable feeling about him. Something wasn't right. Yashi didn't say anything, so I assumed he was okay.

We went ahead and filled out a form and waited until he was done with his phone call. He came out of his office and explained to us the choices we had for available apartments. I looked over the information and made a pick. Yashi agreed it was a suitable choice for me. We asked to see the apartment.

"I can show you the apartment now, if you'd like," Kensley said.

"Sure," I said, "but how much is it per month?"

"Eight ounces of silver per month," he answered.

"Wow," I said. "That's a steal. Can we go see it now?"

"Yes, we can go there now. We can take my car."

We got in his car and drove to the apartment. It was just two blocks from my parents' home and Yashi's apartment. As soon as I walked in, I felt at home. It was a one-bedroom apartment with a large sunny living room and a beautiful kitchen. It had been well kept, and I could see myself living there.

I looked at Yashi, and she nodded. We both felt this apartment would suit me well. I turned to Kensley to close the deal. He said he would draw up the paperwork, and we could come back tomorrow to sign the lease.

Yashi and I left and went back home. I was excited about the apartment, and we talked about buying furniture and decorations.

The next day, we went back to Kensley's office to sign the paperwork. His secretary handed us the lease, and I started to read it over.

"Yashi," I said, "there's a problem."

"What's the problem, Jayna?" she asked.

"Kensley quoted us eight ounces silver per month," I said. "But the contract says ten ounces of silver per month. Let me ask his secretary."

I walked up to the secretary. "Excuse me, I was quoted a price of eight ounces of silver per month for an apartment, but the lease says ten. There must be a mistake."

"Ma'am," she said, "I was told to put ten."

"I would like to speak with Kensley," I said.

"Certainly," she said. She picked up a phone and called him out of his office.

Kensley came out and looked a little concerned. "Yes, Jayna, can I help you?

"Why did you have your secretary put ten ounces of silver for the price of the rent when it should have been eight?" I asked.

"Well," he answered, "we didn't draw up the contract yet. It should be ten. You can afford it. You work on a TV show."

"Do the other renters pay a higher price because of where they work?" I asked.

"Well," he answered, "that doesn't matter."

Then we began to quarrel back and forth, which turned into a heated argument.

"Look Jayna," Kensley said, "it's ten or nothing."

"Kensley, you're price gauging me. As soon as you saw how much I loved the apartment, you raised the price thinking I would take it any way. I'm not playing your game!"

Kensley looked very agitated, and Yashi looked at me. He was determined to get that extra two pieces of silver from me.

"Jayna, I'm not playing your game," Kensley said. "You're trying to take advantage of me. This apartment is worth more than eight ounces of silver a month. You can either get out or I will throw you out!"

I felt my blood pressure rising, and I was starting to lose my temper. I focused on keeping calm and not getting worked up. This man was determined to challenge me, so I decided to call his bluff.

"I'm not going anywhere, because I have a witness. You have to honor the agreement," I said.

With that, his face got red with anger, and I could see his desire to strike me. I just stared back at him. The moment was tense. The situation could escalate at any time, but I had no fear of him. He raised his hands and started to walk towards me as if he were about to grab me. I thought about striking him but instead chose not to.

"Stop, or you will be sorry!" I yelled.

I felt a wave of energy. It released from my forehead and, a split-second later, Kensley stopped dead in his tracks. Seemed the lights were on behind his eyes, but nobody was home. He had a blank stare, his mouth hanging open.

"Jayna," Yashi said, "why did you do that?"

"Did what?" I answered. "I don't know what that was."

Yashi then walked over to him and placed her hand on his head. She closed her eyes and concentrated. "His higher brain activity has stopped. Jayna, you don't know what you did to him. You're going to have to use the Cube quickly to bring him back to normal."

"Okay," I said. "I'll help him, but he should not be allowed to rip people off."

"We'll tell the authorities and they'll deal with it," Yashi answered.

I held the Cube on top of Kensley's head. The Cube lit up, and seconds later, Kensley's face returned to normal. He took a step back.

"What happened?" he asked.

"You tried to attack Jayna," Yashi said. "And that was not allowed."

"I'll go someplace else and get an apartment," I said.

We walked out of the office and down the steps toward the car. As I opened the door, I heard a voice. I turned and saw the secretary walking towards us. She had her purse, and her arms were full of items from her desk.

"I've had enough of him," she said. "He tries to make me his scapegoat. I'm going to find another job. Here's the number to my apartment building's manager; the address is on the back. A couple's moving out into a house because she's pregnant. You can look at that apartment, maybe you'll like it. The manager is fair and the price should be about the same."

The next day, I went to see the apartment and decided to take it. During the next month, I focused on moving my things to my new place and decorating. I loved the rustic look as a theme for my new home. I looked for fire color accessories for pillows and wall hangings and went about creating a space that I was comfortable with. Shopping for unique household decorations was fun for me, and I was pleased with the results when it was all finished. It also took my mind off what could be blocking me temporarily. But still, there was no forgetting it. What could be blocking me?

The Crystal Cube couldn't be used for this type of question. Going back into someone's past could potentially be harmful to the person if they couldn't process the event in their life. The body, in its wisdom, would encapsulate a traumatic memory with a physical membrane sheath around the brain cells if the event was too painful for a person to remember. The event then could no longer be recognized by the person but lay dormant somewhere in their brain, inaccessible to the person. Over time, the membrane would start to dissolve, and the person would experience flashbacks. I did not have any flashbacks, but since I was relatively young, it could be possible there was such a thing hiding in the memories. This was something to consider, but, at the time, I didn't take the possibility too seriously.

The last incident, however, raised another issue for me. I found a new ability, but caution was of the utmost importance. I needed to be able to control my impulse to strike out when angry. Striking out mentally could be far worse than hitting them physically. I could potentially lobotomize someone.

Vacation

I started to feel overwhelmed, so I decided to take a vacation and go back to New York to visit family and friends. I had two months left of time off, and it seemed like the right thing to do.

I contacted the program authorities and made arrangements to go through the Cosmic Fountain and then have a car pick me up when I landed in Ohio. All travel arrangements went smoothly, and I was in New York City in no time. I chose to stay with an old friend of mine, Janet. We were childhood friends and still stayed in touch. She lived in a large apartment in the Flatbush section of Brooklyn, and she had an extra room for me to stay in.

Every time we got together, we have a wonderful time. It was so good to see her! We went out to dinner, reminisced old times, and laughed at our childish antics.

I asked her if she would take a trip with me to see the building that I grew up in as a young child. It was a limestone building in Park Slope, Brooklyn, and was a bit out of our way. She agreed, and we took her car.

Parking was always an issue on this street. There were more cars than there were parking spaces on the block. I remembered my father always having to look for a spot in the evenings when he came home for work. We finally found one a block away and walked the rest of the way.

I loved walking down the streets of Brooklyn. The houses were charming and well built. The old brownstones and limestone buildings on the street I grew up were now classified as historic houses. I still enjoyed admiring their timeless beauty. Having grown up in a limestone house, I appreciated all that they had to offer. They had large spacious rooms, high ceilings, carved wood designs on their door frames, hand-carved wooden spindles on the staircases, and stained-glass windows. Some even had bay windows. The house I grew up in had a dumbwaiter. How cool!

As we walked down the street, I remembered all the houses I used to visit when I was a small child. There were a several children I was friends with, and all the memories came rushing back to me. The buildings were well maintained, and the street looked more beautiful than ever. I remembered when one of my neighbors planted a small tree in front of their house, and now it was huge! So many years had gone by!

We continued down the street and noticed that, even though the buildings were well-maintained, something was different. I then realized no children were playing outside their homes. When I grew up there, there were so many children playing on the sidewalk. Now, there were none. I'm sure that was because of all the child kidnappings taking place since the time I left. When I was a child, parents felt safe, allowing their children to play outside without any worries. In today's world, it just wasn't the case.

My God, I thought, *the Darkness has succeeded in terrorizing the populace.* I looked around and did not see any Darkened people. Thank God! I just wanted to relax on my vacation. My old house was in view.

When I got up to the house, my heart starting racing. I was getting heart palpitations, and there was no reason behind it. I wasn't in any danger. What would cause my body to do this? I immediately began praying and suddenly realized that some memory deep within me that was trying to escape. The memory wanted to surface, but I could not access it still. Why couldn't I remember? Whatever it was, it must have been traumatic. I wished Yashi was here, but she was a long way away.

"Are you okay, Jayna," Janet asked. "You look a little pale."

"Pale?" I said. "I was just remembering my early childhood. This house sure is beautiful."

"Yes, it is," Janet replied. "I bet you have many happy memories here."

"You're right, I do," I said. "It's so good to see it again."

I walked closer to the front entrance and, as I did so, the heart palpitations increased. The closer I got to the house itself, the worse they became. As uncomfortable as I was, I was still happy about one thing. This experience brought me one step closer to finding the origin of my blockage. Clearly, it had something to do with a young childhood memory that I had blocked out. To date, I still haven't been able to solve the mystery of my inability to access my pyrokinetic ability.

Janet and I stayed a few more minutes and then left to go to a neighborhood restaurant for dinner. The walk helped me to recover from my anxiety.

She just started a new relationship with a man named Seth. They were both happy and in love. When she told me about him, I was intrigued. He was a martial artist and taught self-defense at the local YMCA. He was working on getting his own studio. His martial arts style was a Jewish style called Krav Maga, which I had never heard of.

"Janet, what is Krav Maga about?" I asked her.

"Jayna, why don't you go to his classes and find out?" she said.

"Okay, will do," I answered.

We met the following Tuesday night at the YMCA, and I watched him teach a class.

Looks great, I thought. *I need to do this.*

As it turns out, Krav Maga was an Israeli martial arts style that was very efficient and effective.

I signed up for an eight-week course and learned the basic fundamental techniques of this martial arts style. I enjoyed the class; there was so much to learn. And, once you understood the method, there was always the hard work of practice. To become a highly skilled martial artist was no small achievement. It took a great deal of time and energy, there were some financial costs, and one had to stay in shape to be capable of withstanding the physical stress. There was also a psychological benefit. Being able to stop an attacker without freezing in fear was well worth the effort. Fear was replaced with confidence.

I was enjoying my vacation, and all was going well. It was great to see my family and friends and having free time to do as I pleased. One of the things I most enjoyed about New York City was the vast number of restaurants here. Every conceivable style of food was available, and it was most enjoyable to have the opportunity to visit a number of them. I was looking forward to the next four weeks of more of the same.

***

With only four weeks left to go until I was due back on set, I received a phone call. It was John. He told me I needed to pack my bags and get ready to leave immediately for Planet Sekhmet. There was an incident with the Darkened, and it was terrible. They needed me back as soon as possible.

Oh God, I thought, *what now?*

John explained to me what happened. A group of the Darkened, ten to be exact, went to the shopping mall in Sirius and opened fire on the people inside.

My concern was for everyone, but my mind went to Cecilia's shop.

"John, is Cecilia okay?" I asked.

"No, Jayna," John answered. "I'm sorry, she's one of the casualties."

This was devasting news. The entire incident was terrible, but losing my best friend was overwhelming. I started to sob uncontrollably. John tried to comfort me, but I was inconsolable.

We hung up the phone, and I started packing while I remembered all the times Cecelia and I had spent together. I could not think of anything else. The grief was almost unbearable. It seemed like an eternity until John arrived.

When he finally did, my bags were packed, and I was ready to leave. On the drive to the Cosmic Fountain, I still had a heavy heart, and John finished telling me what happened.

They used directed energy weapon handguns, which were easily purchased on Planet Sekhmet. The security guards immediately fired back with their own directed energy weapons, and luckily, some shoppers were armed as well. A colossal battle erupted, and energy beams were going off in every direction. There was a mad rush to the exits. The scene was total chaos. The Darkened were all taken out eventually, and the fighting stopped, but the damage was done. They had succeeded in killing eighty-nine people and left forty-three seriously injured.

The fear, anger, and confusion produced by this event created great energetic food for the evil forces. The

Sekhmetians needed the show to come back on air as soon as possible for some pushback.

But the darkness they sent to us was so powerful, it became harder and harder for me to stay clear in this environment. There was a psychic cesspool on Planet Sekhmet that they created. Our TV show had pushed back the Kemkabi, but they made some headway again in the three-month break. This was what I was afraid of. They took advantage of the show's break to push with everything they had to create more psychic darkness on the planet. In turn, this would make it difficult for me to retrieve any psychic information. Bringing the show back should dispel much of the darkness that they so enjoyed feeding on. Hopefully, now there should be less psychic darkness and less of the Darkened out on the streets.

The question now was how the Darkness could get past my psychic ability and create such a disaster without me being able to see it in advance successfully? The Sekhmetian military contacted Yashi and asked her to work with me to find out what went wrong. Our psychic work had produced good results in the past. What went wrong this time?

Yashi prayed for me as I went through my normal routine of giving updates on the Kemkabi. Apparently, they were directing their dark shadow energy towards me with great intensity in hopes that it would psychically interfere with my work. They did succeed to a degree. Their shadow energy was hampering my psychic ability.

When I got back to Sirius, there was great anger everywhere. The streets were quiet, but I could feel the energy of the people. They had enough of the Kemkabi. The situation with them had escalated, and everyone now was going to move forward, doing anything and everything they could to stop them. Losing my friend made me all the more determined to stop them as well. I was very angry, and at the same time, I had great sorrow in my heart because my best friend from childhood had been killed.

The Sekhmetian military was called in. They patrolled the streets day and night. The army and the citizens actively searched for anybody that had become Darkened. The authorities ordered the military to terminate any Darkened they discovered. The atrocities were no longer being accepted. I was asked to resume my work on the comedy show with the rest of the crew.

We had to come up with a game plan to deal with the Darkness. They were fighting hard. The pushback they received from our show did not sit well with them. They were going to "show us." I turned to Yashi to ask for help to see if there was some way to overcome this psychic interference.

The next day Yashi called me and wanted me to come to her apartment. She said she had something for me. When I arrived, I knocked at the door and she let me in.

"I would like to introduce you to someone Jayna." An Arcturian man standing behind her. She said, "This is my husband, Rahmi."

"Hello Jayna," he said. "It's so nice to finally meet you."

"It's my pleasure to meet you Rahmi." I said. "Yashi told me about your family and your work."

"My work is hard sometimes, but it is rewarding and our family is doing well. I'm only here for a short visit, but I wanted to give you something that I brought from Arcturus."

He reached into his pocket and pulled out a necklace. It was a round-shaped crystalline disc that had geometric shapes etched into it. It had a blue and purple hue with gold wire inlaid around its outer edge, and it was hanging on a gold necklace.

"That necklace is very pretty," I said, "but I sense it far more than just a piece of jewelry."

"It's used to help protect from psychic attacks," he said. "You will be able to tell when someone is attacking you because it will give off a slight hum.

He handed the necklace to me and said, "Jayna, Yashi and I would like to have this."

"Now it should be easier for you to continue your work," Yashi said.

The chain was large enough for me to slip the necklace over my head, and I felt at ease. It began to hum almost like it was singing to me.

"Thank you for such a beautiful gift! The necklace is exquisite."

"Your welcome Jayna," Yashi said. "This necklace should help you in your work."

"I believe it will. I'll see you tomorrow Yashi." Both of you enjoy the rest of your day."

I let myself out and walked back to my apartment. When I arrived home, I meditated for a while and started to feel normal again. I felt ready to go back to work. This necklace was amazing!

It was decided the show would resume immediately, and we would continue to stay on top of their plans through psychic work. Our long-term plan was to bring Landry to Planet Sekhmet, but that was still a very long way off. In the meantime, we had to push them back successfully.

A Sekhmetian military officer named Lieutenant Jagannath was assigned to oversee the situation in Sirius and report back to the Sekhmetian military top brass daily. Yashi introduced me to him, and I immediately felt his energy. He was polite and professional, but I could feel his stern and unyielding demeanor behind his courteous behavior. He was not someone I would want to get into a fight with.

When we were ready to resume the show and start the new season, we all had a sense of apprehension. Never in all the years we'd lived in Sirius did we ever encounter such a violent attack. It was unprecedented. We went about our business, but nothing was the same again. The fun and laughter of last season were gone. Now we were simply doing our jobs. But the show had to go on, and the team tried their best to carry on as usual.

Yashi worked with the military and decided to launch two more comedy shows alongside ours. That way, there was always one on-air to help create positive energy in Sirius.

I yearned for my soulmate! The year was 1981, and it would be 2003 before I could connect with Landry. There were so many years still to go, and it seemed a million years away at this point.

Anticipation

My work schedule was demanding, and there was not much free time for me. This was a good thing because it kept my mind occupied. However, over time, I started to feel lonely, and so I asked Yashi about Landry.

Yashi came over that night, and I opened up a discussion with her about the yearning one feels for their soulmate. We sat on the couch as we always did when there was work to be done.

"Yashi, what about Landry?" I asked.

"It's 1981 and he's only eleven years old. He has no idea about his destiny and what is expected of him. There's much he will have to accept and adjust to, much like you did when you were a child when you were taken into a secret-space program. This will all be a learning experience for him, as you well know. He needs to grow up and become a man, and have relationships outside of you so that he will be mature before you meet him. The two of you were never destined to be together early in life. Rather, you and Landry were destined to meet later on in life so that you both would be mature by the time you met. This would make your relationship easier to work out. In the meantime, we will be focusing on your comedy show here in Sirius. So far, we are successful in creating laughter on the planet."

"It seems like forever until we can finally meet," I said. "What will he look like, Yashi?"

"Jayna," she answered, "he will be 6'3" inches tall, have sandy blonde hair, and light skin with big beautiful blue eyes. He will be very handsome. You will be happy with his looks."

"Will he like my looks, Yashi?" I asked. "I'm afraid I won't appeal to him."

"Yes, Jayna," she said, "you will. Not to worry."

"In the meantime," I asked, "what about me dating other men? Twenty-four years is a long time to wait until we're destined to meet. Now that Conrad's behind me, I've been thinking about dating again. I just don't want to jump into any relationship too quickly, but dating would be fine."

"Jayna, yes indeed," she said. "You are encouraged to seek out male companions as you see fit. In time, you will be okay with getting involved again with someone. Only this time, you attach as profoundly to them as you did with Conrad. You know any relationship you get into won't last in the long run, so you will naturally keep yourself from bonding too deeply with your male companions.

"It's healthy for you to be in relationships. They help you mature and you will go through the ordinary course of development. You should not be frightened to get involved with someone again. It's normal to pull back after a heartbreak. However, it's not advised that you stay completely out of relationships. If this were to happen, you would cave into fear and not develop properly. How could a warrior of the Light be so frightened? Do you see? You are being given opportunities in your relationships to work out your fears. This will help you in your spiritual development more than you know."

"Okay, that's it. I'm going to start dating again and move forward. The only problem is that being on the TV show is very demanding and will take up much of my time, but, hopefully, I'll find someone who will understand."

"You will," she said. "Not to worry. There are plenty of men you can date if you would like to." She paused. "We need to have a serious conversation. I've been waiting for the right time. You're old enough now to be able to handle the information. I'd like to discuss past lives, in particular, one of your past lives with Landry."

"Yes," I replied. "We talked about karma and reincarnation in my spiritual training. All of us are trapped on the karmic wheel until we free ourselves. Any loveless act creates karma and every karma we create further traps us in the physical reality. This, in turn, causes us to need to reincarnate and we are fated to suffer until we learn how to love completely. Therefore, we are bound to the karmic wheel of constant birth, death, and reincarnation until we break the cycle. The path of transcendence leads us to freedom from the chains of the past that keep us in this endless loop of drama. To love all is the answer."

"Correct. And what is the path of transcendence?" she asked.

"Transcendence is the overcoming of the ordinary world and its karmic limitations to step into our divine nature, which is boundless and unlimited. In other words, it is the overcoming of our carnal nature to become a transformed divine being, which is expressing itself in our three-dimensional reality."

"Wonderful!" Yashi said. "You completely understand."

"Yes, I do. You taught me well."

"Okay then, we're ready to move on," she said. "I'd like to start with a past life in ancient Egypt that you had with Landry, your twin flame soulmate."

"What is a twin flame soul mate?" I asked.

"A twin flame soulmate is the other half of your soul. In the beginning, God took every soul and split it in two so that each soul would have its perfect mate. You are the feminine side of your soul, and Landry is the masculine side of your soul. The two of you together are *one* soul. He is your perfect mate, and you are his.

"In ancient times, Landry was one of Egypt's great kings and you were his queen."

I was dumbfounded for a moment and could not speak. Yashi waited for me to respond.

"That is unbelievable Yashi," I said. "But some part of me knows you're right. Please continue."

"Jayna," she said. "It's my mission to prepare you for your upcoming work with him. You are being prepared to help him wake up to his great mission. This is the beginning step for you."

"What is?" I asked her.

"Understanding your past together," she replied. "The two of you will be brought together once again for the greater good of Planet Earth. A brief history of your soul is necessary.

"First, your and Landry's soul originated in the angelic realm. Specifically, you both came from a phylum of angels known as the Thrones, which are warrior angels. Remember the great battle mentioned in the Bible?"

"You mean where the angels and demons fight?" I asked.

"Yes. There was a huge battle in the heavens and the angels fought with the demons. Well, you and Landry fought in that battle, but, unfortunately, the Light lost the war. The battle was fought to keep each soul from having to incarnate into a three-dimensional reality such as this one, where the soul would be trapped on the karmic wheel indefinitely. The object of the Darkness is to trap a soul in matter or on the karmic wheel, which would in turn keep it trapped in matter."

"Why?" I asked.

"Because the Darkness has developed a pathological fear-based defiance behavior against all that is good and Godly. They cover up their fear with arrogance, pride, and haughty mockery."

"Why?" I asked.

"By separating from the Creator, they disconnected from love and, as a result, they feel shame and guilt for doing so. Their prideful and arrogant behavior hides their shame and vulnerability. What they fear most is exposure or, in other words, just simply facing the truth. If you force them to do so, they will more than likely become violent, which is a form of cowardice. This is why they bully so much. They are more afraid of you than you are of them and they overcompensate for their fear with prideful wrath."

"I can see that. There are many bullies on Planet Earth," I said. "They are everywhere. In fact, history is full of them."

"Yes," she answered. "Earth's history is a bloody one. There is no end to the Darkness's fear, shame, and guilt. That is the underlying reason for all such behavior. Selfish, domineering behavior that is not obeyed triggers them to violence. The same story plays out over and over again in your history.

"So, if we go back in time after the Light lost the battle in the heavens, souls began incarnating on Planet Earth, as well as other planets all over the universe because now they *must incarnate.* Soul groups both from the Light and the Darkness incarnated simultaneously on Planet Earth. The ancient continent of Atlantis was a highly advanced culture in your planet's past that had both such groups.

You and Landry both incarnated there as well, and both of you trained in the temples to become High Priest and Priestess of the Light. You both did what you could to keep the Dark ones from furthering their agenda on Planet Earth, which was to pull as many souls into the Darkness as possible.

"The majority of Atlanteans first became indulgent and then corrupted. Eventually, so much corruption existed that Father God allowed the continent to be destroyed through flooding. This was the great flood that is mentioned all over the world in various cultures.

"The ancient Egyptians are the descendants of the Atlanteans. Their culture was advanced by your modern-day terms but was only a remnant of the Atlantean civilization. You and Landry were again trained in the ancient temples and were chosen by Father God to become an Egyptian king and queen in that time period.

"Now it is time for you to further your understanding of your role in life and what is expected of you in the years to come. You and Landry have an old soul and you were sent to destroy evil in this lifetime. Both of you have a fiery temper, with Landry having an even greater tendency towards violence then you. This is all for a reason. Later on, you both will be given the task to destroy all that will seek to overpower you and others, and to absorb you into the Darkness's soul."

"Landry has much work ahead of him!" I said.

"Indeed!" Yashi said. "He's unaware of how the universe actually works."

Yashi looked at her watch and said, "I have a meeting to attend. We can discuss more tomorrow."

Yashi stood up and walked towards the door.

"See you tomorrow," I said.

I closed the door behind her and went to meditate. A soothing sense of peace and calm came over me. I knew I was on the right track. But what subject would Yashi address next? I could only guess.

An Odyssey

Yashi came over the next day, and I made tea for the both of us. We sat down on the couch like we always did when we were ready to have a lesson.

"Jayna," she said, "what would you most like to discuss today?"

"Well, there's so much we are capable of if we apply ourselves correctly, that's a tough question to answer. Let me think about this for a minute... How do we bring about miracles into our everyday experience?"

"I'm so glad you mentioned this because I can now introduce some new teachings to you," Yashi said.

"Like what?" I asked.

"You mentioned miracles. We all are capable of creating miracles if we are taught how."

"But how?"

"These teachings," she said, "are only taught to those who have a guru, or someone capable of passing along such information. Simply put, because we are trapped in a three- dimensional reality that, in essence, is not real, we are trapped by its limitations until we learn how to supersede them. For instance, if I were to jump from a boat into water, under normal circumstances, I would sink into the water. And only if I could swim, would I be able to survive such an experience. Correct?"

"Correct," I answered.

"If I were to practice disciplining my mind so that my ego-mind could no longer overwhelm me, then my ego would be out of the way. With my ego eliminated, there would be nothing blocking me from connecting with the Universal Mind, also known as Father/Mother God. Every thought I think would be a thought in the mind of the Creator. With that being said, every thought in the mind of God is a potential miracle. So, if I were to able to think the ability to walk on water and if I could go beyond the boundaries of ego-mind, then once that thought manifests in the Creator's mind, then that thought could potentially manifest in this world as a miracle. Do you follow?"

"I do. But I have a question."

"Yes?" she asked.

"How does one take control over the ego-mind?

"Good question!" she answered. "Here's where the hard work begins. First of all, it is in the nature of the ego-mind to survive. It does have consciousness; it is the dark energy self. The first issue that you need to realize is that you will have a fight on your hands. Every time you try to discipline the ego-mind, it's going to fight back. The more you fight with it, the more resistant it becomes.

"This is what we teach our young and our students. Rather than be harsh with the ego, we recommend you focus your attention on other things rather than fighting with it. The ego-mind is quite clever, and it will toy with you in many ways. Its main objective is to keep you out of the present moment because that's when you have the most power. Your power is inherently in each and every passing moment. Every moment has the potential to free you from the prison of your ego-mind.

"The ego-mind will constantly pull you into the past and try to convince you that you should be angry about this or that, whatever has angered you in your life. If you dwell on such thoughts, you will never live your life to the fullest – you are too busy living in the past. This is where Yeshua's teaching of forgiveness comes into play.

Whoever you have not forgiven in your life, regardless of what they may have done to you, will fill your mind with angry thoughts of hate and vengeance. If you dwell on these thoughts, you will be consumed by them. By allowing yourself to be hateful and angry, you then wire your brain to such emotions. This becomes a habit if you do it repeatedly. If you don't break this habit, these angry and hateful emotions become trapped in your body, and then a pattern is solidified into your brain chemistry. This pattern now becomes part of your personality. How many people identify with this type of behavior and say, 'Well, that's just how I am!' Is that the absolute truth, or is the honest truth much different?

"If they could see beyond their madness, the angry and hateful part of themselves was never part of their personality. It just got ingrained into their behavior and became a habit. Then, you might ask, 'Well, what's wrong with that?'

"To address that, we must look into the different sides of the issue. First, anger and hatred release chemicals in the body that are harmful and do not contribute to good health. Also, there is the spiritual side of anger and hate. Do they help us in our pursuit of spiritual awareness? What exactly are we aware of in such a situation? How much evil would we like to share with another? Does that help us to connect with the Divine or disconnect? Are these thoughts a complete waste of time when we could be using the same time and thought processes to create positive things in our lives and the lives of others?

"Furthermore, are we being a light to the world when we are hateful and angry? How does harboring such feelings affect other people? Does our hate and anger spill over into other relationships? And, if so, do we just say, 'Well, that's just how I am!' Do you see how important it is to forgive?"

"Yes," I answered.

"Okay," she said. "The ego, in its infinite madness, will also play another game with you. It constantly wants to pull you into the future to create more fear-based thinking, also known as anxiety. How many times have you been worried in your life? Can I do this or that? Will I have enough money to meet all of my needs? Will I be accepted for who I am, or do I need to put on a mask? What if something happens to my loved ones? The ego and its antics are at it once again. It wants to disconnect us from Spirit any way that it can. It was created for this reason. It is now our challenge to overcome it and go back to The Divine.

"The challenge is always to remain in the present moment without any thinking. A mind is simply a tool, and we use it when we need it like any other tool, but no more. We can remain *aware* but not think. Herein lies our freedom. This is easy to say but not necessarily easy to do. Only when a person has developed the necessary discipline can one overcome the mind's desire to drag us into thinking. And once we get dragged in, then one thought will lead to another thought, and we will keep thinking until we realize what we are doing and stop it.

"Not to think is to be aware; not to think is to be awake. Once we are awake, we come into the realization that we are not our thoughts. We are simply consciousness or awareness, trapped in physical matter. When we no longer identify with our egoic identity – meaning the person that we believe we are – we can transcend the limitations of our egoic self. We can even transcend the limitations of this world and we can experience a true spiritual liberation. This is the essence of spiritual transformation. The death of the ego and the birth of the divinely connected self. Or, in other words, death and resurrection."

"You mean like what's in the Bible?" I asked.

"Yes. Yeshua spoke of death and resurrection into eternal life or life in Spirit. Life in physical form is temporary.

But since we got trapped in matter, now we all are on our journey back home to the world of Spirit. When one is in Spirit, they cannot die or struggle to meet the needs of the body. Life in Spirit is perfect, as is our happiness. Negativity does not exist in Spirit. We fell from grace when we disconnected from Source. Arcturians are well aware of these teachings; they have been around on our planet for many millions of years.

"What is different about Planet Arcturus and Planet Earth is the stability of the planet. Planet Earth is an unstable planet. There have been many pole shifts, ice ages, climate changes, and gigantic volcanic eruptions. This has considerably set back the technological and spiritual progress on your planet. Every time your world evolves technologically, its spiritual development does not match the scientific development. Father God purposely allows one thing or another to set back civilization to a very primitive level.

"Planet Arcturus, on the other hand, is a very stable planet, meaning there are not any devasting events in our history to set back civilization to primitive living like there's been on Earth. We have continued to evolve both technologically and spiritually without having to go through periodic planetary devastation.

"By the way, Earth is due to go through another period of great planetary destruction and devastation. This is coming up in the 2020 decade and it will be an uphill battle to keep the planet from being completely destroyed without any hope of recovery. Since the time of the Biblical prediction made in the Book of Revelation, much has happened that was not anticipated at the time of this material."

"Such as?" I asked.

"Many of those of the Light who was destined to fight in this battle for the Light and help turn the tide defected to the Darkness and were corrupted. Too many, unfortunately. Spiritual darkness has gained greater popularity than was expected at the time and it has taken a terrible toll on Planet Earth's karma. The situation is so grave that Planet Earth now is at a crossroads on whether or not it will survive as a planet. The people who reside on this planet must choose to serve only the Light, and the Dark Ones must be brought down. There is no other way. The populace must show their fire now as never before.

"The Darkness has done a good job in brainwashing the various cultures of the planet. The majority of people on Planet Earth are, spiritually speaking, asleep. They must wake up now or they will be heavily disciplined."

"How, Yashi?" I asked.

"By going through great destruction events."

"You mean like nuclear war, pole shifts, famine, pestilence, great volcanic eruptions, tornados, and floods," I asked.

"Yes indeed," she said. "All these things will come to Planet Earth unless we reach critical mass."

"And what is 'critical mass?'" I asked.

"Critical mass means that there must be a certain percentage of the population that wakes up, spiritually speaking. There must be a 25% or more significant percentage of the people willing to be awake and aware for change to follow. If not, things will remain as is with no change.

"Another critical issue is planetary pollution. The Darkness has also done an excellent job of polluting the planet and its life support systems. The air, soil, and water are all polluted. They will continue to spoil them until the people put a stop to it. Terrible poisons being used on crops, and these poisons are throwing off the natural balance of soil microbes and minerals. Furthermore, these poisons make the soil less productive. The ground becomes less fertile, all the while the Darkness makes money from them.

"While there are a few scientists who are calling out the deception of using these products, most of the scientists are too frightened of the Dark Ones to stand up to them. Many in academia cower to them and go along with them so that they don't lose their jobs and their pensions. Very sad indeed."

"How can Landry and I help?" I asked her.

"By pointing to the brave warriors of the Light who are working as scientists and are risking their lives and livelihoods by presenting such information to the public. This job is not for the present, but later it will become a necessary part of your service. There is much to say about environmental pollution, not only for humans, but for all of the wildlife that lives on the planet as well. There is a delicate balance in the web of life and humans must be respectful of this. They too often feel it is their right to dominate the Earth, when it actually is more spiritually correct for them to be a part of nature, not its master. The real master is the Divine, the rest is human folly."

"Isn't that the truth," I said.

Getting Ready

As time went on, my love for my work and the ones I served deepened. I made many friends and had a full life. My parents were happy too. Their restaurant did well, and many community members were appreciative of it. All of us would gather at the restaurant on holidays, and it was heartwarming. Our friends at the TV station joined us as well, making us one big happy family. The community supported the restaurant with regular customers, enjoying the scrumptious meals!

The years went by quickly as there was so much work to be done. We were able to keep the Kemkabi at bay, but just barely. The bigger problem was that the spiritual darkness had taken root in this culture. That was the only way the Kemkabi could get a hold on us. How do you convince someone not to corrupt? Many understood such wisdom, but not all. The Darkness had done an excellent job convincing some that to go "dark" was a wise choice. After all, they promised power, glory, and material wealth. The Light makes no such promises.

I vowed to myself to avoid all spiritually dark and corrupt people. I was careful when dating to be sure the man was not a dark energy soul. Sometimes it was apparent, but sometimes it wasn't. The Darkness was sending their minions to me in hopes of getting the better of me. It did happen occasionally. A dark energy soul would make its way into my world. I found out sooner or later just by their behavior. They were always vain and selfish and could not hide their darkness for long.

I was careful not to get too attached to any one boyfriend. I knew the relationship would never last. But twenty-four years was a long time to wait for someone. It was inevitable that I would have boyfriends and bond with them. Through the years, the relationships played themselves out and t,here was always the pain of break up. When I would go through it, I always swore I would never get involved with anyone again. But in time, I always found a new love, at least temporarily.

When November of 2002 rolled around, I knew it was getting close to the time of my meeting Landry. I had looked forward to this for so long; it seemed almost surreal that the time was almost here. Be that as it may, I still found myself with misgivings. Was he willing to take on a herculean task of fighting to free not only one planet but two? What if Landry decided he didn't want to proceed?

"Yashi," I asked, "there are so many things to consider with meeting Landry, I wonder if it's really worth it?"

"Why do you say that, Jayna?" she asked.

"Well," I said, "he knows nothing about Planet Sekhmet and its problems. Will he be able to handle it? Will he like me? How about a commitment? What if he decides I'm not compatible with him? Also, there it's dangerous taking on the Kemkabi. What if he's not willing to do it? I have so many misgivings!"

"Jayna, this is your insecurity speaking now. Landry had already committed to this work in Spirit before he was born. He will feel comfortable taking this on, I'm sure. Will he like you? I don't think that will be a problem. The two of you are meant to be together. It will feel natural for both of you to bond.

"These feelings you have are normal. There's no reason to be afraid of them. I encourage you to stay on course, and keep in prayer and meditation. Your Higher Self will be leading you to him at the right time. The setup will be perfect. You will enter into his life at just the right time. He's involved with someone right now that's not for him. His relationship is in full swing and if you entered into his life at this time, it wouldn't work. He is in love with a young lady that is lovely in her own right, but she isn't for him. By next year, they'll break up and that's precisely the right time for you to come into his life. There's so much waiting for him here and he doesn't even believe in extra-terrestrial life yet! He'll have much to adjust to."

"I'd say," I replied. "How do I tell him about my work here?"

"Don't worry," she said, "I'll help you. He'll have an initial shock, but then he will simply accept the situation for what it is. He's very pragmatic and down-to-Earth. He also has some very bad habits that you will have to help him with."

"Like what?" I asked.

"He smokes cigarettes heavily," she said. "Also, he does not eat or sleep properly. He's avoiding handling his emotional issues from childhood and he escapes in computer gaming, smoking cigarettes, and poor diet. He needs you to help him take better care of himself."

"I'll do what I can," I said. "Okay, Yashi, I'll proceed. Sounds like he needs a really good friend!"

"Don't worry," she said. "Father God is going to help you with him. I'll also help. You won't be alone in this. We're all here to help you. John too can help if needed. This situation is being monitored very carefully. Both of you were sent to do a job and the situation has escalated. The Kemkabi are fighting hard as the Equinox movement on Planet Sekhmet is growing. More and more are doing what they can to hold them back. Many prayer groups have been started for this reason. This has set them back as well. Every little bit helps."

"Okay. Yashi, how about we start making plans for me to go to River Town? I'll need an apartment, and driver's license. It takes time to get things set up and 2003 is just around the corner."

"Certainly," she said. "I'll contact John when we're done and we can start looking for an apartment for you. You're right, there's much to be done if we are to set this up just right. You'll walk into Landry's restaurant for the first time just as he is breaking up with his girlfriend. The timing will be perfect. The Divine does not make mistakes, you'll see…"

Before I left for River Town, I spoke to the show's program manager and asked to have my character written off.

Meeting Landry

It was January of 2003, and River Town, Ohio, was blanketed with a white sheet of snow. Winters could be very harsh at times. Initially founded by the French, River Town was a quaint town on the Ohio River. Its charm lay in its beautiful buildings, clean streets, and friendly citizens. On Sundays, during the warm months, the town's people would wear their best clothes and come to the riverfront to watch the boats pass by.

There was a park right across the street from the river that had a beautiful white gazebo. On the other side of the park was the business district. Directly across from the gazebo was the Pizza Depot. It had a red, white, and green awning and looked interesting. Under different circumstances, I would have walked in and looked around. But since I was waiting to enter into Landry's life at just the right moment, I resisted the urge to go inside the store. Little did Landry know; I was impatiently waiting for the right moment to enter his life.

I found an apartment in town, and it was close to the restaurant he worked in. I wasn't due to meet him until next month, so I tried to busy myself decorating the apartment and getting my utilities set up. Since I didn't have to worry about doing a show anymore, my routine had changed dramatically. I couldn't help but wonder how everybody was doing, but I knew I had to let it go. They wrote my character off the show and brought in another character to take my place. The show had so many viewers for so long; we became part of their family life. The show needed to continue for the sake of the people of Planet Sekhmet. They had grown used to laughing with our staff for years. It would not have served a positive purpose to cancel the show. Every once in a while, I missed doing the show, but this work with Landry was going to be even more significant for the planet.

February arrived faster than I expected, and it was finally time for me to meet Landry. Yashi let me know exactly when to enter the store for the first time. By following her instructions, I got to hear a very interesting conversation.

"I'm sorry, but a customer just walked in," Landry said while speaking to someone on the phone. "I have to go now....I'm sorry, this is not working out...... There's nothing left to say, I love you still, but this just isn't the right relationship for either one of us.....Please understand......I'll call you tomorrow and we'll talk then.....Have to go, bye."

Landry walked over to me and stood behind the counter, looked right in my eyes, and said, "Hi, can I help you?"

I looked back at him, and his eyes were indeed beautiful. Big blue eyes with a handsome face. I smiled at him and said, "Yes, I'd like a large pizza please."

"Is that a cheese pizza?" he asked.

"Do they not all come with cheese?" I asked.

"I have to ask," he said. "There are some people that order pizza with no cheese."

"In New York, it's always understood there's cheese on pizza, except if you specifically ask that it not be put on the pizza. I've never had anyone ask if the pizza I'm ordering is a cheese pizza."

"This is not New York," he said. "Do you want any toppings?"

"Yes," I answered. "I'd like green peppers, mushrooms, and onions on a thin crust please."

"Got it," he said. "Anything else?"

"No," I answered. "That will be all."

With that, he walked over to the cooking table and started to make the pizza. I could see he had done this job for many years as he was very efficient at it. Within a couple of minutes, the pizza was ready to put into the oven.

He came back to the counter when he was done. "What's your name?"

"Jayna," I said. "And yours?"

"Landry," he answered. "Landry Berkley."

"So, Landry," I said, "are you originally from River Town?"

"Yes. And where are you from originally, Jayna?"

"New York City, specifically Brooklyn, but my parents currently live in Los Angeles. The rest of my family is still in New York."

"So, what brings you down here?" he asked.

"I felt the need to relocate to a small town."

There's no way he's ready to hear the truth yet, I thought.

"And what made you pick this town?" he asked.

Oh God here goes. "Well, Landry," I said, starting my rehearsed story, "I was looking online for riverfront property that was reasonably priced and I saw some beautiful buildings for sale here in this town. After looking through the photographs, I was intrigued and decided to take an apartment here to see if I would like to buy real estate in this town or not."

"Do you have a job?" he asked.

"Not currently. I have an annuity that my grandparents gave me. It gives me the freedom of mobility."

"Did you ever have a job?" he asked.

"I trained as an actress in Los Angeles. But there, you know, actors are a dime a dozen. It's a very competitive business. I like acting in small productions, which can be fun. Hitting it big time is another story. There are many horror stories about it."

"Like what?" he asked.

"Great corruption, prostitution for work, and difficulty in sustaining one's self with constant work. Did you know that only five percent of actors make their livelihoods from acting? The rest of the actors take any acting work they can get and must work at temporary work to support themselves. They call it their 'day job.' It is a very difficult life and all that glitters is not gold."

"I've never thought of it that way. Sounds very difficult."

"It is," I answered. "I realized early on that it was a very difficult life. No matter how well you do in the business, it can't make up for the things in life that are really meaningful, things that fame and fortune can't buy."

"Such as?" he asked.

"Having character, integrity, honor, and being independent. Instead, I would rather not give up any of these things for the sake of success in the entertainment business. There's some real ugliness in the business behind the scenes. You'd be surprised by how much easier it is to live a normal life without all the problems that are created because of fame and fortune. I'm happy with my life as it is."

"That's great, Jayna," he answered. "But would you be happy here in River Town?"

"That all depends, Landry," I said with a smile. "Life can be unpredictable. Let's see if life here in River Town will have promise for me."

With that, I grabbed my pizza and turned around to walk out the door. I glanced back at him over my shoulder. "I have to go now. It was great meeting you. I'll see you again."

"Okay, goodbye, Jayna. Have a great day!" he said as he walked away and went to the back of the store.

I walked out of the store and went to my car.

That didn't go too bad; I thought as I walked away. But it didn't match up to all the fantasies I had about our first meeting. I guess I was a romantic fool, but, all in all, I'd say it went okay.

There was so much I would like to tell him, but only God could know how he would react if I even tried to tell him all about the government's secret space program and my life back on Planet Sekhmet. Imagine me telling him about being chosen by Father God as His choice for an incarnate and leading a battle against the Kemkabi?

Oh Lord, I thought, *how do I explain all of this? I'm going to have to keep praying...*

I waited about a week before I went back to Pizza Depot. I didn't want to appear too anxious to connect with Landry. I thought it best to keep my conversations with him casual for now.

But this time, when I walked in, something seemed different. He was busy working, and when I walked in the store, I saw he had someone take over what he was doing, and he came right up to the counter to wait on me. He did seem like he was happy to see me again.

"Jayna, hello. What can I get for you today? A large thin crust pizza with onions, mushrooms, and green peppers?"

"Landry, you remembered!" I said. "That's great.... Sure, I'll take one of those please."

He seemed happy to see my pleased reaction. I watched him as he went about his job, managing a store and preparing food. He looked exactly as Yashi had described and indeed was a handsome man.

He worked quickly and efficiently. Within a few minutes, he had my order ready, and I was good to go. This time, after paying for my order, he took my pizza and walked me out to my car. I was surprised but not displeased.

"Jayna," he said, "I was hoping you would stop by the store again. I enjoyed talking to you. Can I call you? I'd love to talk some more and get to know you better. You're an interesting person. I liked some of the things you said."

"Like what?" I asked.

"Like having integrity and so on," he answered. "So many people don't have those kinds of values. I like people who are honest and speak their mind."

"Sure," I said and proceeded to write down my phone number for him.

"Do you stay up late at night?" he asked.

"I stay up to about 2:00 a.m.," I said.

"Good," he said. "My shift ends at twelve midnight on weekdays, and one o'clock on Fridays and Saturdays. I can call you after work."

"Don't you go home and go to sleep?" I asked.

"No," he said. "I like playing video games and I stay up all night. But I enjoy talking to people after work. I usually stay and talk to the other employees after work, and don't get home before 2:00 or 3:00 a.m. anyway. I'd love to talk to you if you're okay with me calling you that late."

"No, it's okay. I stay up late anyway. Please feel free to call anytime."

"Great," he said, "I'll call you later."

He handed me my pizza as I got into my car. "Talk to you later," I said and smiled at him as I drove off.

I felt happy but a little nervous. This was the man I dreamed about and waited for all these years. It was finally happening! We were connecting, and now things were moving. He wanted to communicate with me too and seemed happy to do so.

I called John to give him the update. He was pleased that we were moving forward. He would provide the update to his superiors.

Landry called about 1:30 a.m. He didn't sound tired at all; he sounded energetic and full of life. He was just chatting about various things, and I could see he enjoyed talking to people and was a good conversationalist. He was quick and responsive to me, and I felt we had a great connection. I realized things had to happen in progression. First, our relationship had to be established even before we could step into our divine roles. A friendship between us was being formed, and I felt this was the right way for our relationship to develop. Our friendship would be the foundation of our relationship, and a romance could be built on that.

We spoke for about two weeks on the phone, and we started to develop a natural rapport. I stopped by a couple of times a week for pizza, and he always seemed happy to see me walk through the restaurant door.

One night at the local supermarket, we bumped into each other. We got our groceries and went to the checkout line together. We then stayed in the parking lot for about an hour before going our separate ways. But that night at the supermarket, something was different.

"Jayna," he said, "I love talking to you. Why don't we meet for dinner this week?"

"Sure, Landry," I answered. "I'd love to

I smiled at him, and he smiled back. *This is good*, I thought. *We're going to the next step…*

We met for dinner, and all went well. Our relationship was getting off the ground. We decided to meet again for dinner the next week, and then the next, and then the next.

One day Landry and I met for lunch at a little diner, a couple of blocks away from the park. He had to work later that evening, but he wanted to eat here so I could try the homemade vegetable soup that was rumored to be the best in town. He checked and made sure it was vegan. How thoughtful of him!

"Have you found any interesting properties?" Landry asked.

"Oh, I'm still looking," I answered. "I haven't found anything that I like yet."

"If you don't like any in the city, there's some really nice houses in the country. I think there's one for sale where I grew up. Do you want me to get the information for you?"

"Sure," I answered. "I'd love to check into it."

Landry continued, "When I was a kid, Mom and I woke up one morning, and there was a big ring on our front lawn. It was oval-shaped. The grass was all smashed down, and there was fine ash all around it. We showed the ash to the neighbors, but nobody had ever seen anything like it before. One of my friends, Davie, said, "It must be a UFO landing that landed in your front yard. You're lucky you didn't get abducted!"

I told him, "Why would aliens want to take some redneck that was out in the sticks?"

Davie answered, "The aliens abduct people like us all the time!"

I said, "How did you learn the word 'abduct?' Did you watch that UFO show again?"

"Yup"

"I think it's unlikely that a highly advanced alien species would want to have anything to do with this planet," I replied.

"Why?" he asked.

"Because if," Landry said, "we have limited space travel, we really don't have anything to offer them."

"I never thought about it like that!" Davie said.

Our food arrived at our table, and we began to eat our dinner. Landry looked deep in thought.

"What do you think about aliens, Jayna?" Landry asked.

"That's a pretty interesting story," I said. "I believe that extraterrestrial life exists."

Landry replied, "Not really. I've never seen any convincing evidence."

"What about the story you just told me?"

Landry answered, "I just think that some of the kids on the street were trying to play a prank on me. But it sure freaked Mom out for a while. She didn't know what to make of it!"

I smiled. If he only knew what was going on…

A few days later, I stopped in The Pizza Depot one night, and could hear Landry's voice from behind the counter. He seemed to be engaged in an argument with someone. I heard Landry say, "I really don't care if you own this place or not, you're wrong."

I heard another man's voice say, "The inventory is messed up so I'm gonna figure it out."

Landry answered, "I work here forty hours a week, and you think working here two mornings a week you can figure everything out?"

The man answered, "Yeah, I can do that."

"Sure you can," Landry said, "so you say. The only thing you do is come in here, rile up the crew when everybody was doing a good job, and then you leave, and I have to get everything running smoothly again.

You're really starting to get on my nerves. You don't think I know about the inventory?"

I noticed Landry's big blue eyes turn ice cold. He looked seriously aggravated.

He continued, "One of us has to leave now. You can go home, or you can work open to close today. You can make the choice."

I heard the man answer Landry, "You had better figure that inventory out."

I saw the man come out from behind the door to the kitchen. He walked past me and swung open the front door, and left.

I walked up to the counter, and Landry saw me standing there and walked up and said, "Hi, how are you doing, Hon?"

"Hello dear…that sounded like fun."

"Yeah," he said, "I'm kinda used to him by now. That man would complain if his ice cream was cold."

"He sounds difficult to work with."

"I already know what's wrong with the inventory," Landry said. "I just wasn't going to tell him that."

"You looked really mad," I said.

"Yeah, dealing with him, that happens quite a bit. I really don't want to talk about him anymore."

Landry reached out and took my hand, and said, "You look really pretty today. I like your outfit. How about I call you later?"

"Sure," I answered.

Landry called me that night after work, and we spoke for an hour. The sexual tension was starting to kick in. We now held hands when walking together, and we kissed each other good night. I knew one night that the tension would be unbearable. We were building up to that moment quickly.

After a couple of months of hanging out, the tension was rising through us both. One night, he placed his hand on my back to step behind me, and all of a sudden, I had an experience I would never forget. His energy opened up my every chakra, and I felt like I was flying high. I felt as if I had died and gone to heaven. It was such a blissful moment! I had never experienced anything quite like that before. Even my experience with my first love couldn't compare to this. It was like being drunk or drugged, but this intoxication was even more blissful. This was what people were singing and dancing about, I'm sure.

I looked at Landry to see if he had the same experience, but he did not look like he was aware of anything extraordinary. He seemed wholly natural and unaware of the experience I just had. I acted normal but did not feel as I usually do on the inside. That moment was a great epiphany for me! This man was part of my karma and life's work, and now it was apparent to me. I didn't have to take anyone's word for it. I could see it for myself now. He was for me!

I felt ready to make love with him now but had to wait for the right moment. Landry seemed interested, and our bond was growing stronger.

One night he kissed me and the passion that we held back was coming to the forefront. I could feel the electricity between us, and it was overpowering. *Oh God,* I thought, *here it comes!*

We were passionately kissing and made it to my apartment. We started on the couch, and got up, and walked to the bedroom. As we stood kissing by the bed, Landry looked into my eyes and held my face, and said, "I love you Jayna."

"I love you too Landry."

We then started kissing and fell onto the bed. There was no stopping us now. We made love that night; he ignited the passion in my soul. I was the happiest I had been for a long time. There was a profound joy that flowed through me. I felt so deeply connected to Landry. He was my soulmate; I was so sure. Our love was so meant to be; it couldn't be more obvious to me.

When he left the following day, I felt like I was flying high. For the next two weeks, I could barely function. Typically, I was swamped, taking care of everyday chores. Now I felt utterly overwhelmed by my feelings for him, and I felt madly in love. I could think of nothing or no one else.

We spent time at each other's apartment. If he was not at my apartment, I was at his. We spent a lot of time together. We watched movies some nights while we cuddled on the couch, we cooked together, and there was no lack of action in the bedroom either. On his days off, we would go to the mall shopping, and then we would go out to dinner. When he was working, I would visit him and bring him something to eat. We saw each other every chance we could. This went on for about six months.

Landry seemed happy with our relationship. However, it made sense that we would have an easier time seeing each other if we shared the same apartment. So, one night I invited Landry to move in with me.

"Jayna," he said, "are you sure you'd like to share an apartment with me?"

"Yes, Landry," I said. "I'm sure. How about you?"

"Yes," he said. "There are definitely advantages to living together. First, we would save money. I could leave my apartment and would not have to pay a second set of bills. And, as you say, it would make our lives easier if we lived together. We would be able to see each other all the time and not have to try to make time for our relationship."

"Yes," I said. "It would have its advantages. Would you please think about it?"

"Sure."

About two weeks went by, and Landry finally gave me an answer.

"Jayna," he said, "I've been thinking about your offer to move in with you."

"Yes?"

"I thought it through and you're right, there are advantages to moving in together. I wasn't sure if I wanted to go to the next level of a relationship so quickly, but we seem to be so happy together, it would make sense to do so. If I gave up my apartment, we could combine expenses and it would give us more money for savings. Also, it would give us more flexibility about spending time together. And I'm ready to move on. My last relationship didn't work out. I just knew, as nice as a person she was, she just wasn't for me. Now it all seems to make sense. So, the answer is, sure, Jayna. I can move in anytime."

"Great, Landry!" I said. I reached up and kissed and hugged him. I was so happy! I felt as if his presence in my life was having such a positive effect on me. I would never want to be with anyone else.

"Hey Landry," I said, "let's go out to eat to celebrate!"

"Sure," he said, and off we went.

***

My life took another turn when Landry moved in. We had a small apartment, his things barely fit in my one-bedroom apartment, but I didn't care. I was so happy we were living together. It just *felt* so right.

The more I got to know him, the more I realized how talented he was. He loved fantasy games, and he made up adventures to play with his friends. He would tell me about his made-up characters, and I listened intently. I realized that he didn't understand this dynamic about himself. But, if the truth be known, I'd say *he* wanted to be the fantasy hero, and he was projecting himself into his role-playing game characters and adventures that he created. They all had some special ability and had a combination of both human and mystical traits.

I kept praying that the right way to introduce him to all that was waiting for him in another solar system would happen.

Landry Goes to Sirius

One night, while Landry was out with his friends, I practiced with the Crystal Cube. I made it a point to practice with it when he was not around. It had been a part of my life for so long; I couldn't imagine my life without it.

On that particular night, I had the house to myself and decided to do some work. I went through my routine exercises with the Cube while I sat on the couch. I had it floating in the air when Landry walked in unexpectedly. I stood up quickly, grabbed the Cube, and put it behind my back. I slowly backed up towards my handbag that was lying behind me on the chair.

"Landry!" I said. You scared me. I wasn't expecting you home so early. What happened?"

"Jayna," he said, "what's going on? What was that thing floating in the air?" Landry looked puzzled.

"What thing, Landry?" I said as I stepped away from him to get to my handbag.

"Jayna, something was floating in the air when I walked in the door! Now, what was it?" What's in your hand?" he asked

I caused the Cube to levitate behind my back so that Landry couldn't see it, and I then presented my hands to him. "See, I don't have anything in my hands."

Landry turned and looked at the couch, and that was when I lowered the Cube into my handbag. He inspected the couch briefly before sitting down.

"Landry," I said, trying to change the subject, "what happened to your game?"

"My friend's kid was sick and he decided not to show up tonight. He's playing the Healer in the adventure and we can't play without him. The rest of the guys decided to wait until next week to play again when everyone was there. So, I decided not to stick around and talk to the guys. I thought we might go out to dinner. How's that sound?"

"Great!" I answered. "Would love to. Let's go."

I was so glad he let me off the hook and didn't demand an answer. I wasn't prepared to answer his question, and he wasn't ready yet to know about the Cube.

We then left the apartment and drove downtown.

Landry and I entered the restaurant.

"We should've made a reservation," Landry said.

"You're right, but we didn't know that you would be free tonight for dinner."

Landry looked around the restaurant. "This place is still kinda new. It's really busy."

The greeter walked up to us. "How can I help you?"

"We would like to get a booth," Landry answers.

"We're full right at the moment," the greeter said, "but there'll be an opening in 30 minutes."

"That would be fine," I answered. "Landry, we can walk to the new shop that just opened last week."

"It's closed now," Landry answered. "But if you'd like, we can window shop."

"Sure," I said.

"Window shopping it is," Landry said to the greeter. "We'll be back at 10. See you then."

We took a shortcut through an alley. As we walked into it, I got a strange feeling, as if we were being watched. Something felt off on this back street.

As we got halfway down the alley, two figures stepped out from behind a dumpster. Immediately, I saw that they were the Darkened. Landry had no idea about any of this. The alley was dark, and they couldn't be seen clearly. One of them was armed with a strangely shaped blade and moved to intercept us.

Landry put me behind him. As we moved, the men had to adjust their path to attack us. Landry launched a fierce front kick with his left leg, striking the first man in the solar plexus. The man bent forward. Landry followed the strike with a downward hammer fist from his right hand, striking the man's neck at the base of his skull. The man dropped to the ground; Landry had broken bricks with this technique. The man would not be getting back up again.

The second foe attacked Landry with a hard-right-handed strike towards his head. Landry raised his left arm, placing his left palm over his temple, blocking the incoming blow with his forearm. Stepping forward, Landry slammed his forehead into the middle of the attacker's face. Before the foe could land his attack, Landry grabbed the opponent behind the neck with his left hand and slammed his right elbow into the man's neck. Then with a spinning step to the right, Landry hip threw the attacker to the ground. It was over for him.

Bending down to grab the attacker's knife, Landry suddenly turned and saw a third person enter the alley with his right hand inside his coat. The man produced a weapon and aimed it at me.

"Get down, Jayna!" Landry yelled.

He lunged towards me as the man opened fire. The pistol made virtually no noise, and projectiles flew towards us. Landry grabbed me and pivoted, shielding me with his body. I heard some of the shots hit objects in the surrounding area as they missed us, but three of them hit Landry in the back, causing him to cry out in agony. His scream seemed to pierce my very soul. Then his weight shifted towards me as he started to fall forward. I supported him, but as the strength in his legs faded, he sank to his knees. I saw our foe, felt a rush of rage, and my blood started to boil. This intense emotion released energy from deep within me. My gaze locked on the man as he began to reload his pistol.

"Jayna," Landry said as he tried to stand up, "your eyes are glowing with golden light!"

With that, I felt the fiery energy within me come forth. I concentrated and focused the energy towards the attacker's core. The man at the end of the alley screamed as light erupted from his body. There were cracks of light coming through him as he was engulfed in flames, burning him from the inside out. His body burned up instantly and transformed into fine ash, which was gently carried away by the wind.

A fourth attacker ran towards us from the opposite end of the alley and lunged at me with a knife. Landry gathered his strength and rose to his feet. He then moved past me with the knife he had picked up from the ground. He put up his left arm to block the blade coming at me, which protected me. However, the knife pierced through Landry's left forearm and was embedded there. A savage guttural yell filled my ears. Landry, even though injured, still managed to use the knife to stab the fourth attacker through the heart. The attacker fell backward to the ground.

Landry seemed to blackout and he collapsed on top of the attacker. I could see three projectiles protruding from his back, and his arm was bleeding. I immediately took a shirt from one of the attackers and used it to stop his arm's bleeding..

Oh my God, I thought. *Cell phone, where is the damn thing?* I scrambled for my phone in my purse. I speed-dialed John.

"Hello?" John answered.

"I need help now!" I cried. "We were attacked by the Darkened. Landry's hurt. He needs immediate medical attention or I'm afraid that he'll die. They shot their poisonous projectiles at us and Landry got hit with three. He also took a knife to the left forearm, which is still embedded in his arm. I used clothing to stop the bleeding, but he needs medical attention fast. The problem is there's no way the medical personnel here in River Town would have ever seen this type of poison. Their technology won't be able to save his life. It's imperative that he be taken to Planet Sekhmet immediately. The Sekhmetians are well aware of the Kemkabi's poison. He can be treated successfully there."

"I'm on my way," John said. "We have a lock on your cell signal. ETA fifteen minutes."

John always seemed to be calm no matter what the circumstances. His voice never conveyed emotion.

"Thank you, John," I answered.

I had seen pictures of this weapon before; it was in files about the Kemkabi. It fired long crystalline darts filled with a toxin. One by one, I pulled them from Landry's back. I thanked God that the dart under his right shoulder blade did not break, which would leave the poison projectile inside him. The dart just a few inches from the left side of his spine had not broken either. But, the one in his left shoulder blade was broken. Oh no, the poison was beginning to spread. I could see gray tendrils were starting to appear in the tissue near the wound. A cold chill ran down my spine.

Reaching out with my mental power, I felt the dart, and I telekinetically pulled it free from the wound. I needed to slow the poison. The Crystal Cube was the only way to do that. I pulled the Cube from the hidden compartment in my handbag while rolling Landry over. I held the Cube close to his heart. The Cube slowed Landry's bodily functions and gave its power to him. I was shown this technique before. The life force in the Cube kept Landry alive until we could get him medical attention.

Concentrating my energy into the Cube, I then placed it first on Landry's wounded arm. The bleeding stopped. I then put the Cube on his left shoulder blade. The spreading poison stopped as well. I had never used the Cube in this way before, and this was the right time to do so. I was deeply grateful for such technology. This was the only chance that Landry had to survive.

Suddenly, there was a screech of tires on the pavement behind me. I heard a voice that sounded like John as well as other male voices as well. They were talking about the Cosmic Fountain and keeping the Cube powered to keep

Landry stable. Could he survive that long of a drive? I heard John's voice, but what was he shouting?

"Get them into the van," John said. "We'll take them to the Fairgrounds where we can land the helicopter."

There was a ten-minute drive to the Fairgrounds, where the air ambulance was waiting for us. Landry, John, and I boarded the helicopter, and we took off.

"John, I need to talk to you. Could you please give me a minute?" I said.

"Yes, Jayna?"

"John, we need to find a way to communicate with Landry's employer and landlord about his disappearance. His family and friends will be worried about him too. What would you suggest?"

"No problem, Jayna," he replied. "We have a holographic cloaking device, also known as a holocloak. I will use it on myself to disguise myself as Landry while he's away. I'll tell his friends family that you had a family emergency in Los Angeles and Landry went with you, and you both may have to stay there a while. We'll handle it, not to worry."

"Thanks so much, John," I said. "As always, you are always there for us. Bless you!"

"You're welcome, Jayna," he replied.

Within a half-hour, we were at the tunnel entrance that led to the Cosmic Fountain. "We're here," John said. "Get Landry and Jayna on the cart. Go, go, go."

As we traveled, the lights along the top of the tunnel passed by quickly. I heard the electric motor's hum at maximum output on the cart, which was taking us deeper into the mountain.

I looked down at Landry. He was so still, barely breathing. The discoloration of the poison seemed to have stopped, at least where I could see. Using the Cube worked. I breathed a sigh of relief, but I kept praying for him. I knew the danger he was in was not over yet.

Two men lifted Landry onto a stretcher. I walked alongside them down the stairs with my hand still on the Cube as we entered the Cosmic Fountain. The men parked the stretcher in the middle of the platform and then turned around, leaving us behind.

I turned my attention back to Landry. He did not look good, but he was momentarily stable. I needed to get him medical attention immediately.

I stepped on the platform, and the Fountain came to life. The prismatic energy rose all around us and transformed into the dancing multi-colored energy. No matter how many times I had been through this process, it was still breathtakingly beautiful. But this time, the circumstances didn't allow me to take in the moment.

Landry and I arrived. Haneul and Najma were waiting at the top of the stairs with a few other Sekhmetians. The team rushed down to us and tended to Landry. Haneul injected Landry with a compound to start the poison neutralization process. Najma placed two small-pyramid shaped devices on Landry, one on his forehead and one on the center of his sternum. Both lit up with a blue light.

"You can remove the Cube now," Haneul said to me.

"Welcome back, Jayna." Najma said.

"Yes, it's good to be here again, but not like this," I said in a shaky voice as I fought to hold back my tears.

"How did this happen?" asked Najma

"Landry and I were attacked by four of the Darkened," I said. "They were able to hide what they were from me. Landry killed two of them at the beginning of the fight. I dealt with the third one. Landry killed the fourth one despite being shot. Even though he was injured, he put up his arm to block the knife coming at me. He saved me. I never thought I would ever see someone do that."

"Someone that loves you would do that," Haneul said.

"Yes, and a warrior would as well," Najma replied.

Landry's Hospitalization

L andry was placed in a Biobay at the local hospital in Sirius, which was the equivalent of the Intensive Care Unit in hospitals on Planet Earth. Dad and Mom came to visit Landry. They looked shaken up. I think they dreaded the possibility of Landry not making it. Their daughter would lose her soulmate, and there would be a massive defeat for the Light as well.

A week passed by, and Landry was still unconscious. The Healer said if we had arrived fifteen minutes later that Landry wouldn't have made it. The hospital gave me a room across from him to stay there with him until he recovered. Watching Landry go through this was very hard on me. I waited so long to be with him, and now he's almost dead.

Landry was going to have to deal with several issues when he woke up. The gravity on Sekhmet was more substantial. A person gained about ten pounds automatically just by their bones having to adjust to the new gravity. But the good news was that the bones adapted and became denser. Landry would have to go through this process while he was recovering from his wounds. But this would help Landry when he went back to Planet Earth. His body would have grown stronger, which would make him an even greater warrior than he already was.

There was another issue to be dealt with as well. Landry knew nothing of Planet Sekhmet and the human settlement here, not to mention the lion people. This would be a bigger shock because he did not believe that there was life on other planets. He had to be introduced into this situation gradually. We decided not to tell him that he was on Planet Sekhmet right away. Landry would go on red alert seeing lion people.

One night, the sound of an alarm woke me from my sleep. I heard loud talking and realized it was Landry. I opened my Biobay and rushed to see him, and he was sitting with his legs hanging from the bedside. The doctors were blocking his view, but I could see him just fine. He looked good. He wasn't pale, and his eyes were bright as they always were. I could hear Landry asking about me, but he did not receive an answer.

Then I glanced over at him, and there was what I call "the look." That was when those pretty blue eyes of his turned ice cold, and he was going to someone where to go.

I stepped up, so I was in front of the doctors. Many things had to be explained. But where should I start?

"Where am I?" Landry asked.

"Well, dear," I said, "you're in a hospital. You were hurt when we were attacked."

Landry reached out and pulled me to him and said, "Are you okay honey?"

"Sir, you are lucky to be alive," one of the doctors said.

"I'm not talking to you," Landry spouted angrily.

"Doctors, you should probably leave and let me handle this," I said. "Landry's confused right now."

The doctors exited the room. I walked over to Landry and took his hands into mine. The wound on his left arm healed well. The Biobay did a great job healing him.

"Okay," he said. "This is not a normal hospital bed. The bed has a cover on it, much like an iron lung. Where are we?"

"You're right, Landry," I said. "Remember me telling you there's life in other planets?"

"Yes."

I smiled. "Well, Landry, we're on one."

"You're joking, right?" he said with a puzzled expression.

I looked at him with a straight face. "No, Landry, I'm not."

"Then how did we get here?" he asked.

"There's a device," I said, "called the Cosmic Fountain. There are four of them on Planet Earth and they appear on planets all over the universe. The device was designed by an advanced ancient culture to allow space traveling. It folds space-time from one fountain to the other one. This is the device that we used to teleported us here. That was the only way I knew how to save your life."

"I know you wouldn't lie to me, but it's still hard to believe," he said.

Someone came into the room, and I turned to see who it was. It was Yashi, thank God. She was smiling as always. Her skin was almost luminescent in the light.

Landry stared at her and followed her with his eyes as she crossed the room. It seemed as if he wasn't sure if what he was seeing was real.

"Jayna," Yashi said, "it's good to see you again." She turned to Landry. "It's a pleasure to finally meet you. We've waited a long time for this moment."

Landry stood up slowly and extended his right hand to Yashi. "I'm still feeling a little weak."

"Gravity on this planet is greater than you are accustomed to," Yashi said.

"You seem to be fine," Landry said.

"My race is from a planet with much less gravity than Planet Sekhmet. When we visit planets like this, we wear devices to counteract gravity's effect.

"I come from a planet called Arcturus. We're a highly advanced culture, both spiritually and technologically. Our race transcended our collective ego eons of years ago and we incarnate in physical form to serve the Light. In fact, our entire culture comes from the Light. I was assigned to work with Jayna first and, eventually with you as well."

"The Biobays will help you acclimate to the gravity quickly," Yashi said. "Exercising will help you as well. Your strength and speed will be enhanced from training on this planet, especially when you return to Planet Earth. The Biobays repair genetic damage and diseases."

"That is so amazing," Landry said. "But how is it possible that a device can do such a thing?"

"This is advanced technology, Landry," Yashi answered. "There's much that the doctors and scientists of your world don't understand about the disease processes yet."

"She can tell you quite a bit about this, Landry," I said. "This subject is fascinating to me. They have a completely different outlook on diseases here on Planet Sekhmet than we do back on Planet Earth. Our doctors and clinical scientists look at the physical causes of disease that can be seen under a microscope. But what if the true cause of the disease was not located in this dimension? That would give a completely different perspective on the situation, wouldn't it?"

"I'd say," Landry said. "That is interesting. I never thought of diseases that way. How is it possible that the cause of disease could be located in another dimension?"

"Yashi," I said, "do you think Landry's ready to hear this?"

"I am!" Landry answered. "Please continue."

"Jayna," Yashi said, "it's okay. He's interested in the subject material; it won't overwhelm him."

"Okay," I said. "Landry, all diseases that are caused by pathogens are actually the physical manifestation of an evil entity in another dimension. These demonic entities all have an energy signature. They are angry, hateful, malicious, and spiteful. The energy of these emotions has a specific vibratory frequency. If any sentient being exhibits such hostile behaviors, then they retain the negative energy in them. Since the law of attraction is that 'like attracts like,' the energy of anger and hatred will attract a demon from another dimension that has the same energy. Certain demons can manifest in the third dimensions as pathogens and cause great suffering to those who succumb to them through illness. These demons feed off the suffering that follows and delight in the emotional pain that is created."

"What?" Landry asked.

"There are evil beings that exist in other dimensions that desire to create suffering in sentient beings," Yashi interjected. "They are so cruel that this pleases them. They also energetically feed off the energy that negative emotions produce. This is their sustenance. Since they disconnected from the Creator, which is an infinite energy source, they must get power from somewhere to sustain themselves. They create suffering so that they can siphon off the dark energy.

"If someone experiences pain, but does not get upset about the discomfort of the pain, these evil beings can't feed off the situation. Suffering is the emotional component of pain. Pain is physical; suffering is emotional and subjective. If a being experiences pain and becomes emotionally upset about it, then they experience both pain and suffering. The Biobays can heal the body of this dysfunction, but the negative emotions are our responsibility to address."

"That's very interesting, Yashi," Landry said.

With that, Landry turned to me and said, "Jayna, why are you here? Why are humans here?"

"I'm a psychic," I answered. "My family and I were brought here years ago. Yashi trained me when I was young and helped me develop my abilities. I can use the Crystal Cube to see events as it is happening. The other humans here are all talented in one way or another. The purpose of the human settlement is to exchange their technology for our cultural gifts."

"What is the Crystal Cube?" Landry asked.

"It's a device created by The Arcturians," I said.

Yashi joined in. "Landry, if you are willing, I can now start to train you as well. You also have spiritual gifts."

"I don't know what you are talking about," Landry said. "I'm not sure if I have anything like that golden-light-eye thing Jayna did."

"Jayna had that ability locked away for many years," Yashi said. "Her fear to use the power was what had been stopping it from manifesting. It was her love for you and the anger of seeing you hurt or possibly killed which removed that barrier. Landry, I heard what happened back down in the alley. How did you know there was an attacker at the other end of the alley?"

"I saw him there."

"How did you know to look there?" Yashi asked. "How did you know that the last attacker was trying to attack Jayna with a knife?"

"I just knew," Landry said.

"Jayna tells me that you have had dreams that came to pass when you were a child."

"Yes," Landry said. "I had a dream once we were going to get a new dog. Then two days later, the same dog that was in the dream showed up at our house!"

"That's a form of precognition," Yashi explained.

"That's interesting," I said.

"Landry, we need to talk," Yashi said. "Jayna, you need to join us as well. We're going to have to make a plan, especially since Landry's here with us now. There's no time to waste, the Kemkabi are fighting hard. We can't afford any more incidents like last time."

"What happened?" Landry asked. "And who are the Kemkabi?"

"That's what we need to talk about, Landry," I said. "There's a war going on, and we all need to join forces. These entities are pure evil, tough to fight, but not impossible. We need to talk to the doctors about when you can be released."

"We can talk here, can't we?" Landry asked.

"Yes," I said, "we have much to share with you."

"I'm listening," he said.

"Yashi," I said, "could you please tell him about the Sekhmetians? I don't know how to explain all of this!"

Landry looked right into my eyes and stared at me for a moment. "You know, Jayna, I knew you were hiding something. When I came home and saw that cube floating in the air, I realized there were many things you hadn't told me. I didn't push you that night because I could see you weren't ready to share it. Something *very big* was going on behind the scenes. Now I know why you hid this from me!"

"Landry," Yashi said, "Jayna couldn't tell you about any of this because you weren't ready. If she tried to tell you, you would have written her off as a nut. This incident actually worked in our favor because it pushed Jayna to bring you here so you could see it for yourself."

"Ready?" Landry asked. "I don't have a choice in being 'ready.'

"I understand that you couldn't tell me everything, Jayna, but that doesn't mean I have to like it.

He drew a deep breath and paused a moment and then exhaled and asked, "Where exactly am I?"

"Well, Landry," I said, "that depends on your perspective. Right now, you're in a hospital, you know that. The city you're in is named Sirius and the planet you're on is Planet Sekhmet, which is a planet located in the Alpha Centauri solar system. This planet revolves around its sun, which is Proxima Centauri."

"What?" he shouted.

Oh, dear Lord, I thought. *This must really be hard to process.*

"Landry, please relax, it's okay," I said softly.

"What's okay, Jayna?" Landry said. "I'm in another solar system and don't remember coming here. I'm in a hospital that doesn't look like any hospital I've ever seen before. There are humans here, but our government has never told us about human settlements on other planets. And why hasn't our government told us about life on other planets? And then there's a blue woman standing here to beat it all. Am I supposed to be okay with all of this?

You all ought to be happy I haven't had a nervous breakdown!"

"Landry," I answered, "I know you're overwhelmed right now, but there are answers to all of your questions. It will just take some time to explain each part of this story."

"Well," he said, "I'm not going anywhere, so shoot!"

"Then what should I start with?" I asked.

"Why don't you start with the Kemkabi?" she answered.

"Yes, Jayna, tell me about the Kemkabi," Landry said.

I proceeded to do so and told him everything, including who the attackers were in the alley. He listened intently and never uttered a word. When I was finished, he said nothing. He just looked at me with a straight face. I waited for him to give me a signal that he was okay to continue. It never came.

"Landry, would you like me to continue?"

"Yes, Jayna," he said, "I would. This is the most fascinating story I've ever heard. I would never have imagined anything like this could happen to me."

"Okay, great," I said. "We can continue as long as you are okay with it. If you feel overwhelmed, please let me know and I'll stop."

"Okay," he said.

I then proceeded to tell him about the history of Planet Sekhmet in its entirety. It was inevitable that he would have to see the Sekhmetians, and it was probably a good idea to prepare him now so that he didn't freak out too much. I remember the first time I saw them. It was a little shocking if you were not prepared. After that story, I proceeded to tell him how the humans got here, the story of the city of Sirius, and how I got here as well.

Again, he listened intently and never said a word. He never showed any emotion on his face, and it was hard to tell how he was feeling about all of this. He was a warrior through and through. He's just dealing with the unexpected as best he could.

When I was finished explaining the whole story, he finally said something.

"Jayna, are there any Sekhmetians around that I could meet?" he asked.

I looked at Yashi in hopes she would answer the question. She picked up my request immediately and responded to Landry.

"Landry, we can take you back to Jayna's apartment and ask Lieutenant Jagannath to visit us. He's in the military, and he's been assigned to Sirius to watch out for any more attacks from the Darkened or any possible developing issues from The Kemkaba People.

"Sounds good to me," he said. "Can you get the doctors to release me in your custody?"

"Let me talk to them," Yashi said.

She came back and motioned for us to leave the Biobay and follow her. Landry looked at me, and I could see the excitement in his eyes. He was over the initial shock, and now he's starting to feel good about being here. We followed Yashi and get in her car. She drives us back to my apartment. Landry is quiet for the entire time in the car. Yashi and I don't speak so he could have time to process what was happening to him.

When we arrived at my apartment, Yashi left us alone to unwind and go to sleep. We both know it's been an eventful day, and now it was time to go to bed. I bought new clothes for him, so he could shower and go to sleep comfortably. I handed him a towel, and he took a long shower. When he was finished, he sat down next to me on the couch and wanted to talk.

"Jayna," he said, "How about my job in River Town? My employer, co-workers, friends and family will be upset and worried if I just disappear one day. What do we do?

"Landry," I said, "We've got that covered. A government agent will use a holographic cloaking device, also known as a holocloak, and change his appearance to look like you. He's going to tell everyone that I had a family emergency, and we had to go to Los Angeles and might be gone a long time. He's going to gracefully create an exit for you so that no one will worry about you."

"That's crazy, Jayna," he said.

"That's life, Landry," I answered. "Life is crazy."

"No, Jayna," he said. "*You're* crazy!"

"Okay, okay," I said, "come on. Let's get some sleep. All of this is exhausting."

"Okay, Jayna," he said. He then leaned over and kissed me. "I love you."

"I love you too, Landry," I answered.

Lieutenant Jagannath

The next day, we got a knock on the door. It was Lieutenant Jagannath. He immediately came over to introduce himself to Landry.

I watched Landry's face as the Lieutenant entered the apartment. Landry knew what to expect, but he had never seen a Sekhmetian before. He handled it well. He didn't look too surprised. But then again, with Landry, not much seemed to unnerve him anyway.

"Landry, it's a pleasure to meet you," said Lieutenant Jagannath.

"Thank you," Landry said, "and you as well."

"Landry, we have much to discuss," Lieutenant Jagannath continued. "There is a war going on and we need all the warriors we can get, especially warriors with special abilities."

"But I don't have any special abilities, Lieutenant."

"Yashi has informed us of your potential," he said. "She can work with you to help activate your power. However, you must first decide if this is what you want to do."

"I guess I can try," Landry said.

"You didn't 'try' against the Darkened when they attacked you and Jayna," Lieutenant Jagannath said. "You did what a warrior does, win at all costs, even if you don't have the strength to carry on."

"But this is a little different," Landry answered.

"Landry," I said, "remember what Yashi said to you? She reminded you that you knew what to do and when to do it. That's not luck! You've used this ability before and you didn't even know it. She is just going to help you refine your abilities."

"You're right, Jayna," Landry said.

"Tooth and claw," Lieutenant Jagannath said.

"What does that mean?" Landry asked.

"It's a saying for using everything you have to get the job done," I said.

Lieutenant Jagannath smiled. "Your mate is honored among my people and I think you shall be too, but it must be earned."

330

With that, the Lieutenant turned around to head for the door.

Landry followed him. "Okay, let's get this done!"

"This will be a difficult and painful process, training with Sekhmetians while being human," Lieutenant Jagannath said.

Landry grinned. "I'll take it easy on you."

The Lieutenant chuckled. "We will see." He then stepped out the door and closed it behind him.

I turned to Landry. "And you say I'm the crazy one?"

"You say like attracts like!"

By the next day, Landry's strength was starting to come back. His training would start soon. We walked through the streets of Sirius, taking in the surroundings. We watched the vehicles as they pass by, and the people would greet us in passing. He always noticed things, things I missed or that seemed insignificant to me.

"So, are there any military personnel from Earth here?" he asked.

"No," I answered, "the Sekhmetians protect the planet."

"Who polices this settlement?" he asked.

"We have our own police force," I answered. "There's no serious crime, just some minor offences. Someone may be drunk or loud or drive fast, but nothing worse than that. Our police are basically 'peace officers.' They help to settle disputes and assist in medical emergencies, but they are always ready if there is an attack of some sort, like from the Kemkabi.

"Almost everyone in the city has a job. Humans have businesses here just like on Earth. Some people have a per diem from the American government. These are the people who are retired and want to live here."

"Can we go to another city?" Landry asked. "I want to see what it's like."

"Sure," I said. "We'll need a vehicle. The closest city is twenty-five miles away. I'll call Yashi and ask to borrow her car."

"Why don't you have your own car?"

"Well, maybe it's about time I get one. I have some savings. How about we go looking for a vehicle?"

"Sure," he said. "Let's go."

We walked downtown and found a used car lot. There were about ten cars to choose from. The cars all looked like vehicles from Planet Earth. Landry looked around and found a small white car. He liked it! He looked under the hood to check the fluids and the engine and remarked how he never saw a machine like this.

I explained that the cars on Planet Sekhmet were powered by magnetics. The Sekhmetians developed a motor that functioned by using the fluctuating magnetic field of the planet. Landry looked puzzled for a moment and then asked the salesman about the car's issues. He had a way of knowing things without being told. He often made very wise choices.

The salesman started asking Landry about the cars on Planet Earth. He has been on Planet Sekhmet for twenty years and was wondering about any new innovations. They probably would have talked for hours if I hadn't said anything. Landry was quite a talker and made friends quickly.

We paid for the car, and drove off and headed for the nearest city. It was a reasonably large city with about 50,000 people. The drive was through the countryside, and Landry was amazed to see the Sekhmetian landscape. There were no homes to be found on the flat terrain until we came into the city limits. I loved to go to Ceres. There were charming shops and good restaurants there. The architecture was different from Sirius. The Sekhmetians lived in dome buildings, which seemed to be the theme of their architecture. They had large arches inside the homes, and buildings were split-level with the bottom floor underground. The buildings were of different heights. Four strong columns supported the vast domes, the more massive central column had large doors and windows.

These cities were designed with dome structures to withstand the storms that raged through the towns. The planet was about fifty percent water and could have violent storms and high winds. The buildings were attractive and functional at the same time.

Since the buildings in Sirius were like the ones on Earth, the Sekhmetians had designed an energy shield that would protect the city from these storms when necessary.

We spent the whole day window shopping and walking around the city. The weather was lovely, and Landry seemed to enjoy himself. We both needed a break from the trauma of the attack. Spending a day relaxing and talking did us both a world of good. By the time we went home, we were relaxed and tired, but in a good way. Landry looked like he had made the transition to his new environment and was ready to take on the challenges given to him.

When we got back, we went to Mom and Dad's restaurant, and Landry got a chance to meet my parents.

They were happy to see us both and waited on us hand and foot. Landry enjoyed the Italian cuisine, and I enjoyed all of us being together. We were coming up to a challenging chapter in our lives, so this pleasant break helped us recharge our batteries. The next step would be to begin Landry's training with Yashi and the Sekhmetians. I knew this would be tough on him, but he had the will and the spirit to take on such a difficult task. The Sekhmetians were known for being fierce warriors and tough trainers. Landry said he wouldn't have it any other way!

When we got home, Landry went to my computer to play video games, and that gave me a chance to sit quietly and process the events of the last two weeks. I was so focused on Landry that I forgot about the significant breakthrough of my own. I had tapped into my pyrokinetic ability, and I hadn't thought about it until now. When Landry was in the hospital, I was so consumed with concern for him. I forgot to meditate on this to see if I could access a distant memory in my childhood that caused my fear of this ability. Now in the quiet peace of the moment, I could focus on this question and see if I could remember what caused the problem.

I began meditating and became very still. I asked to be shown what happened that caused the problem.

Suddenly a memory came back to me. It hit me like a lightning bolt! Oh my God, now I remembered!

I was five years old and living in Brooklyn with my parents. It was Christmas day. I was focusing intently on our Christmas tree, which was lit up beautifully. The lights and decorations were colorful, which set a festive mood. I was so engrossed in my study of the tree that I didn't even hear my mother calling for me. She finally got me and asked me to come to the dinner table since it was time to eat.

I was enjoying the moment, and I didn't want to be disturbed. Dinner wasn't appetizing to me at this time. I was annoyed that Mom wanted me to end this moment. I wanted to stay and look at the tree and not come to the table. Mom called again. I tried to resist her directive. I was still intently focused on the tree, and suddenly there was a feeling of a powerful energy inside of me. It felt like a heatwave, and, if directed, it could easily kill. In my inexperience, I used the energy I felt and aimed it at the tree. The tree burst into flames.

I screamed. Dad and Mom came running into the room. Mom grabbed me and ran outside while Dad tried to fight the fire. Mom told me, later on, he picked up a rug from the floor and tried to snuff out the fire with it.

He did get the fire under control; however, he suffered a first-degree burn on his left forearm. Our dog was barking and whimpering.

We had to take Dad to the emergency room on Christmas day. Luckily, the burn wasn't as bad as it could have been, but the experience left me terrified. I felt guilty and couldn't process the fear I had felt at the time. I cried and told Mom and Dad that I was sorry, that I didn't mean to set the tree on fire; it was an accident. They were dumbfounded by what I had told them. They knew I had spiritual gifts, but they had never encountered anything like this in their life.

I realized I didn't know how to handle this fiery energy within me. That fear stayed with me for decades.

***

During the attack, my love for Landry motivated me to burst through my psychological wall and reconnect with my power again without any fear. It was evident that Yashi had been right. Pyrokinesis was one of my gifts, and Landry was the catalyst for me to unlock it.

I felt relieved. It was all okay!

Comfortable tiredness came over me, and my eyes grew heavy. I felt as if I weighed twenty pounds lighter.

The emotional release of that fear was liberating but tiring. I had been carrying all of that pain with me all those years. That had been my blockage. Now, I could relive that experience without being frightened. Dad was okay, and the situation didn't escalate. There was no reason to be afraid of this memory anymore.

I got up and made myself a cup of chamomile tea. Mom used to make it for me as a child; it helped me relax. I checked on Landry. He was engrossed in his video games.

"Landry," I said, "I'm tired. I'm going to sleep."

"I love you," he said.

"I love you too," I said,

I went into the bedroom and laid down in bed. Tonight, I would sleep peacefully.

Tooth and Claw

The next day, Landry began his training with Yashi. She scheduled his hand to hand combat training with the Sekhmetians the following week. In the evenings, he would train at Talther gym in Sirius. His schedule was now set, and he would be busy.

Landry and Yashi would work on prayer and meditation, just like she did with me. When Landry was comfortable with this routine, she then started him on exercises that taught him how to move his energy within his body. Landry also was able to enhance his physical strength and speed using this technique. When he was young and studying martial arts, he was taught the basic version of this exercise, but now he had mastered the complete version of this power. Now Yashi was training him to learn the telekinetic ability. He was a natural at this.

This was going to help him with his training with the Sekhmetians as well. If he could efficiently move his energy, he could deliver more brutal strikes and could accurately use weapons. Naturally, he was very agile. She was setting the stage for him to become a great warrior of the Light. But he was still needed to prove himself. No warrior was respected unless respect was earned. He would have to hold his own under tough circumstances. Father God would do His part, but Landry would have to remain committed to the cause. This was the moment where the rubber met the road. He had to be able to perform.

My role was to support Landry in any way I could. My training was over, and now that I had gotten in touch with my pyrokinetic ability, I was ready to help him master his abilities. I attend his meetings with Yashi and with the Sekhmetians as well. Landry was doing very well, but I sensed there was something he wasn't telling me.

One day, he finally came out with it.

"Jayna," he said, "you know I love you, right?"

"Yes," I said.

"Well, if I ask something of you, please don't take it the wrong way."

"Okay," I said. I felt a little apprehensive but tried not to show it.

"I would prefer if you did not attend my training sessions. You being there distracts me and I feel I would be more comfortable if you weren't there. Could I ask this of you without you being upset with me?"

"No problem, Landry," I said. "I can always find things to do. I'll keep myself busy. Not to worry."

From that point on, we changed our routine. He trained with Yashi by himself.

For months, Landry trained with Yashi every morning and with the Sekhmetians in the evenings. Sometimes he returned bruised and battered. I would ask him what happened, and he would grin and say it was only training. Then he hugged and kissed me before laying down in the Biobay that we brought home. It had become part of our nightly routine. Much of the time, Landry came home bruised and battered, always needing the Biobay to heal.

That night, I wanted to talk to him. I was unsure how I should approach him as I want to know what progress was being made. I decided to wait until the morning.

I woke up early, but he was already gone. I took a shower, washed my hair, and got ready for the day.

There was a note on the refrigerator that said, "knock, knock." There were two knocks at the door. I went to the door and opened it. It was Yashi.

"Jayna, where's Landry?" she asked.

I went back to the note again. I looked underneath the first message to see that it said, "Tell her I'm at Talther."

"Jayna," she said, "I believe Landry thinks he's ready. We should go now, he's expecting us." She paused to smile. "I see that Landry's precognition is getting sharper."

"I believe so," I answered.

We arrived at the gym and a Sekhmetian warmly greeted us. He motioned to follow him, and he led us to seats overlooking a training area.

Landry was crouched down, sitting in the center of a sunken arena about twenty feet across. There was a rim around the depression about two feet high. Seven Sekhmetians standing, waiting for something.

Landry stood and motioned to one of them. The Sekhmetian jumped from the edge of the pit and rushed towards Landry. The Sekhmetian attacked with two clawing swipes. Landry dodged the right and parried the left. He kicked his opponent with his right leg, hitting him on the back of his head.

His opponent tried to claw-kick his abdomen in return. Landry stepped forward and blocked the kick with his left shin, cutting the kick short in the air. Landry then struck out with a right-handed clawing motion across the face, hitting the eyes and nose. The Sekhmetian attacked with a right over handed clawing motion. Landry stepped diagonally to his left, blocking the strike, circling partly behind his opponent. He grabbed his opponent's neck under his outstretched arm. Landry slammed two elbow strikes onto the Sekhmetian's head. Landry slightly squatted down and picked him up before slamming him on the ground. The Sekhmetian landed on his back with a hard thump. Landry paused, judging that the Sekhmetian was down for the count.

I leaned over to Yashi. "Landry is doing well, but I'm still concerned. Why isn't he using all of his abilities on this opponent?"

"It was part of the agreement he made with Jagannath," Yashi said. "Landry would not attack opponents with his telekinetic ability."

"I see," I said.

Landry motioned to the Sekhmetians again. Two of them dropped into the arena. They were armed with some kind of training weapon. The weapon looked like a khopesh. The blade came out twelve inches and then dropped like an upside-down sickle. Landry moved towards them, circling to the left. The Sekhmetian on the left adjusted and attacked his stance to attack Landry with his sword in a left to right horizontal cutting motion. Landry grabbed the Sekhmetian's wrist and kicked him in the face. He disarmed his opponent and knocked him into the other Sekhmetian.

The second Sekhmetian threw his partner to the side, but it was too late. Landry wielded the sword from the first Sekhmetian and closed the distance. He struck the forearm of the second Sekhmetian, sending the sword flying from his grasp. Sliding to the right, Landry extended his left hand. The blade seemed to dance in the air and land in his hand. Landry then spun around and made a right-handed horizontal cut to the head of the second opponent. The first Sekhmetian turned toward Landry. Landry then made a left-handed diagonal attack against the chest of the first of the pair. Both now lay on the ground.

"Landry can enhance his speed as long as it's not faster than this opponent," Yashi said.

"Well," I said, "how about manipulating the weapons with telekinesis?"

"Landry is allowed to use his abilities on weapons only as long as he faces multiple opponents, or opponents with projectile weapons," Yashi said. "But he can't manipulate the weapon to attack on its own."

Landry motioned again. Three Sekhmetians entered the ring armed with spears, moving towards Landry. One circled to the right, the other to the left, and the third held his stance in the center. Landry moved forward as the three spearman attempt to stab him. I gasped in fright for him. Landry dodged the center attack and parried the other two. He quickly threw one sword to the right and the other to the left. The swords hit his opponents in the chest and dropped them to the ground. The last spearman attempted to stab Landry. He parried the attack with his right hand, grabbed the spear and drove it into the ground. With his left hand, he forced the spear shaft under his opponent's armpit. Pivoting slightly and twisting the lance, he threw his opponent on his back and struck the fallen foe in the chest with the spear. Now there's only one left on the rim of the arena.

The last Sekhmetian dropped into the arena behind Landry. He produced a Kemkabi pistol. Landry turned as the Sekhmetian fired. Landry knocked the dart aside with his spear and moved forward so fast that he was just a blur. Deflecting the second projectile, he edged closer to his foe, throwing his spear at him. Landry dodged the third projectile and threw the javelin at the Sekhmetian. His opponent barely dodged the spear; it grazed his left shoulder. Landry, still moving forward, extended an empty right hand. One of the swords leapt to his hand from the ground. Dodging left, Landry avoided the upcoming projectiles and effortlessly wielded the sword to point at the opponent's throat.

Landry had done it; he defeated six Sekhmetian warriors in combat. The last warrior seemed surprised in defeat. Landry was also the only person who had defeated an opponent armed with a projectile weapon.

"I told you I would go easy on you, Jagannath," Landry said as he stepped back from his opponent.

Jagannath looked Landry in the eye and made a lion sounding grunt. All of the Sekhmetian stood up, including the ones in the arena. A moment later, in unison, they all made the same sound again, a lion's grunt. Jagannath stepped up to Landry's right side and raised his hand. In unison, all the Sekhmetians roared. The first human had passed the Trial of the Warrior's Last Stand.

Time To Step Up

Yashi and I waited for Landry to leave the arena. I could see that he was trying to process all that he had done by just looking into his eyes. His hard work had paid off. He now had earned the respect of the Sekhmetians. There was no turning back from here on out. He had awoken and was now prepared for his next challenge. No more making pizza for Landry. He was ready to be trained by the Sekhmetian Military.

Yashi congratulated Landry and drove us home. She was happy. I could see it in her eyes. Landry was her student and he must have felt proud of him. He had lived up to all of the expectations. This was his right and he had stepped into the ring. She was thrilled for both of us.

We were getting closer and closer to the ultimate challenge: taking on the Kemkabi. Preparations for the next phase of our battle were necessary, but not before we celebrated.

I called my parents and asked if we could have a party at their restaurant. They were thrilled to hear the good news and accepted. Of course, all our friends were invited, as well as Yashi. We planned the party for the next night.

The party was fun. Dad wrapped up the party by making a toast to Landry.

"Landry," Dad said, "here's a toast to your continued great success! Cheers!"

"Cheers!" everyone shouted.

I looked at Landry and I could see this was one of the happiest moments in his life. He was so thrilled that the joy was in his eyes. He waited until the toast was over to give a short speech.

"Thank you, everyone. Coming to Planet Sekhmet has been the most incredible experience of my life. First, I'd like to thank you all for being so kind with your well wishes. It's been an incredible experience just getting to know each one of you. The circumstances that we've all met under are absolutely extraordinary. I could not have imagined such an environment in my wildest dreams. However, now that I'm awake, I see the greatness and grandeur of God's creation. It's such an honor to be here, I thank you all for welcoming me into your world."

Landry sat down and I sat next to him and cried. I was so happy! What a beautiful moment. Landry held my hand and kissed me. Our hearts touched and everyone was deeply moved as well.

On the drive home, Landry and I had a conversation about more training with the Sekhmetians. He wanted to ask Yashi more questions.

"I'm not quite finished training with the Sekhmetians," Landry said. "I have to complete their small arms training. Jagannath tells me the female instructor is a hardcore fighter. She expects excellence from her trainees. They don't want me to use any of my powers during training, like how I did in the arena. They don't want me cheating because I can change the trajectory of a bullet or projectile in flight. I guess I've always done that, but not known it. When I would target practice or hunt, I was always a perfect shot."

"I didn't know you hunted," I said.

"When I was young, we were poor, and that's how we foraged for food."

"Did you enjoy hunting?" I asked.

"I liked being close to nature," he answered. "I really didn't enjoy taking an animal's life, but everything eats something. If you're not going to eat it, you shouldn't kill it,"

"So, why don't you hunt now?"

"We have enough food, so there's no need."

"Yes, I agree. No need to kill unnecessarily."

"Landry," I said, "I'm going to bed."

"Okay," he answered.

I changed into my nightclothes and went to bed. A few moments later, Landry laid down beside me.

"I had to get my pillow," Landry said as he scooted closer to me. "You said you were going to bed. I didn't hear you say were going to sleep."

"Whatever do you mean?" I replied with a smile.

Landry moved closer to me and embraced me. He started to lightly kiss my neck while lightly stroking my hair.

"I've missed being with you," Landry said. "It not that late and we need time for us."

"How right you are," I said as we kissed passionately.

Needless to say, it was a great night…

I woke up, but Landry was nowhere to be seen. A delicious smell came into the room. Oh my, he made us pancakes! A few minutes later, the bedroom door opened slowly. Landry carried a tray with a small table tucked under his arm. He was trying to surprise me with breakfast in bed.

"Here you go, my love," Landry said. "I made your favorite, blueberry pancakes."

The phone rang and disturbed a perfect moment. Landry put the small table on my lap and placed the plate of pancakes and a bottle of syrup on top of it. He then rushed to answer the phone.

"Hey, Jagannath, what's up?" he said. "Okay.....I think we can do that.....I'll ask her to make sure this is something she wants to do.....Right, I'll call you back in a few."

Landry walked back into the bedroom. He gazed at me with a pondering look.

"I guess those were good," he said, nodding to my plate. "They're almost gone. I wasn't on the phone that long, I guess you worked up an appetite last night."

"Yep," I said with a smile and a wink.

Landry sat down on the bed by my feet. *Something is going on,* I thought. After hearing part of that conversation, it had to be important or Jagannath wouldn't have called.

"Jagannath said the small arms instructor wants to train you and me," Landry said. "What do you think about that?"

"Sounds like it will be challenging," I replied. "It's something I need to do anyway."

"Awesome, I'll call him back and let him know," Landry said.

Landry called Jagannath back. They talked for an hour or so. That man of mine can talk without a second's pause. It seemed like he could talk to anyone, even someone from another planet.

I listened to them talk while I cleaned up the kitchen. If he cooked, I cleaned up afterward. Landry was a good cook. Dad used some of Landry's recipes in his restaurant. I think Dad wants him to eventually work there, but I wasn't sure if Landry had enough of that kind of work.

Landry hung up the phone, telling me that our training will start in two days. Uniforms would be dropped off at the house soon. Jagannath had arranged for Landry and me to be trained with a smaller group of trainees. During the three-week course, both of us would stay at the facility. Our stay in the barracks with other trainees would help us learn more about fighting skills.

A few days later, there was a knock at the door. A delivery company dropped off a package. When we opened the package, there were two Sekhmetian uniforms inside. The uniforms included a shirt, pants, and a sleeveless vest. The vest was put on over the shoulders and fastened on the sides, so it covered front and back. The material on the front and the back of the vest was a hard substance that had a small hexagonal pattern over the surface. Between the hexagons, there was a wire mesh integrated into this material.

There was other equipment in the package as well. There was a belt that had a holster for a sidearm and other places where things could be attached. There were also a pair of boots and a pair of gloves with reinforced knuckles and palm protection.

It looked like we were ready to go. The Sekhmetians were a warrior race and this was their forte. Landry and I were looking forward to the training. It felt wonderful to move forward together.

Later in the day, I received a call from Yashi. She asked to meet us tomorrow to go over some material she would like to share with us before our training begins. She said she was going to expound on spiritual warfare. We agreed to meet at her at Sirius Botanical Gardens. It was July of 2004 and the flowers were in full bloom. It would give us all the chance to meet under pleasant circumstances.

The next day we met Yashi promptly at 1:00 pm. The weather was perfect. The sun shone brightly in the sky. Proxima Centauri was a beautiful star and looked magnificent across their landscape. With a red core, the sun sported a white and yellow-colored band around it. It was a spectacular sight and it graced the skyline with its majestic beauty.

"How are you two lovebirds doing today?" Yashi asked.

"We're doing well, thank you," I answered. "And you?"

"I'm doing well," Yashi answered. "I wanted to go over some material with you today. I thought this might be a pleasant way to spend some time together."

"It is, Yashi," Landry answered. "Thank you for inviting us."

"My pleasure," Yashi replied. "Now, I know you both are scheduled to start your training with the Sekhmetian Military tomorrow. I wanted to be sure you both are prepared. They are known for their stern discipline and you will come out of the experience a far greater warrior than you were when you started. Still, you have to accept how things roll here."

"And how's that?" Landry asked.

"The Sekhmetian military is adamant about their rules. They will administer stern discipline if you don't follow their rules."

"That sounds a lot like the military from Planet Earth," Landry said.

"To some degree, you're correct," Yashi responded, "but the difference is their level of discipline. They don't have a legal system of military justice. There are no court-martials. They terminate anyone who is a threat to their people or to their planet. If anyone in their military demonstrates an unwillingness to act on behalf of the greater good of their people or their planet, they will destroy them. It literally is that simple."

"That's a good thing," Landry said. "I agree with their thinking. If you allow evil to spread, it will destroy all that it can destroy. This is the nature of evil. It wants to suck everyone and everything into it. The Sekhmetians don't allow evil to spread like a cancer. They nip it in the bud, so that it is no longer a problem."

"I would agree as well," I said. "The Sekhmetians got it right. Evil cannot be tolerated. It's unfortunate that everyone does not desire to serve the Light, but that's how it is."

"Good," Yashi said. "I just wanted to be sure you both understand how their military operates."

"We're okay with it," Landry said.

"Wonderful," she answered. "Now, we can move on. Landry, do you know the difference between a dark energy soul and a psychopath or sociopath?"

"Landry," I said, "be careful, that's a trick question!"

"It's okay, Jayna," he said. "I get it."

"I wanted to talk to you both today about the spiritual aspect of being a warrior. The dark energy souls are what your culture calls 'psychopaths or sociopaths.' Planet Earth authorities cannot see into the bodies of those who are spiritually dark. If they could, they would see a dark energy soul, which has infinite physical variations. Every physical being has a genetic make-up and genetic predisposition. This being can express evil in every genetic expression. Therefore, it encourages the spread of unimaginable evil throughout the physical universe. There are entire races of humanoid beings that are dark. For example, the Draconians. They are all an expression of one evil being."

"You mean like a hive mentality?" Landry asked.

"Exactly," she said. "All evil beings are simply tentacles of one being and they are all controlled by the same entity, the one I call the Dark One. They all exhibit the same basic personality traits. They're selfish, vain, manipulative, greedy, arrogant, and insensitive to other's needs and feelings. They act as if only they matter as though there's no room for anyone else in their way of thinking. They are incapable of true love but very capable of special relationships. They blame you for their bad behavior. They never admit to error and they don't take responsibility for their actions. They're never at fault. They're pathological liars and should not be trusted. They are the biggest hypocrites you will ever meet. There's always a double standard with them. They can do whatever it is that they please, but they always point fingers at other's bad behavior. What about their own?

"They're also duplicitous. They'll pretend to be your friend to your face, but will talk behind your back. They're great lovers of gossip and evil speech. They always try to make it look like everyone else has the problem, but not them. Gossip is an avoidance strategy for them. They want the focus on someone else's shortcomings and issues, never on their own. They enjoy creating a sense of superiority over someone else and cannot see their madness. They have no inherent superiority, they just think that they do.

"They also will turn people against you if you stand up to them. This is to be expected. They don't even care about the validity of their speech. They will say anything to put you or anyone that stands up to them in a bad light. This is why you have laws on Planet Earth that protect whistleblowers. You can always count on the Darkness retaliating. It is correct to protect whistleblowers."

"Yashi, question," I said. "The behaviors you are describing are simply bad human behaviors. Can a light energy soul exhibit such behavior too?"

"Good question, Jayna," Yashi answered. "Yes, a light energy soul can also behave badly. There is the capacity for egoic behavior or spiritual darkness, if you will, in all of us. The difference is that light energy souls will be able to overcome their immature behaviors much more easily than dark energy souls. Remember, there is dark energy in all of us. Still, the light energy souls are not consumed or absorbed by it, so they can overcome such foolishness without too much trouble. The dark energy souls can also do this, but not easily. That dark energy keeps pulling them back. It's quite a struggle for them to be able to come back to the Light. The Darkness does everything it can to keep them in its grip.

"The battle for the emancipation of the dark energy soul must be fought and won. It is entirely possible to bring them back, that is if they haven't destroyed their soul already. This is the process of spiritual healing that is essential to take place in every soul when it journeys back to its Creator.

"In the meantime, while we are all in our life process, the Goddess allows the Dark ones to drag us down as a learning experience and also as a way of speeding up our spiritual healing process. They serve the Light indirectly by giving the rest of us an opportunity to forgive and let go. Their manipulative behavior gives us ample opportunity to pull us into drama. They do this quite well.

"If you should happen to have a relationship with a dark energy soul in some way, they always follow the same pattern. If you give them what they want and if you please them, they will show you love and favoritism. If you don't give them what they want, they withdraw their love from you as a punishment for not giving them their way. This is the manipulative game they play. Many people suffer emotional problems by parents who are dark and are incapable of raising children properly. They will manipulate their children to no end. Those young ones will grow up with psychological problems."

"Could the family dramas that result from such parenting be considered a form of spiritual warfare?" I asked.

"Yes, Jayna," Yashi answered. "There are many from the Light who are sent to spiritually dark parents to demonstrate that the Light's power is greater than the Darkness's. They can develop some issues around this kind of mistreatment, however, unless they are corrupt, they will always find their way to healing and positivity. The experience, in turn, makes them stronger and they overcome victimization. They also make good counselors themselves because of what they have lived through. This type of situation is known as the Wounded Healer. Through their own suffering, they are able to help others to heal."

"If that is the case," Landry said, "then it stands to reason that the entire physical universe is one large battleground. Spiritual battles are being played out constantly by all the beings in the universe, be it a light energy soul or a dark energy soul."

"Both light and ark energy souls," I said, "desire to share. The only difference is *what* they desire to share. The light energy soul wants to share love and healing, while the dark energy soul wants to share evil and desires to capture your soul."

"You just mentioned a very important topic to discuss," Yashi said.

"What's that, Yashi?"

"Capturing a soul," she said. "This is an important topic for any spiritual warrior. If a person should corrupt, then their energy will reflect this evil intention. This in turn will attract an evil being to it with the same evil intention. The Creator allows a demon to possess someone if they are corrupt. The demon desires to express evil and find an avenue of expression through a corrupted being. In these cases, the person loses control over themselves, and the demon is allowed to take over them. The person would then become more corrupt and dishonest than they were previously. A period of time is always given in these cases to allow the person to correct their behavior. If they should do the necessary work, then they will be given the means to exorcise the demon and they will be free. That is, providing they learned the lesson.

"Over time, if the person never corrects themselves, the Creator allows the person's soul to be absorbed by the Dark One. They literally lose their soul. So many from the Light have fallen to the Dark One. It is of the utmost importance that one never corrupts, because if one does, the price is unimaginable."

"You mean they lose their soul?" Landry asked.

"Yes, they lose their soul. They get absorbed into the one dark soul and they no longer have any autonomy, even if they think they do. Very, very sad."

"Is it possible to gain one's soul back after they've been absorbed?" I asked.

"Yes, Jayna," Yashi said. "It is possible. They must completely give themselves over to the Light and never slip back into their bad behavior. It's best if they go through Yeshua and vow to eternally serve only the Light. He can bring them back.

"If a soul fails to come back to the Light, the karmic consequences are indeed serious. After they die in physical form, they get thrown into a fiery pit and literally suffer hell's wrath. It's a blessing that you cannot hear inside the gates of hell. If you could, you would hear the screams of the damned. So many are burning in hell right now for their past mistakes. Some do learn from the experience and desire to come back to the Light. They are then released from their suffering and move on to other beautiful and peaceful dimensions. Their soul can then find rest. But for those who willingly serve the Darkness, it is damnation they experience. Not eternally, but long enough to learn a very painful lesson. In the most extreme cases, the soul is destroyed."

"How gruesome!" I said. "Why would the Creator do such a thing?"

"Dear one, in these extreme cases, the karma that these souls have created is so severe, it would take thousands of lifetimes of great suffering to balance out their karma. The Creator destroys their soul, only for them to be reborn again like a newborn baby. They have no memory of their past evils and their slate is wiped clean. They are beautiful and innocent just like a newborn baby. It's in their best interest to be destroyed. It would be too cruel to allow them to continue with such a heavy karmic load.

"The Darkness' people are the ones who are running Planet Earth right now. They are more than likely going to have their souls destroyed. They have created unimaginable karma for themselves. We'll have to deal with them at a future date, but not for the moment. Planet Sekhmet needs us right now."

"Yashi," I asked, "is there a difference between souls that have given themselves to the Darkness of their own free will between souls that get captured and then absorbed?"

"Yes, there is. Those who give themselves over to the Darkness willingly are usually eviler than their captured counterparts. The ones that have had their souls captured still have the instinct to do good. They usually are not quite so evil and are a mixture of both positive and negative qualities. It's usually easier to bring someone back from the Darkness if their soul was captured than if they willingly decided to become evil.

"And in the cases of extreme evil, there are some who are incarnations of Satan. Just like Father-Mother God can have incarnates, the Dark One can have his own as well. They are so evil that they are the embodiment of Satan himself. There are a few around in your world today. None of them reside here on Sekhmet. The Sekhmetians would have destroyed anyone of this nature.

"The problem here on Sekhmet is that the Kemkabi are working through the Darkened. They literally are the hunters for the Darkness. We're getting ready now to take on the Kemkabi once and for all and banish them from the planet!"

"Absolutely," Landry said. "I'm looking forward to beginning my training. I can't wait to see what kind of weapons the Sekhmetians have. I bet they're very powerful!"

"Indeed," Yashi said. "Firepower is indeed powerful. This is the next subject for me to discuss with you."

"That's my shtick," I said.

"What does shtick mean, Jayna?" Landry asked.

"Shtick is a Yiddish word. It means a routine that someone uses to make people laugh."

"I saw what you did that night in the alley," Landry said. "And I didn't think it was funny."

"Landry," Yashi said, "you saw Jayna's power with fire. That's her gift from the Goddess. She was a fire high priestess of the Light in ancient Egypt. She can summon its power when she needs it."

"I noticed!" Landry said.

"To the ancient Egyptians," Yashi continued, "the Goddess was the Eternal Flame. Fire possesses great power and every spiritual warrior needs to understand its attributes. Fire is the Creator's power. It is a symbol of the Divine. Fire embodies various elements of the Divine. Physically, fire gives light, which enables us to see. Spiritually, we need spiritual light to help us understand life's lessons. Physically, fire gives heat so we can survive. Spiritually, fire gives us the warmth of love to nurture our souls. Physically, fire explodes to give us firepower weapons. Spiritually, fire gives discipline when necessary.

"When we use firepower as a warrior, we are using the Creator's power that was bestowed to us. Firepower is deadly and should never be used for destruction unless instructed to so by the Divine. There is a time and place for everything, even for firepower. We should not abuse its power, nor should we refrain from using it if it is necessary.

"The Sekhmetians are very sensitive about this subject. After their emancipation from the Draconians, they vowed to never allow themselves be enslaved ever again. They take firepower very seriously and will not hesitate to use it when the situation warrants it. Jayna's firepower is what interested them in the first place. Her parents told the government agent about the first instance when she unleashed her power. Little Jayna once started a fire with her mind. That, along with her demonstrable psychic ability, made Jayna a candidate to come here and assist with the Kemkabi issue."

"Oohh, you're hot baby!" Landry said.

"Don't mind him, Yashi," I said. "He's a real wise guy."

"Not me!" Landry replied.

Yashi smiled. "It's okay, Jayna."

I looked around and saw we had completed our walk around the gardens and we were back to where we started. Time had gone by quickly. We walked over to the picnic tables that were under a shade canopy by the garden's entrance and sat down. I could see Landry was deep in thought. This topic was a very relevant one for both of us. Yashi looked beautiful and radiant as always.

"Yashi," Landry said, "I have a question."

"Yes?" she answered.

"What are the Dark ones most afraid of?"

"Good question, Landry," she said. "The Dark ones' greatest fear is exposure. They live in a world of lies. They lie to others and they also lie to themselves. In their minds, they have conceited beliefs about their greatness, which helps compensate for their deep sense of inadequacy. But deep down, they're petrified and vulnerable. If anyone tries to show their bad behavior or their hypocrisy to them, they will become uncontrollably angry and violent. They are extremely dangerous and it isn't a wise idea to provoke them unless you are completely prepared for what will follow."

"What will follow, Yashi?" Landry asked.

"Landry," Yashi said, "what they will do to you will be unimaginable. They will either beat you to a pulp or humiliate you in the most despicable way, or sometimes even both. Only the most formidable and skilled warrior should try to take them on. They will have the strength of a madman, who is completely lacking in compassion and empathy. Their fear is so overwhelming to them, they cannot see their own madness. They literally go insane."

"I'm not afraid of them," Landry said.

"Nor should you be," I said.

"There's great complexity in standing up to the Dark ones," Yashi said. "Each situation is different and that's why a daily practice is so important. When you encounter a similar situation, your practice will help you make those important decisions. The Dark ones are extremely dangerous when challenged."

"So am I," said Landry.

"Indeed," Yashi answered.

"This should be interesting," I said.

"We should be going now," Yashi said.

With that, we got up and went to our car. Yashi said her farewell as Landry and I headed for home. We changed into our uniforms. We packed our gear, got into the car, and made our way to the military base. We were scheduled to stay in the barracks that night. Tomorrow was going to be a big day.

Not So Basic Training

When Landry and I arrived at the guard post of the Sekhmetian Army base, he shut off the car as the sign on the gates instructed. The ground was well lit. The guard post stood twenty feet from the fifteen-foot walls that surrounded the perimeter of the army base. The mesh metal boundary surrounded the facility. A slight breeze moved across the surface of the wall and the mesh gave off a faint glow. There was a large gate with two doors and both doors were mounted to large concrete pillars. On the top of these pillars, there was a turret with some type of weapon and surveillance system. In front of the gate, five-foot-tall metal poles were protruding from the ground. The poles were about two feet across. These poles stopped us from driving past the guard post.

The guards were wearing the same uniforms we were wearing, but just with a helmet. They were armed with a rifle, pistol, knife, and sword. One guard was standing inside of the guard building and he was examining a group of monitors. I could see him moving his arms as if using something, maybe a keyboard. Then the turret started to move, emitting a green light, which slowly moved over our car. The guard inside of the building gave the all-clear signal to the other guard. The guard standing along the side of the building where we were sitting walked over to the car.

"What is the reason you are here?" she asked as she looked down at us and into the car.

"We're here to have small arms training," Landry replied. He retrieved the pass card and IDs from the pocket on his shirt. He held our paperwork out the window so that the guard could check our documents.

She looked at us with a strange, questioning look as she took the documents from his hand. As she looked them over, her eyes widened. She motioned to the other guard and he left the building to walk over to our car. He looked at our IDs as well. They snapped to attention and placed their right over their forehead.

"Welcome to our base, sir and ma'am," she said. "It's a privilege to meet both of you."

She handed back our paperwork as the other guard returned to the building. The gates opened, with the metal poles disappearing into the ground. A blue line lit up on the ground in front of the car. I could see that the line of light lead into the base.

"Follow the marker line to the parking area," she said. "From there, two new marker lines will appear. You may proceed." She stepped back and saluted again.

Landry revved the car and followed the blue marker line into the Army base. The Guard saluted as we passed the guard post. As we drove past the on-duty Sekhmetians, they stared at us with the same look we received at the gate. Moments later, we arrived at the parking spot. I had not been around guns much in my life, so this would be interesting.

I paused before leaving the car. Landry was looking at the rear-view mirror.

"Do you know why the Sekhmetians are saluting you?" I said.

"When I passed the Trial of the Warrior, it was more than just a test," Landry explained. "Only one out of ten pass the trial. I could hold rank in the Sekmetian Army if they would allow it."

"You didn't tell me that it was that big of deal," I replied. "They won't allow you to hold rank in the army?"

"No, I'm not from Sekhmet," he said. "They allowed Draconians in their army and were betrayed by them."

"Oh, now I see why. So why do they salute?"

"Their pay me respect for my accomplishments. You never know though, things might change." He grinned at me and leaned in close. "Give me a kiss. This one will be the last that you'll get for a while."

"It might," I said before kissing him.

We exited the car and started following the lighted path markers. At one point, we had to go our separate ways. I found my way to the women's barracks, walked in, and looked around. There were only Sekhmetian women there. I had not spent much time with Sekhmetians outside of working with them and visiting their cities.

A woman approached me after I entered the barracks. She was a little taller than me, about 5' 8" inches, but about the same weight. Like all Sekhmetians, she was lean and muscular, yet still feminine. The female facial features were softer than the males of their species. They were very pretty but still deadly.

"Hello, how can I help you?" she asked. "I'm Sergeant Kabira."

"Hello, I'm Jayna," I replied. "I'll be training with your group."

"This is called a squad and the combined squads are called a platoon," she said. "You're the seer? And call me Sergeant."

"Yes, Sergeant, I am," I said. "Thank you for the information, Sergeant."

"Private Tabassum will show you to your quarters," the Sergeant ordered.

The Private led me to the end of a row of cots. There was a footlocker at the end of the cot that had my name on it. She nodded and walked away. I didn't think they liked me very much. I wasn't military, which didn't help. I opened the footlocker and found new clothes, undergarments, socks, and a training uniform.

A voice crackled over the intercom. "Lights out in five minutes."

I went behind a screen and changed into what everyone else would be wearing. I sat on my cot and meditated. As the lights went out, I went to sleep.

I was woken up by a buzzing sound on the intercom. I got up and looked around to find that everyone was changing clothes, so I followed suit. All of us stood in front of our footlockers. Sergeant Kabira did roll call as we were leaving the barracks. I followed the person in front of me and mimicked what they did. We went to the cafeteria. It was called "the mess" and we had our breakfast.

After everyone was done eating, we left. The squad went to another building. It was a large single-story building with double doors, with two windows on the sides. As we entered the building, I started to look around. At the front of the room, there was a large whiteboard. A desk was set up to the left and a female Sekhmetian stood there. We all took our seats. I could see Landry. He winked and I nodded back.

"I am Master Sergeant Rhiannon," the Sergeant said. "I'll be your instructor for small arms training. Over the next three weeks, you will learn the following: week one will be operation, assembly, and repair. Week two: weapon handling, marksmanship, and maintenance. Week three: close quarter combat, water training, climbing and repelling, helicopter rope training, and sniper training."

And so we started our first day of training. There was so much information to remember. The rifle and sidearm was covered the first day. The weapons functioned with magnets, not gunpowder. This weapon was more durable than directed energy weapons. It was called rail gun technology.

I knew all the specifications of these weapons because I had to disassemble and reassemble them hundreds of times. On day four, I had to do this blindfolded. I was one of the fastest in our squad, but another trainee, Dameka, had me beat. She was quick and smooth with this task. One minute and forty-five seconds was her best time. My time was five seconds slower. Dameka always said, in a half-joking manner, that I used my powers to keep up with her. Everyone believed that I wouldn't do that.

One day I asked the Sergeant if I could have a demonstration and she agreed to do so. On the sixth night, she brought a rifle to the barracks. The rifle was placed on the cot next to mine. Dameka looked at me and grinned. I closed my eyes and drew in a deep breath, then smiled and opened my eyes again. I levitated the weapon from the cot. Each component detached from the rifle in unison and floated in the air. Then each component broke into smaller parts. I reversed the process, making the rifle whole again. I lowered the rifle to the cot. The Sergeant announced the time: forty seconds. The squad whispered among themselves as they looked at Sergeant Rhiannon. Dameka smiled and nodded to the Sergeant. Sergeant Rhiannon walked over and picked up the rifle.

"Sergeant," Dameka said. "That's probably not as easy as it looked."

"It is very difficult," I replied. "It takes years of practice."

"You beat your mate's time by five seconds," The Sergeant said. "Well done."

"I have trained longer than Landry with this ability," I stated.

"Females are nimble and more cunning," Dameka replied. "The males have strength and power. This is the balance."

"We are all equals in different ways," I said. "Two halves of the Whole."

Then lights out was announced over the intercom. Everyone dispersed and got ready for bed. Tomorrow was the last day of the week. Tests would begin after breakfast. I believed I will do well.

***

After the day of testing was over, I ranked second in our squad. Dameka was first. Landry scored high as well. He secured firth position in his squad. Not bad for someone that wasn't educated on Planet Sekhmet.

The second week was interesting. We started handling live weapons. We also had to wear a helmet on the range. I had night and thermal vision on the visor of my helmet. The schedule was at the same intensity as the previous week

Range time was intense. Making sure you knew how to handle the weapon safely was a priority. Firing a weapon that could punch a hole through a half-inch of steel was sobering. I had to learn to fire the weapons standing, kneeling, and lying down. I thought that if the weapon didn't use any chemical propellant it wouldn't recoil that hard. I was wrong.

The first time I fired the rifle, I missed the center target by ten inches at one hundred yards. The projectiles had hit all over the target. The Sergeant instructed me on my grip and stance. I improved and could hit the center ring seven out of ten shots by the end of the week. The sidearm or the pistol took longer for me to handle. I didn't hit the target the first time I fired it. The Sergeant was so helpful through my training. She was always very professional and courteous. By the end of the week, I could keep six out of ten shots in the center circle of the target.

Parisa was the trainee that bunked next to me and she was the top shot in our squad this week. I talked to Dameka the most, but Parisa was the nicest by far. They asked questions about Planet Earth, our culture, and customs. We all became good friends.

Dameka was the more boisterous of the two, while Parisa was the quiet and thoughtful one. They were both fierce warriors, but more importantly, they were great friends. I learned more about their lifestyle and culture. Going through this training was good for me. This time was helping me to be a more adaptable warrior.

The penultimate day turned out to be my best. The platoon came together to qualify on marksmanship. There were five lanes set up to shoot at our practice distance. Everyone in the platoon qualified and I was finally able to watch Landry shoot. He was really good. His stance and grip were perfect. His shot placements were all in the center of the target. He was shooting fast and accurately, and he didn't even use any of his mental abilities. I figured he would do well because he had started shooting when he was only eight years old. The Sergeant was impressed by his technique and performance, but Parisa moved on to sniper training.

The last week of training was very group intensive. On the first day of the week, the only gear we trained with was our defensive vest and helmet. The helmet contained a heads-up display, known as HUD for short. The HUD assisted the soldier in aiming their weapon. This feature was displayed as a green dot when the visor was down, covering the face, and moved wherever the weapon was pointed. It made hitting a target much easier. I wish we had this during weapons training. But if your helmet was ever disabled, you'd better know how to shoot without it. I understood why we were trained to shoot like that. The helmet also contained communication devices built into it so troop action could be guided and monitored, and also so soldiers could communicate with each other.

We were also issued forearm guards and shin protection to add to our equipment. The vest had more to it than I originally thought. The vest, the arm guards, and the shin guards could protect the wearer in two ways. It could stop piercing, slashing, and blunt force strikes. The vest also added to survivability. The vest could be connected to a power cell that was attached to our belt. This created an energy barrier that could deflect projectiles fired at the wearer. Our training also covered the repair and maintenance of the shield array and power cell.

Parisa was present for this part of the training. After lunch, she departed to start sniper training. This was the last time I saw her until the end of the week.

After lunch, we went to the firing range and were issued live sidearms. The Sergeant explained the specifications and limitations of the protective gear. She went into detail on how the equipment would react when taking fire. The power cell is the limiting factor. The more damage the barrier takes, the faster the cell is drained.

The Sergeant asked for a volunteer. Landry and Dameka stood up at the same time. The Sergeant asked them to come up to the front. She instructed them to stand ten feet apart, then had both of them power up their vests. The Sergeant commanded them to draw their weapons and fire at each other.

"Want a gun fight, killer?" Landry said.

Without blinking an eye, they both drew their weapons. Landry fired first, shooting from the hip, like a cowboy from an old Western movie. Dameka went for the full draw. Landry's shot hit first and would have hit the heart if not for the shield.

The impact on the shield caused Dameka to stumble backward. As she returned fire, this caused Dameka's shot to strike Landry's shield on his left thigh, making him lose balance and stumble. I winced when I saw this happen, but the two of them chuckled. The Sergeant reprimanded them, saying that this was no laughing matter. She made Landry and Dameka do one hundred pushups and squats in full gear.

The Sergeant then told everyone left to pair up and activate their shields and fire one round at each other. So that was what we did. It was disconcerting to have someone fire a weapon at me, shield or not. Sometimes I thought Landry was not right in the head and it seemed that Dameka might not be very far behind him.

When the squad returned to the barracks, Dameka and I talked the rest of the night. Other members of our squad gathered around and listened to our conversation. It seemed that I had earned their respect and they have mine.

The day after was all about how to cover, conceal, ambush, and how not to get ambushed. We practiced how to ambush another squad and they practiced on us. Attacking a squad from concealment was considered an ambush. And when another squad would do it your squad, it was the worst day of your life.

We trained inside structures like houses, apartment buildings, and such. We were taught how to move around corners and enter doorways.

On the fourth day, we were trained to climb and repel on natural and constructed surfaces. This was my least favorite part of everything so far. Climbing up a cliff face with rocks and dirt falling on you wasn't fun at all. Dameka liked climbing and she was much better at it than I was. The Sekhmetian trainees didn't seem to mind at all. I knew Landry didn't like it much, since he didn't like heights. He said as long as he has something to hold on to, he would be okay. His Sekhmetian friend, Okoth, always teased him during training and made funny comments about him being afraid of heights to help him overcome his fear. I could tell that they were becoming good friends.

The fifth day was focused on rope training with a helicopter. The Sekhmetian helicopters were different from those on Earth. Two large rotor fans spun in opposite directions and were mounted on both sides of the extended cabin. The crew could drop ropes from the back of the helicopter to deploy or retrieve troops. The rotor fans were enclosed inside protective guards. The motor ran off of a self-recharging battery system. The weapons were mounted underneath the cockpit of the aircraft.

We trained on how to quickly attach ourselves to the ropes when they were dropped down from the helicopter. Some ropes could hold the weight of as many as five people, but more often than not, each person had their own rope. I found this interesting and enjoyable.

On the sixth day, we learned water operations. We learned the basics of how to board a watercraft and how to swim with all of our gear on. I also enjoyed this part because I loved the water. Landry, however, didn't swim very well and looked agitated most of the time.

On the seventh day we were dropped from a helicopter by a rope and we had to make it back to camp in under ten hours. There were many obstacles in our way that we had to overcome. There were buildings set up with different scenarios we had to face. Inside the buildings, robotic soldiers would fire marker pellets. If you were hit, you could not continue through the rest of the course. If you hit the robot, it would be deactivated. The squad I was on only lost one person. We did very well. Landry and his squad didn't lose anybody. Landry had problems with the river crossing, but his teammates helped him. Everyone who made it back passed. And we made it with plenty of time left.

At the end of all three weeks, we received a patch, provided to us by the Sekhmetian military. Even though we were human, we received the same status, but technically, we were still not members of the military.

Military personnel had their weapons and gear in their homes. They normally had a safe installed someplace in their dwelling. To my surprise, the military allowed us to do the same.

This was the last time I saw many of the people we trained with, but I intended to stay in touch with my friends. Landry also wanted to stay in touch with his friends as well.

Wedding Bells

After our training, Landry and I wanted to take a break. We were exhausted. The training was awesome; however, we needed rest to recuperate. Landry was tired but in good spirits. We decided to take some time to be alone and enjoy our lives. Yashi agreed, so we took a month off. She said a rest period would refresh us and sharpen our senses.

It was a happy time for us. We went shopping, exploring, and even made it back to River Town for a three-day visit before our vacation time was over. Landry got a chance to see his family and friends, and we kept up our Los Angeles cover story. The time off deepened our relationship and our bond was stronger than ever.

The trip ended on a happy note. Little did I know what he had planned for me. When we were done visiting in River Town, John picked us up and drove us to the Cosmic Fountain. Landry seemed to be in an upbeat mood and I sensed there was something about to happen, but I didn't know what. The two of them chatted happily on the ride to the Fountain and John dropped us off there.

Landry took my hand and we walked down the stairs together. We usually didn't hold hands as we walked down the stairs, but on this night, Landry seemed to be acting differently.

Just before we got to the platform of the Cosmic Fountain, Landry got down on bended knee and said, "Jayna, will you marry me?" His face was loving and beautiful. I could tell that he wanted to create a romantic moment for me.

I waited a moment to answer. I looked directly into his eyes – those big, beautiful blue eyes – which were sparkling with the joy of love.

"Landry," I said, "I would be honored to marry you and become Mrs. Berkley. The answer is yes, yes indeed."

With that, Landry reached in his pocket. He pulled out a small ring box and handed it to me. But before I could open the box, he took my other hand in his and guided me onto the platform. Our weight on the platform activated the machine and the multi-colored energy surrounded us.

"Destination please?" the Manjin asked.

"Planet Sekhmet," Landry answered.

With that, the energy engulfed us with beautiful swirls of prismatic colors and we were transported back to Planet Sekhmet.

Still holding my hand, Landry guided me up the stairs with him. When we got to the top, there was a crowd of people waiting for us, both friends and family. I was momentarily shocked.

Landry reached over and grabbed the ring box from my hand. He pulled out the ring and held it up so I could see it. It was so beautiful! It had a diamond in the middle of a setting with three smaller diamonds around it, which formed a pyramid. I had never seen an engagement ring like this one before, it was so different.

Landry took the ring and placed it on my ring finger. We both just looked at each other. The moment was so profound. We both felt that the other was our perfect match. The connection we had was so deep; we both knew we belonged together.

I hugged and kissed Landry and began to cry. This was one of the happiest moments of my life. I felt light as a feather. Everyone began to clap.

"Come on everybody, let's go back to the restaurant to celebrate!" Dad said.

With that, everyone got in their cars and drove off. Landry and I went with Mom and Dad in their car. The mood was a happy one. We all talked and laughed. When dinner was over, Dad stood up.

"Here's a toast," he said, "to my wonderful daughter, Jayna, and her future husband, Landry. May your marriage be a long and happy one, with great success in your work. Cheers!"

"Cheers!" everyone answered.

We were all in a happy mood and the party ran late into the evening. Landry and I slow danced at the end of the night. Some of the Sekhmetians were trying to slow dance as well. It was quite a sight to behold. I made a mental note that night, don't dance with people that have claws on their feet, retractable or otherwise. When the party was over, we drove home with Yashi.

"I'm so happy for both of you!" she said.

"Thank you, Yashi," I said. "This is one of the happiest days of my life."

"I know," she said. "Landry, her wait for you was long and hard. She struggled with her desire to meet and know you many times throughout her life. It was harder for her than what she lets on."

"Well now," he said. "She's going to be my wife. The wait is over."

Landry reached over and kissed me. I put my head on his shoulder and just rested for the rest of the drive home.

Yashi dropped us off at our apartment. I asked her if she would like to come inside, but she declined. She said she would come by tomorrow. Our vacation time had come to an end and we knew it was time to get to work again.

Yashi came by the next day and we started to go through our exercises again. Both Landry and I had our practice. It was of the utmost importance that we stayed ready for whatever may come.

We got together with Jagannath and decided to train together with the Sekhmetian military three times a week to keep ourselves in tip-top shape. We went back to the military base to conduct our training exercises. Landry and I worked with the Crystal Cube at home.

Everything seemed to be falling into place. The show was still going strong and everyone still loved it. It helped to keep the negativity at bay. But still, the Equinox movement was growing due to spreading corruption. We did have occasional incidents with the Darkened, although not as severe as the shopping mall incident. We never let our guard down and we were vigilant.

Landry and I decided on a date to get married. We picked May 1st of the next year, 2006. That gave us enough time to get all the arrangements made. I decided to have red and blonde highlights put into my brown hair since Landry's favorite color was red. He was pleased with the results.

We decided to be married outdoors in a forest clearing. When I was a child, I enjoyed going to the forest with my parents. It was my favorite spot. We would drive into the forest and go down a dirt road and park our car right in the middle of the forest. Alongside the parking lot was a row of bushes. Just a short walk away, there was a hidden garden, one that I always thought of as "a secret garden."

After our training, Landry and I wanted to take a break. We were exhausted. The training was awesome; however, we needed rest to recuperate. Landry was tired, but in good spirits. We decided to take some time to be alone and enjoy our lives. Yashi agreed, so we took a month off. She said a rest period would refresh us and sharpen our senses.

It was a happy time for us. We went shopping, exploring, and even made it back to River Town for a three-day visit before our vacation time was over. Landry got a chance to see his family and friends, and we kept up our Los Angeles cover story. The time off deepened our relationship and our bond was stronger than ever.

The trip ended on a happy note. Little did I know what he had planned for me. When we were done visiting in River Town, John picked us up and drove us to the Cosmic Fountain. Landry seemed to be in a really upbeat mood and I sensed there was something about to happen, but I didn't know what. The two of them chatted happily on the ride to the Fountain and John dropped us off there.

Landry took my hand and we walked down the stairs together. We usually didn't hold hands as we walked down the stairs, but on this night, Landry seemed to be acting differently.

Just before we got to the platform of the Cosmic Fountain, Landry got down on bended knee and said, "Jayna, will you marry me?" His face was loving and beautiful. I could tell that he wanted to create a romantic moment for me.

I waited a moment to answer. I looked directly into his eyes – those big, beautiful blue eyes – which were sparkling with the joy of love.

"Landry," I said, "I would be honored to marry you and become Mrs. Berkley. The answer is yes, yes indeed."

With that, Landry reached in his pocket. He pulled out a small ring box and handed it to me. But before I could open the box, he took my other hand in his and guided me onto the platform. Our weight on the platform activated the machine and the multi-colored energy surrounded us.

"Destination please?" the Manjin asked.

"Planet Sekhmet," Landry answered.

With that, the energy engulfed us with beautiful swirls of prismatic colors and we were transported back to Planet Sekhmet.

Still holding my hand, Landry guided me up the stairs with him. When we got to the top, there was a crowd of people waiting for us, both friends and family. I was momentarily shocked.

Landry reached over and grabbed the ring box from my hand. He pulled out the ring and held it up so I could see it. It was so beautiful! It had a diamond in the middle of a setting with three smaller diamonds around it, which formed a pyramid. I had never seen an engagement ring like this one before, it was so different.

Landry took the ring and placed it on my ring finger. We both just looked at each other. The moment was so profound. We both felt that the other was our perfect match. The connection we had was so deep; we both knew we belonged together.

I hugged and kissed Landry and began to cry. This was one of the happiest moments of my life. I felt light as a feather. Everyone began to clap.

"Come on everybody, let's go back to the restaurant to celebrate!" Dad said.

With that, everyone got in their cars and drove off. Landry and I went with Mom and Dad in their car. The mood was a happy one. We all talked and laughed. When dinner was over, Dad stood up.

"Here's a toast," he said, "to my wonderful daughter, Jayna, and her future husband, Landry. May your marriage be a long and happy one, with great success in your work. Cheers!"

"Cheers!" everyone answered.

We were all in a happy mood and the party ran late into the evening. Landry and I slow danced at the end of the night. Some of the Sekhmetians were trying to slow dance as well. It was quite a sight to behold. I made a mental note that night, don't dance with people that have claws on their feet, retractable or otherwise. When the party was over, we drove home with Yashi.

"I'm so happy for both of you!" she said.

"Thank you, Yashi," I said. "This is one of the happiest days of my life."

"I know," she said. "Landry, her wait for you was long and hard. She struggled with her desire to meet and know you many times throughout her life. It was harder for her than what she lets on."

"Well now," he said. "She's going to be my wife. The wait is over."

Landry reached over and kissed me. I put my head on his shoulder and just rested for the rest of the drive home.

Yashi dropped us off at our apartment. I asked her if she would like to come inside, but she declined. She said she would come by tomorrow. Our vacation time had come to an end and we knew it was time to get to work again.

Yashi came by the next day and we started to go through our exercises again. Both Landry and I had our practice. It was of the utmost importance that we stayed ready for whatever may come.

We got together with Jagannath and decided to train together with the Sekhmetian military three times a week to keep ourselves in tip-top shape. We went back to the military base to conduct our training exercises. Landry and I worked with the Crystal Cube at home.

Everything seemed to be falling into place. The show was still going strong and everyone still loved it. It helped to keep the negativity at bay. But still, the Equinox movement was growing and spreading their corruption. We did have occasional incidents with the Darkened, although not as severe as the shopping mall incident. We never let our guard down and we were vigilant.

Landry and I decided on a date to get married. We picked May 1st of the next year, 2006. That gave us enough time to get all the arrangements made. I decided to have red and blonde highlights put into my brown hair since Landry's favorite color was red. He was pleased with the results.

We decided to be married outdoors in a forest clearing. When I was a child, I enjoyed going to the forest with my parents. It was my favorite spot. We would drive into the forest and go down a dirt road and park our car right in the middle of the forest. Alongside the parking lot was a row of bushes. Just a short walk away, there was a hidden garden, one that I always thought of as "a secret garden."

There was a beautiful pond with lily pads on it, with three cement steps leading into the water. All around the pond were various types and colors of flowers. The floral smell was heavenly. There was a pink flowering tree with large blooms on one side of the pond and its branches hung down over the water. On the other side of the pond, there was a different type of tree, with blooms that I had never seen before, but were very beautiful. The flowers had long thin petals and were a combination of pastel colors of yellow, white, blue, violet, and pink. The tree was large and full, which created a beautiful kaleidoscope of soft colors.

On the opposite side of the steps stood a white pillar with a beautiful white flower pot, which almost looked like an ancient Grecian pot. White and pink flowers sprouted out of the top and it added charm to the environment.

We planned to have about fifty guests and the space seemed just big enough for a crowd of that size. We decided to have the ceremony with our backs to the pond so that the camera would pick up the beautiful colors and scenery behind us. When the ceremony was done, we would stay at that spot to take pictures.

We made all the preparations and arrangements as time went by quickly. Planning a wedding was fun, but was very time-consuming. There were many details to work out. Yashi would marry us and fill out the paperwork for the US government. We would receive a legal marriage license.

After the ceremony, we would come back to my parents' restaurant to have lunch. After lunch, we would go through the Cosmic Fountain and travel to the Bahamas for our honeymoon. After we were done in the Bahamas, we would take a flight back to River Town and visit with Landry's family and friends. When we were done there, we would come back to Sirius and resume our normal routine.

When our wedding day finally arrived, Landry left early to meet with Jagannath. I got ready and went with Yashi to the garden. The weather was perfect. The sun was shining and all the preparations were made. I was a little nervous, but I tried to not let my anxiety get the better of me. Yashi had a short ceremony prepared and it would only take a few minutes. I had a fairly simple pretty white dress, with a beautiful pearl necklace around my neck. Landry had on a black suit with a tie. This was the first time I had ever seen him in a suit. He was not one to dress formally. Casual dress was his style, but it suited him.

We planned the wedding to start at 1:00 pm, and Yashi and I arrived fifteen minutes early. Landry and Jagannath hadn't arrived yet. Lorraine would be the matron of honor, and Jagannath would be Landry's best man. Emma, Parisa, and Dameka were in the bridesmaids, and Todd, Bradly, and Okoth were the groomsmen. The bridesmaids' gowns were soft lavender, and the groomsmen wore black suits.

The guests were arriving, everything was going smoothly. Landry and Jagannath showed up at the last minute. We were ready to begin.

Yashi looked beautiful as always, and she wore a long flowing silver-colored robe. It gave her a goddess-type look, and she wore it well. I could see the joy in her eyes, I know she loves Landry and I like her own children. This was a very happy moment in her life as well.

When the ceremony began, Dad walked me down to the pond where Landry met us and they exchanged places. Landry and I stood in front of Yashi and we were ready to exchange vows.

As we did so, I couldn't keep from crying. The love of my life, the man I had waited for so long! We are being married, I thought. What a moment!

We kissed, and it was done. We were *married!* We turned around and faced our guests and they all threw flowers on us. Landry and I were overjoyed, and they shared our joy with us.

The photographer had been taking pictures all along, and he asked us to pose for pictures. We did, and then Mom and Dad joined us in the pictures, and so on.

Everything had gone smoothly, we were taking pictures, when all of a sudden, I heard a crash. The next thing I know, some of our guests are screaming, "NO!" I was shocked for a moment and was having trouble processing what was happening. It all happened so fast. Landry looked to see what was going on, and the next thing I know he jumped into the bushes and was running through them. I was not able to speak; I was trying to process all of this. Landry, I thought, *why are you running through the bushes? Are you crazy? Why are you doing this?* But Landry couldn't hear my thoughts. I just watched in horror.

Kensley, the man who tried to overcharge me for an apartment, decided he and two of his friends were going to ruin my wedding. While everyone was occupied with the wedding, they tried to put a bomb underneath our car. Some of the guests heard them talking. When they went to see what was happening, the man underneath the car quickly came up from under the car. He accidentally ran into one of the other men. He tripped over the bag of tools, and the first man knocked into the second man. He fell, and his elbow broke the glass of the front passenger side window.

Landry ran through the bushes to ambush them, but he didn't catch them because they ran into their waiting vehicle. They tried to speed off, but they had to drive on an access road to make it to the highway. Dameka saw them enter the car and start driving away, so she ran across the grass to intercept the car. Landry had to follow suit and adjusted his path, running after the car as well. Dameka made it to the highway first and picked up a large rock that ringed the trees on the side of the highway. Landry used his mental energy to augment his physical prowess to run and catch up to the car. Landry and the car intersected on the highway. He then punched through the rear side glass with so much force, his fist hit the man in the head and killed him. As the car pulled away, Landry extended his hand and caused the car to veer off the highway into the guardrail. Dameka, still standing in the road about twenty feet away, threw the large stone at the man in the passenger seat. The side glass shattered, and the stone smashed into man's head. He slumped over in the seat.

The driver tried to open the door of the smoking vehicle. The crash caused the door to be jammed, and the car to start smoking. Kensley climbed from the car and tried to flee, but only made it six feet from the car. Landry rushed him and kicked him in the chest, which knocked him off his feet. While Kensley was still in the air, Landry stepped forward and grabbed him by the ankle, pivoted, and slammed him into the side of the car.

Apparently, Kensley and his friends became Darkened. This entire episode was ugly; it was my wedding day! I tried not to show my real feelings; I didn't want to deal with such violence today, but The Darkness had other ideas. They were trying to assassinate us on our wedding day. This was especially meaningful since Landry and I were warriors of The Light. This was their way of saying they were going destroy us, and we couldn't stop them from doing so.

The only way out of the situation was to resume our wedding celebration and put this behind us. Landry was upset too. I saw in his eyes "the look." When he looked this way, he's capable of killing someone, and that's what happened twice today. I had to work very hard to hide my emotional state.

"We know that was Kensley, do we know who Fluffy and Feefee are, I mean were?" I asked sarcastically.

Landry just stared at me and said, "No."

Jagannath jumped in and said, "We'll call the police, they'll find out for us."

The police arrived and began their police work. Pictures were taken, forms were filled out, statements were made, etc.

When they were done, I felt defeated. Landry held my hand and consoled me. He reminded me that we could put this behind us and continue our celebration. Yashi tried to console me as well. I felt overwhelmed.

After about an hour or so, I started to feel better. Once the police work was finished, it was easier to move forward and not let this incident ruin our day.

We all went back to the restaurant, and the mood was starting to lift. Dad and Mom hired people to cook and clean up for us, so they could join the celebration with us.

We stayed at the restaurant for about two hours, and then said goodbye to our guests, and left for The Cosmic Fountain. We booked reservations in a hotel in the Bahamas and had to be there before 10:00 pm.

When we got there, it was a very beautifully decorated lobby, with a live parrot out of his cage as the star attraction. He stayed on a stand and was quite large and beautiful. He was well behaved and ate seeds as the guests looked on.

There were pictures on the walls, all colorful and tasteful.

Landry and I were tired, but not disheartened. The owner of the lobby was very kind and sent us a bottle of champagne. Our hearts were at peace. The day ended gracefully, no more incidents, only joy. We made passionate love that night; it was a special occasion never to be forgotten.

We spent a few days there sightseeing and enjoyed our vacation. When it came time to leave, we took a plane to River Town and continued the rest of our honeymoon there.

We rented a motel room, and went to visit Landry's family; they were all happy for us. We also stopped at his old job at Pizza Depot and visited there as well. He called his buddies and told them the good news.

Our stay there was a pleasant one, but it came time to wrap things up and leave. We said our goodbyes and John came and picked us up.

We made it back to Sirius late and went right to sleep. The traveling was exhausting. The next morning, Landry made me breakfast in bed, and we rested for the rest of the day. The following day, it was back to work.

The Kemkabi Strike

That morning, we received a call from the TV station. They said they had bags full of wedding cards for Landry and me. They asked us to come by and pick up the mail.

We got ourselves together and went down to the station. Six large sacks of mail were waiting for us. We sat down in the conference room and started to go through the mail. There were all kinds of wedding cards and handwritten notes on stationery, all with kind wishes for us and our marriage.

We spoke to the manager of the TV station. His name was Anmol and he was a third-generation child from the original group from Planet Earth. He was of Indian descent and was dark-haired, brown-eyed, with a medium-dark complexion. His demeanor was kind and professional, and it was obvious he was very good at his job.

"Anmol," I said, "is it possible for us to make a public statement on your Public Broadcast Channel, thanking all the people who sent us wedding cards and kind wishes?"

"Sure, Jayna," he said. "I'm glad you asked. We need to address a couple of issues publicly. This would give us an opportunity to do so."

"Like what?" Landry asked.

"Well," he said, "first, we have to address all the mail the station received on behalf of your marriage. We estimate we received about six thousand cards and letters congratulating the both of you. It would be advisable to address that first. Then we could address the incident on your wedding day. This caused quite a stir in Sirius. The Sekhmetians are starting to get agitated as well. This is clearly a part of the Kemkabi's scheme. They have every intention of succeeding in their plot and they're letting us know, in so many words, that they do not fear us."

"But," I said, "they failed in their attempt to assassinate us. Does that not speak of their incompetence?"

"Yes," Anmol answered, "and no. Yes, they did not kill you, and no, they did disrupt the wedding and cause a ruckus."

"We need to address the Equinox movement," Landry said. "We can use this incident to unite all the people of Planet Sekhmet. Hopefully, this incident will work in our favor."

"I agree," Anmol said.

"Let's come up with a game plan," I said.

"Okay," said Anmol.

"Sounds good, Jayna," Landry said.

We went into the conference room and began brainstorming. The other TV staff members joined us as well. We worked through the rest of the morning, working on Landry's speech and what we needed to do to move forward. When we were done, we ordered lunch and ate in.

We decided the most efficient way to address the Kemkabi's challenge was to galvanize the energy of the masses and create resistance so strong, they could not possibly overcome us. We needed to encourage participation in the Equinox movement.

Landry rehearsed his speech until he mesmerized it and he went live on the air at the next available opportunity.

"Good day, everyone," Landry said. "My wife and I would like to take this opportunity to thank everyone for their cards and notes. Jayna and I are deeply touched, and want everyone to know how much we appreciate your kind words. It's such an honor for me to be here with you. Words could never express my deep gratitude and appreciation for having this opportunity. I am indeed blessed.

"The incident on our wedding day was a challenging one. The attempt to assassinate us on our wedding day failed, which is the good news. The bad news is that the Kemkabi are sending a message to the people of Planet Sekhmet. They have every intention of succeeding in their mission to pull this planet into the rift, which would take us into their evil dimension. All of us here at the TV station have agreed that the best course of action would be to unite the people of Planet Sekhmet in the Equinox movement.

"The goal of this movement is to assert that all beings are sovereign and have the right to self-determination. The people of Planet Sekhmet do not desire to serve the Darkness. We will do whatever it takes to put a stop to the Kemkabi and stop their evil intentions. We urge everyone to be united in prayer and, under no circumstances, feed into the darkness. The more light we share, the harder it is for them to succeed in their goal. The Sekhmetian Military is ever vigilant; we are prepared. On behalf of all of us of the Light, we thank you for your participation in the Equinox movement."

With that, Landry ended his speech and we left. The mood in Sirius was getting somber. You could feel the tension in the air. This was all coming to a head, I could feel it.

We drove home and didn't speak during the car ride. Landry was deeply upset. He could feel the tension in the air as well and he was not handling it too well. After we got home, he went on his computer for a while to relax, but could not. He told me he was tired, then he went into the bedroom and closed the door.

After about a half-hour, he burst out of the room and looked upset. "Jayna, I have to tell you something!"

"Okay, what is it?"

Landry told me the dream he just had.

He was looking at the night sky full of stars, but there were more than stars in the sky tonight. Spacecrafts were moving across the heavens so fast that the eye could hardly follow them. There were bright flashes of exploding spacecraft outlined in the darkness. Some of the Kemkabi's ships had been able to break away from the battle. This group of Kemkabi ships was heading to attack the planet. The defense shield, paired with the planetary energy cannons, could deal with this threat if both were functioning.

He saw a horde of dark creatures and humanoids battling with the Sekhmetian army forces on the ground.

The dark creatures were devastating the formations of the army. These creatures were jet black and had a sleek hairless body. Their bodies resembled a large wolf that was close to the size of a horse. On the top of their shoulder, an arm was ended in a large scythe-like crystalline blade. The head of this monstrosity framed a cavernous mouth, with two-inch-long curved razor-sharp crystalline teeth behind the wide flat canine-like nose. They had four eyes, a pair of milky white eyes that sat parallel to each other on each side of the creature's head. Its ears were long and ended in a point.

These creatures were sent in first, causing chaos by brutally mauling and slashing the Sekhmetians in their path. They were followed by the Darkened firing their weapons. The Kemkabi were mixed in with all these dark beings, comprising their army so they could telepathically command their forces. The power station fell dark as the last of the Sekhmetian defenders drew his last breath.

The Kemkabi spacecrafts were now bombarding Sirius. Fires rage throughout the homes and streets as people fled in terror, but there was no place to hide. Cars exploded with their occupants trapped inside. One of the Kemkabi's crafts positioned itself directly over our home and fired. Everything became dark and silent. Planet Sekhmet had fallen.

After Landry had finished his recount of the dream, he ran to the phone and called Jagannath and told him about it.

"I dreamt that the Kemkabi were already here," Landry said. "They've already sent the Darkened to carry out a mission."

Just as Landry finished the phone call, our lights started to flicker. The phone went dead. Luckily, Landry had finished his call. Now it was up to the Sekhmetian Military to complete their mission. The Kemkabi must be destroyed now.

Landry went to the walk-in closet and opened the door. He stepped inside. Ten minutes later, he emerged carrying my gear. He was ready for battle. He was armed with his rifle, sidearm, and sword. He was wearing the gear from our military training. I could hear that the communication devices in the helmets were active. The lights flickered again as Landry handed me my gear.

"We'll be ready in ten." Landry said to whoever was on the other end of the conversation. He turned to me. "Jayna, there's a helicopter on the way. It'll arrive soon. It won't be landing and they'll be dropping two ropes. Remember helicopter rope suspension technique?"

"Yes, I do remember that. I liked that part of the training," I replied. "You and Dameka didn't."

I started to put on the gear. He helped me by handing me the items in the proper order and making sure my vest was plugged in. Then he gave me my weapons. It occurred to me I needed to get the Crystal Cube, so I went to my meditation room to grab it from its stand. I placed the Cube in a pouch that was attached to my belt.

I heard the aircraft arrive, so we went outside. The whine of the rotor fan blades turning was loud. The downdraft caused dirt and debris to blow around under the helicopter.

The ropes were dropped and we attached them to our belts. We told the pilot that we were ready. The rope became taut, lifting us off of the ground, and away we went. The crew started using the winches to reel us into the helicopter. I enjoyed flying on the drop line. It was what I thought an angel or bird would feel when they flew. I liked to feel the wind on my face.

When we boarded the helicopter, there was a squad of Sekhmetian soldiers with their leader. There was a familiar face with them as well, Parisa. She was a sniper attached to the squad.

"We're on our way to Nekkar," Landry said. "Jagan-nath was able to figure out which power station was being attacked from my dream. It's about two hundred miles away."

I heard Jagannath over my comm. He was explaining that the Sekhmetian spaceships were moving into position between the planet and the rift. Some of our space fleets were engaging the Kemkabi ships, but the Kemkabi had a large armada of spacecrafts. As Jagannath was speaking, we could see the power station in the distance.

Landry told the pilot to drop the squad and Parisa on the roof of the facility. We could see from the helicopter that their Dark army was inside the entire walled perimeter. The Sekhmetian troops on the ground were barely holding their positions at the front of the facility. Landry then instructed the pilot to open fire on them.

The pilot dropped us on the side of the building. There was some cover in this area and the cover provided safety for us to drop down from a rope off the helicopter. The Sekhmetians were holding this area a little better and we positioned ourselves to enter the facility.

Landry turned to me. "This is a bad deal. We have to stay close to each other. I love you, dear."

"I love you, too," I said. "We got this."

We moved to the doors of the helicopter and hooked onto the ropes. Then we stepped through the door. The line slowed our descent, which was twenty feet from the helicopter to the ground. Projectiles and energy blasts missed impacting our surroundings, but some hit our shields. I heard a voice calling the helicopter away. Then the comm went dead.

The helicopter hovered over us, firing at the enemy until it flew away. This gave us enough time to get behind cover. Landry looked over the battle zone.

"Are you good?" Landry asked the Sekhmetian commander. "Is there enemy inside?"

"We can hold this area for now," he replied. "Some have slipped through the front of the power station. All of our comms are down; they must be jamming them."

"Give me eight soldiers," Landry commanded. "We need to move."

"You're not a member of the military," the Sekhmetian commander said. "But I do know the two of you are working with us."

"We're going in with or without them," Landry stated. "The rest is up to you."

The Sekhmetian commander pointed to eight soldiers and motioned them to go with us. Landry and I moved towards the door. The Sekhmetians fell in line behind us and Landry motioned for me to open the door to the facility.

I paused and grasped the Crystal Cube. I reached out with my mind and scanned the area inside the door. I saw a hallway. There was no one inside, so I peered further into the facility. The hallway branched off to the left and the right. I saw movement to the right and followed the movement to its source. There was a group of Sekhmetians engaging the enemy inside the facility. They were trying to keep them at bay. The Sekhmetians were firing from makeshift cover. Two Kemkabi and twenty Darkened fired back at them.

I turned my attention to the other hallway. There was a sign on the door that said, "Control Room." I saw down that the hallway was strewn with bodies of fallen Sekhmetian soldiers and slain Darkened and Kemkabi enemies. There was a portion of the door missing. I could see inside the control room. It was the same as the hallway; there were corpses on the floor as well. There were only two Sekhmetian soldiers left. One of the soldiers was sitting against the base of a control panel. He had a pistol in each hand. He was missing his right leg below the knee, which has been temporarily treated. The second Sekhmetian was crouched down, looking through the hole in the door.

I broke contact with the Cube and relayed the information to Landry.

"Jayna," Landry said, "open the door."

Landry was the first one to enter the facility, followed by the Sekhmetians, and with me close behind. I closed the door after we entered. We headed to the end of the hallway. Landry told four of the Sekhmetians to go to the control room. The rest of us headed to reinforce the group to the right. We reached the Sekhmetians at the barricade.

Landry looked at me. "Now is the time to do it, Jayna. Burn them."

I stepped forward and could feel my eyes change into pools of golden light. The heat rose from my core. The energy built as an orb of heat hovered in front of my face. It intensified and became a burning yellow-orange fiery orb. With a single thought, the orb hurdled toward the group of enemies. When it reached its destination, it exploded in a bright fiery flash. The enemies were incinerated. I had to take a moment to recover. It took intense energy for me to do this.

Landry told the Sekhmetians to hold the control room. One of the Sekhmetians told us that they were low on ammunition. Landry handed the man his rifle and all of his ammunition. Landry told the Sekhmetian soldiers to check the fallen and see if any were still alive and to gather their weapons and ammunition.

Landry and I were standing behind the barrier alone. Landry told me we needed to get to the front of the facility to help them. He first drew his pistol and placed it in his left hand. He then removed his sword with his right hand. We moved forward, past the barrier, into a large room. This was a large storage area, with crates that lined the floor. Landry and I moved down a pathway that was created by a wall of crates on each side.

One of the huge canine creatures jumped down from the top of the crates and charged towards us down the hallway. This hideous beast is even more terrifying than how Landry described it. He moved very fast and tried to pounce on Landry. I had to push my fear aside and keep my focus. I stopped the monstrosity in midair with my telekinetic ability. Landry fired into its open mouth. It tried to attack him with one of the blades from its back. Landry blocked it with the sword and fired four more times into the creature's head. It stopped moving and went limp. I let it fall to the ground.

Landry did not seem to be affected by all the stress of the situation. He was treating everything like it was just another job. He asked me, "Are you okay?"

"I'm okay."

We moved past the beast and continued towards the front of the facility. We could hear the battle still raging ahead. I moved quickly to keep up with Landry. Suddenly, two jet black humanoids appeared, emerging from the shadows. They were wearing a form-fitting black and dark gray padded bodysuit with a black belt. The dark gray area covered their chest, forearms, and shins.

One of them attacked Landry with a long black blade. It was a three-foot-long, single-edged serrated blade, similar to a Falchion-style sword. Most of the Kemkabi seemed to be armed with this type of sword. He sliced his foe from the right side of his neck to halfway down his torso. Landry kicked the lifeless body from his sword. The second attacker rushed towards me and I used my telekinetic ability to pick him up and slam him to the ground. I walked up to him and fired my rifle into his back.

Multiple Darkened appear at the end of the remaining portion of the hallway. Landry fired his pistol, hitting two of them multiple times in the chest. I fired at the other two, hitting one in the head and hitting the second one in the abdomen multiple times.

I saw another Darkened looking at us around the corner. He threw an object toward us, which bounced on the ground. It was some type of grenade. Landry picked up the grenade with his mind and tossed it back. The grenade exploded and multiple Darkened fell from both sides of the hallway. Huge chunks of the crates turned into splinters by the explosion.

We continued on our path. We reached the front of the building. Landry quickly turned to the right and fired at a hidden enemy at the top of the crates. A Kemkabi fell, landing on the floor with a thud. Multiple Darkened charged us from the left. I stepped forward and released a vicious psionic wave of energy. The Darkened screamed and grasped their heads, falling to their knees. They slumped lifelessly to the ground.

Landry and I pressed forward. We arrived at the front of the facility. The battle's intensity was still high. Waves of enemies attacked the Sekhmetian forces. They had fallen back to the hastily constructed barriers created by moving anything they could find that would create adequate cover. The helicopter had created a small window of opportunity that allowed them to use this time so this could be accomplished.

A Sekhmetian military officer approached us.

"How can we help?" Landry said.

"Landry and Jayna," he said, "I'm Master Sergeant Ajani. Find out where these hostiles are and eliminate them."

"Right away, Master Sergeant," Landry answered.

I retrieved the Cube from the pouch on my belt. I expanded my consciousness to be able to see and hear more of the battlefield. I saw a squad that had pushed into the enemy's territory. They were moving towards the rear of a parking garage. I looked into the half-empty garage. There was a rift being created by a strange Kemkabi device. Kemkabi, Darkened, and creatures were exiting from this rift. An alpha Kemkabi commanded the group inside the garage.

This aberration was more horrific than the Kemkabi we had already encountered. It looked to be about seven feet tall and powerfully built. It had four arms and it looked like there was a top part of a torso attached to another torso. There were two sets of shoulders and collar bones. At the end of these arms were hands with three fingers and a thumb ending with six-inch-long crystalline claws. It had a six-foot long tail that ended in a sharp spike, which was attached to the back of its pelvis. This Kemkabi had a large mouth full of shark-like teeth. It had no nose, unlike the others of its species.

It was giving orders to the group inside the garage. It looked right at me with its lifeless white eyes and snarled. How did he know that I was there? I quickly pulled back to the outside of the building and viewed the surroundings. The squad had detected the lookout and the Darkened waiting to ambush them. They had fallen back behind some trees for concealment. I pulled back further to get a wider view. There was a group of enemies just outside of the wall. It seemed that they were guarding a tall glowing spire made of crystal. This had to be what was jamming our comms.

I released my grip on the Cube and returned my attention to where I was standing. I told Landry and Master Sergeant Ajani what I had seen. They started making plans. Landry and I would engage the target in the parking garage with the squad that was already there. A team would be sent to take down the communication jamming device. The Master Sergeant assembled a six-unit team of the best-trained soldiers in his command. Landry recognized two of them He had trained with them since he had trained with more elite groups than I had. The team left for their objective.

Landry and I made our way to the squad by the parking garage. I used the Cube to guide us. We joined up with them and waited for the comms to reactivate. About twenty minutes later, there was chatter on the coms again. The strike team leader said that they would create a diversion.

Moments later, a large semi-truck slammed through the gate. It immediately started taking fire from the enemies nearest them. The truck started plowing through the enemy's army towards the front of the power station. The driver turned the truck sharply to the right and the trailer of the truck swung around. The sound of screeching tires and the smell of smoking rubber filled the air as the trailer hit the larger enemy group. Some were thrown twelve feet into the air, while others fell to the ground after being hit by the trailer. The trailer detached from the truck and rolled over a group of Darkened. The driver turned the truck, circling the area, and ran over more Darkened. The truck tires were going flat and the truck started to smoke. The truck just barely made it back to the gate. The six-man team exited the truck and returned fire as they moved to use the walls for cover.

I grasped the Cube to see inside but saw nothing but darkness and I heard nothing. The alpha Kemkabi must have possessed formidable psychic powers of its own. It was blocking me from being able to psychically see it. We had to go in without any information.

Landry and I sprang into action. There was a group of Darkened that was hiding to ambush us and I blasted them with psionic energy, destroying their minds.

Landry pulled the lookout from the two-story roof with his psychokinetic ability. The Darkened fell and hit the railing of the steps below him with a loud crash.

The squad rushed forward. One of them kicked in the door and they entered through the back door. There were cars on this end of the building to give us some cover. I heard gunfire erupt seconds later. Landry and I entered through the doorway. We located the rift generator and its power source. I focused my pyrokinetic energy into the power source and it went ablaze. The rift closed.

The rift generator was made out of shiny black metal and had strange writing on it. The writing looked like some ancient language that used geometric shapes to communicate.

There were Kemkabi returning fire with blasters at the soldiers. These blasters were made from the same black glossy material as the rest of their gear. There was a crystal that extended from the front of the L-shaped weapon. When the weapon was grasped, it wrapped around the hand, hiding it completely.

Two of them had crafted square shields from the shadow essence nearby to deflect the projectiles that were fired by the soldiers. The shields were two-foot by three-foot rectangles that were pot marked by the Sekhmetians' weapon fire. The pattern looked like the shields had been interlinked by the edges to intercept the projectiles.

The alpha Kemkabi was behind the two other Kemkabi. Inky-black tendrils of energy stretched out from the shadows. He was forming armor from the shadow essence. This armor reminded me of European knights. The armor solidified and had a glossy black finish.

We had already lost two from the squad, but they had lost more. Ten Darkened were on the ground. The soldiers pushed forward, using the vehicles as cover as best they could. Then the Kemkabi teleported through the shadows. They materialized on the car roofs above the soldiers. The Kemkabi opened fire at point-blank range. Their weapons were different than the dart weapons. These weapons fired a green energy blast. These blasts depleted the Sekhmetian shields quickly and tore through their bodies, killing them instantly.

Landry used his mental energy to augment his strength and speed. Within a blink of an eye, he moved towards the car on the right and used his sword to cut the Kemkabi's legs off from the knee down. The Kemkabi fell forward onto the shield it was carrying. Landry slashed through the Kemkabi's back, killing him instantly. I used my mental energy to wrench the shield from the second

Kemkabi's grasp and then I fired my rifle into his chest. He fell to the other side of the car.

Landry and I moved in unison to attack the alpha Kemkabi. It moved toward us in response, releasing a blast of dark energy. The blast drained the power cells of our gear and weapons.

Landry and I paused. Landry extended his hand toward one of the fallen Sekhmetians and pulled the sword from the scabbard. I summoned the fiery energy from within me to burn this aberration from the inside out. I tried to focus the fire inside the Kemkabi. It was like there was nothing there, no life energy to target. It must have been using its psychic ability to counteract mine.

"We will have to work together," Landry said. "The flow state is the only way to win."

"We will," I stated.

Landry charged forward, but I didn't move. Landry dodged under the two claw attacks from the alpha Kemkabi's right pair of arms. Landry took a sliding step to the side and slashed at the bottom of the creature's torso with his sword. He attacked the back of the Kemkabi's leg with his other sword. The black armor protected the creature from these attacks.

I blasted the creature with fire from my hand as a coordinated attack with Landry's. Parts of the black armor turned bright from my blast for a moment. The creature growled with pain. I could tell he wanted to attack me, but Landry moved between us. It attacked with the pair of arms on its left side. Landry blocked one of the claw attacks with his sword and ducked under the other attack. He then slashed the inside of the creature's left thigh, but the armor stopped the blow from landing once again.

The creature clawed at Landry with a right, then a left claw. Landry avoided both of these attacks. The creature grabbed hold of Landry's arms, using its bottom set of arms, and quickly held him up to its mouth to try to bite his head off. I restrained the top set of his arms with my telekinetic ability. Landry pushed the creature's head back with his mental energy and then kicked it in the face with both feet. The Kemkabi released Landry and, as Landry fell, the creature kicked him away, sending Landry flying backward into the side of a parked van. The side of the van was dented where he impacted.

The Kemkabi tried to step towards Landry. I used telekinesis to pick up a motorcycle and hurled it at our enemy. The motorcycle hit him in the chest with a loud crashing sound. The Kemkabi staggered backward and fell to the ground, with the motorcycle on top of him. Landry stood up slowly and he spotted the opponent. He raised the motorcycle into the air with his mind. He ran to the suspended vehicle, grabbing it and slamming it onto his enemy with both his psychic ability and physical strength.

The creature attacked Landry with its spiked tail, which pierces his left shin. He fell to the ground. The creature pushed the motorcycle from its chest and stood up. Its armor was bent and shattered in multiple places. The creature moved to pounce on Landry. I restrained it from reaching him with my psionic ability.

I noticed that Landry's eyes were glowing an ice-cold blue. He began to stare intently at the creature. He reached out with his right hand, fingers spread wide. He slowly closed his hand as the creature's armor and flesh started to frost over. The ice grew whiter and whiter, and colder and colder. The creature had slowed in its movements.

The creature was completely frozen.

"Drop it," Landry said.

I telekinetically raised the creature twenty feet in the air and dropped it. The creature fell. When it struck the ground, it shattered into hundreds of pieces.

We did it! The Kemkabi had been disabled. Now the other Darkened would scatter like their broken leader.

I walked over to Landry and used the Cube to mend his wounded leg just enough so that he could walk. He winced in pain, but the Cube's healing energy kicked in and the pain passed quickly.

We exited the front of the parking structure. The Kemkabi forces were still trying to engage the Sekhmetians in the power facility. We heard on our comms that we had helicopters inbound. Landry asked to speak to Jagannath over the comm.

"What message should I relay to Lieutenant Jagannath?" asked the controller.

"We may have the means to close the rift," Landry answered.

The helicopters arrived with reinforcements and started providing air cover for the troops. The enemy troops crumbled without the leadership of the alpha and the snipers were able to remove the few Kemkabi that was commanding the Darkened. The enemy troops soon were overwhelmed.

Lieutenant Jagannath contacted Landry. He had a helicopter bring us, with the rift device, to the Military Weapon Development Facility. They had their researchers start analyzing the device.

The defense grid of Planet Sekhmet remained functional so the Sekhmetian space fleet was able to defend the planet. The Kemkabi ships returned to their Dark dimension. Now we had to use the technology we captured to seal the rift. Many Sekhmetians laid down their lives in this battle. The human settlement of Sirius was kept safe. This was greatly appreciated by all that lived within the city and the US government as well.

Closing the Rift

The next day, Landry was called by Jagannath. He said the Sekhmetian Military was not able to reverse engineer the rift device. The technology was based on a dark energy matrix. They did not possess the equipment to analyze their generator and they did not know how to duplicate the device.

Landry and I were on a conference call with Jagannath. He explained to us about the dark energy matrix. All physical matter was comprised of dark energy. This device manipulated this energy and could tap right into its matrix. It changed the order of molecules and could be used to manipulate a tear in the space-time continuum.

Jagannath suggested to us that we contact Yashi and ask her to go through her channels to see if the Arcturian scientists could help us.

I called her and explained the situation. She said she would see what she could do. Two hours later, I heard back from her. She said Planet Arcturus was sending one of their top military scientists to address this issue with us. He would be arriving through the Cosmic Fountain tomorrow morning.

We went to the Fountain to meet him. He arrived promptly at 9:00 am. We exchanged pleasantries and headed to the Sekhmetian military base. Jagannath was waiting for us and we headed to a conference room.

The scientist's name was Mabon and he was about six-foot-tall, slim, and had blue skin. His scientific genius was well respected on Planet Arcturus and if anyone could help us, he could.

He examined the device and looked as though he was deep in thought. This was a great challenge for him. I prayed that Father/Mother God would enlighten his mind and bring the necessary information to him.

"Jayna," Mabon said, "this device has undecipherable writings on it. Can you please check the Cosmic Cube for further information on these sets of symbols? Let's see if we can decipher the writing on the device. That should lead us in the right direction."

"Will do," I answered.

I held the Cube in my hand and asked for further information on the writings that were on the device's face. The information that came through was not what I expected.

The Cube first showed me what could not be seen with the naked eye. The round-shaped black disc that was in front of us was not the entire device. There was an energetic component to it, which sat on top of the disc. The device worked inside the darkness of this unseen dimension.

I described to them the device's energetic components. First, four bars that were six-foot-tall and were placed on each quadrant of the base and then tapered from the edge of the base to an intersecting point in the disc's center. There were two rings. The first ring, two feet from the base, and then the second ring, two feet higher than the previous one. In the center, there was a foot-wide hexagonal column that was three feet tall. This column had energy moving along pathways of dark conduits. Their surface looked like it was covered with some kind of printed circuitry. On top, there was a sphere that floated above the intersection bars. This sphere was comprised of channels and markings that also looked like printed circuits.

The Cube took me into the dark dimension of the Kemkabi. I saw a group of them weaving dark energy into physical form and using the soul energy that was stolen from the Darkened to create the disc and the device.

This was mind-blowing! The Kemkabi was able to weave the corrupted soul's energy into a living dark construct. This dark soul energy was then trapped forever until the way was made for their release. Therefore, the machine itself was a form of hell, where the soul was in a constant state of torture. This explained their fear-based reality.

The only way to change the dark energy matrix was to infuse it with light energy. By doing so, the dark energy would be transformed into light energy so that the soul energy was no longer trapped in a hellscape. This would change the dark energy construct of the device to light. There were many souls that were trapped in it and were used to create this device.

Then the question now became, what was light energy? All of a sudden, I flashed back to the teachings of Yashi. She taught me that the Creator was the Light. Then what was the Creator? The Creator was love. Then, the Light must be love. What was love? According to Yeshua's teachings, all positive qualities were the many attributes of love. Therefore, all light energy was a manifestation of love, or a manifestation of light energy, which were the same. If we followed this line of thinking, then the energy of love could heal the energy of darkness.

When I had finished searching the Cube, I relayed the information. Mabon was intrigued. He asked to meet with us again tomorrow. He wanted to have time to think about it. I asked if it was okay to invite Yashi to the meeting and he agreed that it would be a good idea.

***

The next morning, Yashi came by to pick up Landry and me for the meeting. I sensed she was happy about something, but then again, she was always positive and in good spirits. Maybe I was imagining it or maybe she had an answer to our dilemma?

When we sat down for the meeting, Mabon opened the discussion and suggested that the Cube be placed on the device and used to infuse it with positive energy. Yashi agreed and we came up with a game plan.

We decided to place the Cube on the device and then the four of us would connect our energies to the Cube at the same time. Since all four of us were light energy souls, the Light could use us as conduits for its light energy power.

Jagannath knocked on the door and interrupted our meeting. He opened the door and walked into the room. "Excuse me, I have an important message. There's an armada of the Kemkabi ships approaching our planet. They have returned."

The armada of ships moved toward the planet from the rift. There are large ships, the largest ships that have ever been seen by the Sekhmetians. These ships were even larger than the ships of the Draconians. They were comprised of the same black glossy substance as all the constructs of the Kemkabi. The ships were a mile in length. The main hull of the ship was an oval-shaped tube. Two smaller oval tubes were embedded into the hull of the ship. From the front of the tube, a large crystal protruded. Surrounding the large crystal, there were two large spikes on each side. Connected to both sides of the tube were three bat-shaped wings. These wings fanned out, one in the middle, with one above, and one below. A sphere sat in the middle of the top and bottom wing. There was an oval-shaped dome on top of the body of the ship. It was located just behind the crystal.

The Sekhmetians' spacecrafts were no match against the larger Kemkabi spaceships. One blast from the large crystalline cannon and their shields were gone. The second blast would destroy the ship entirely. On the smaller ships, only one blast was necessary to destroy the craft.

The Kemkabi fleet moved toward the planet. They left destruction behind in their wake. Parts of ships that had exploded were everywhere, floating lifeless in space. This time, no stealth or subterfuge tactics was being used. Today, they came in the daylight. The destruction of the planet was now their goal and nothing would stand in their way.

Their ships were now starting to bombard the planetary defenses. The secondary shields around each city had been deployed, but the imminent destruction of this world had begun.

We all looked at each other. Now is no time to let fear control our actions. There were no coincidences or mistakes made by the Light. The time was now to put our plan into action.

We took the Cube and placed it in the middle of the black Kemkabi disc. Each one of us formed a circle around the device and connected our energies to the Cube. We all then pictured the best and happiest times of our lives. Like a slideshow, our minds were filled with the scenes from our lives that brought us immense joy. We allowed ourselves to be filled with the love and laughter created by these situations. Within seconds, the Cube began to glow. We all felt connected to an infinite source of love and healing, which was, of course, the Creator.

The Cube then began to levitate on its own and the light from it was growing even brighter. It started spinning in the air, all the while growing brighter and brighter. The invisible outline of the dark construct became visible, but I could feel resistance of the evil from within the construct. It wanted to maintain control over the ones trapped inside of it.

Torturous scenes and screams tried to assault my mind. The device itself seemed to be a malevolent entity battling for its survival. It tried to flood my mind with images of the ones closest to me suffering and dying. The others were having the same struggle, but we persevered, drawing strength from each other, and forced the negative emotions to dissipate. We focused past the device to contact the ones inside so that we could help them destroy the fear and negativity that they had suffered in life. Some still tried to blame others for their painful experience. Slowly, they began to understand what caused them to be in their condition and what created their own personal hell. They started forgiving themselves and others. This allowed them to join us. They were able to experience compassion and divine love.

The dark energy started expelling from the device. The more dark energy that was expelled, the easier it became to infuse it with light energy until the room was filled with light. Moments later, the construct had completely transformed and embodied the light energy rather than the dark.

We focused our attention on repairing the tear in the fabric of the space-time continuum. The device blinked out of this reality for a moment and then returned. The light then moved to the dark matrix within the rift.

We immediately went into the war room, where Jagannath and his staff were watching a large screen that had the Kemkabi fleet firing into the planet's protective shields. There was a burst of light in the distance, behind the Kemkabi armada. The ships slowly began to get pulled toward the rift as they continued to fire at the planet. The hulls of the ships seemed to be buckling under an unseen force as the ships tried to hold their position. The crafts were colliding with one another as they were drawn back into the rift. Parts of them were being pulled off and were moving towards the rift, striking whatever was in the way. It was reported that the bodies of dead Kemkabi and Darkened were disappearing from the surface of the planet as well.

It appeared that the Light had cleansed Planet Sekhmet from these parasitic entities. There was stillness in the room for a few minutes, while the intensity of the situation was fully realized.

Slowly, we all began to speak. The shock was wearing off.

General Zuberi walked in the door. Jagannath addressed him formally first, and then we all followed.

"Great job, Jagannath!" the general said. "I think you deserve a promotion."

"It wasn't me, sir," he replied. "It was them." He motioned towards us.

"That would be us, General," Landry said.

"Ugh," the general said, "two humans with two Arcturians saved the planet?"

"Yes, sir," Landry said.

"I can't give you a promotion," the general said.

"That's fine," he said, "it's our pleasure to serve." Landry turned to the group. "I'm hungry. Does anyone else want to come with me to the restaurant? I'm cooking."

"I'll be a while, but yes, I'll be there," Jagannath said.

"I would like to attend as well," Yashi said.

"I will attend," the general said.

"That is great idea," Mabon said. "I've never had authentic Earth dishes prepared for me."

"Jagannath," Landry asked, "can we send some food here for your staff?"

"Certainly," Jagannath replied.

Landry took my hand and we walked towards the doors. In the background, we heard the general ask Jagannath to update him on all the events of our work together.

We all met at the restaurant and had a wonderful time. This was a day that would go down in Sekhmetian history. There were celebrations everywhere on the Planet. Sirius was all lit up and the mood was joyous. Praise the Lord!

Landry and I went home. We decided to take a vacation. We chose to go back to River Town to visit our loved ones there.

A Secret Program

I called John to let him know that we were coming to River Town. He was briefed on our success by channels in the US government, so it was not necessary to explain what had happened when we got there.

"John," I said, "I wanted to ask you a question, if you don't mind."

"Sure, Jayna," he said. "Proceed."

"Well, I've noticed that throughout all the years I've known you, you never seem to age. I was wondering if you'd share you secret with us."

"He's a vampire, Jayna," Landry said.

"Wise guy!" I replied.

"Okay, you two," John said. "I can address your question, Jayna. Just like you and Landry are part of a secret program, so am I. There was technology that was experimented with in the 1950s, with regards to the merging of human consciousness and machines. The government had robots created that were unbelievably humanlike and could easily pass as a human. But the challenge was how to automate it with human consciousness and merge it with a machine.

"Well, a very brilliant scientist gave us a technique to do this. He hooked up a robot to a special machine that could hold a life force in it. He ran the machine through the robot and focused his consciousness through the machine. The nature of consciousness is to be self-aware. With the life force running through the machine while infusing it with self-awareness, the life force became aware of itself and the birth of the first android took place. This android became self-aware and now could function as a human. It was capable of performing tasks, as well as communicating. The android was given information in its memory banks that would be necessary for it to function, depending on what job it would be given.

"As an early model android, I was constructed in 1965 when the technology had developed a little more. A government agent's job was given to me that specialized in secret programs such as the one that the two of you belong to. There are many secret government programs and they keep me busy. I've been upgraded throughout the years and I only need to be maintained. I don't tire or age like a human does. My existence is quite pleasant actually."

Landry and I were speechless. This was not the answer I expected.

"John," I said, "you mentioned that there were many secret government programs. Can you tell us more about them?"

"Jayna," John replied, "our planet is such a mess and there is so much to say on this subject that I literally could write a volume of books about it. Suffice it to say, the environment is on its way to collapse unless it's stopped. There is an evil group of people who control the planet that is from the bowels of hell itself. They are so evil that they cannot be understood by the average person. They have created cyborgs to carry out heinous crimes against the public. I was created by a group of people who only wanted to serve the Light, so my jobs are all of a positive nature. But this is not true of all androids or cyborgs.

I've told you all I can...."

"I think Earth is more dysfunctional than Sekhmet, and, for the most part, humans are to blame," I replied.

(To Be Continued)